PRAISE FOR *BONEY CREEK*

"*Boney Creek* is a captivating page-turner with enough small-town suspects and secrets to keep you guessing till the very end. A master of mystery, Gleeson crafts compelling characters alongside her well-paced clues to create an enthralling tale that can't be missed."

—Megan Davidhizar, author of *Silent Sister*

"An aspiring investigative journalist is led (or misled!) to a small, rural town where she might have the best vantage point to a headline story, but at what cost? Is it worth her marriage? Her career? Her life? You won't be able to put it down until you find out. Gleeson has done it again in this taut page-turner!"

—Carinn Jade, author of *The Astrology House*

"A married couple moves to a secluded small town to recover from a trauma—only to discover their most frightening days are still ahead of them. If you're looking for a smart, twisty, slow burn of a thriller, you won't want to miss *Boney Creek*."

—Sarah Pekkanen, #1 *New York Times* bestselling author of *House of Glass*

"With a fully immersive setting, a town plagued by mysterious deaths and brimming with secrets, Gleeson's *Boney Creek*, much like her debut, expertly delivers one shocking twist after another and had me racing to the end!"

—Marlee Bush, author of *When She Was Me*

T0402326

PRAISE FOR *ORIGINAL TWIN*

"Swift and immersive, *Original Twin* is sure to mesmerize and keep you guessing. In her brilliant debut, Gleeson weaves a compelling net of secrets, lies, and dangerous family drama. This deftly paced thriller is a sinister kaleidoscope of suspense! I dare you to put it down."

—Katya de Becerra, author of *When Ghosts Call Us Home*

"Razor sharp and deftly plotted, Gleeson's debut unfolds like a feature film. The twists hit one after another until reaching a heart-stopping crescendo that left me gasping for breath. I couldn't put it down!"

—Marlee Bush, author of *When She Was Me*

"Paula Gleeson's debut, *Original Twin*, is a clever whodunit loaded with hidden clues and twisted family secrets. This thriller—where no one can be trusted and everyone could be guilty—will keep you guessing until the very last page."

—Ashley Tate, author of *Twenty-Seven Minutes*

"Paula Gleeson will keep you on your toes with every twist and turn. If you love a mystery where each piece of the puzzle calls into question what came before, pick this one up. *Original Twin* is utterly unpredictable!"

—Tracy Sierra, author of *Nightwatching*

"*Original Twin* weaves together twist upon twist, creating a tapestry of intrigue and deceit. Gleeson deftly spins a tale of family secrets, sibling rivalry, and simmering resentment—all laced with her unique brand of wry humor. An effortless, page-turning pleasure read."

—K. T. Nguyen, author of *You Know What You Did*

BONEY CREEK

BONEY CREEK

PAULA GLEESON

This is a work of fiction. Names, characters, organizations, places, events, and incidents are either products of the author's imagination or are used fictitiously. Otherwise, any resemblance to actual persons, living or dead, is purely coincidental.

Text copyright © 2025 by Paula Gleeson
All rights reserved.

No part of this book may be reproduced, or stored in a retrieval system, or transmitted in any form or by any means, electronic, mechanical, photocopying, recording, or otherwise, without express written permission of the publisher.

Published by Thomas & Mercer, Seattle

www.apub.com

Amazon, the Amazon logo, and Thomas & Mercer are trademarks of Amazon.com, Inc., or its affiliates.

EU product safety contact:
Amazon Media EU S. à r.l.
38, avenue John F. Kennedy, L-1855 Luxembourg
amazonpublishing-gpsr@amazon.com

ISBN-13: 9781662519550 (paperback)
ISBN-13: 9781662519567 (digital)

Cover design by Faceout Studio, Jeff Miller
Cover image: © Bjanka Kadic / ArcAngel; © Andrius_Saz, © Jurgens Potgieter / Shutterstock

Printed in the United States of America

For Gwen,
my agent, advocate, and friend

It's dead.

Has been for some time. Its branches twisted, bare. Some broken, unmoving on the ground.

A man sits on one of them. His chainsaw at his feet. A cup of hot tea from the thermos in his hand, the steam rising like the heat haze coming from the arid land around him. He swats a fly. Another lands in its spot. He curses the midday sun and all the bullshit it brings every summer.

If he's caught out here cutting wood in fire season, he'll be fined, but he couldn't give a rat's ass. No one around here would dare tell him what to do. Especially now he's back to stay.

He throws his tea away, too bloody hot. The land guzzling the liquid as soon as it hits the ground.

He's already polished off his ham-and-pickle sandwich, and all that's left is the brownie Mary made down at the general store. She'd kept it for him. *No charge,* she said, teeth brown and lips thin.

Most days her words are like venom. Piercing to start, then slowly sinking in, impossible to shake loose. Other days she's as sweet as her baked goods.

Like today. Clearly wanting something by not taking his money. He'd figure out what soon enough by way of her telling him. Mary might be delicate in her withering frame but not in her delivery.

If she knows already, I'm screwed, he thinks.

He bites into the dense chocolate texture, needing that tea after all. Mary always heavy handed with the cocoa. No matter, the sugar will get him through the rest of this tree, cutting it early to sell for firewood.

Dead trees are not hard to come by around here, just depends on whose property they're found on. Firewood is easy money if you own the land—which he doesn't.

He knows he's pushing his luck being out here so late in the day. But this tree has been a bastard, and the sun hasn't helped. Plus he's miles from anyone; they'll be lucky to hear his chainsaw this far out.

His truck stands close by. The flatbed already packed with his other cuttings. Just this last one and he's out of here.

He shoves the rest of the brownie into his mouth and coughs a little at the loose cocoa powder going down his throat. *Mary'll kill this town with her cooking,* he thinks. Knowing full well he'll pick up whatever she's baked tomorrow and all the days afterward.

Unless she knows.

He dismisses the thought, wipes the sweat from his brow and his hands on his jeans, pushing the wide-brimmed hat onto his head. Just get this last tree down and he can be home in plenty of time to have a shower and a beer before the kid comes over.

Get himself right—in the mirror and in his head.

It's a relationship he's been wanting since forever, and he's not going to screw this up. Not again. Three little words and he'll be free. Finally.

I'm your father.

He smiles a little. Not common but it suits him. It's lost out here with no one to notice.

His grip on the chainsaw is firm, and he only needs one pull to get it started. It's something he prides himself on. A few crows land on one of the branches overhead as he moves to the tree trunk. One of them lets off a wet shit, but it misses its mark. No good luck for him today.

He steps closer to the trunk, sizes up his first cut so the tree will fall just right. Felling them is a dangerous business.

A loud crack pierces the quiet of the bush.

Followed soon after by another.

One of the crows squawks, stumbling as the branch that's been hit begins to fall. The birds screech as they all take flight, knowing their temporary resting place is no longer.

He looks up, distracted by the movement.

Not from the birds but the branch now falling from the sky.

There's a thud as it cracks his skull just so.

He's dead before he hits the ground.

The chainsaw rattles away for a while longer, until it, too, dies.

Chapter One

DAY ONE

The sign hints at all the deaths.

BONEY CREEK
POPULATION 217

Except the *217* has been spray-painted out in red and left with two question marks.

Addie flicks her eyes to her husband. Nope, no reaction to the ominous sign. Acting like seven tragic deaths here in the last three months is no big deal. She fidgets in her seat. They've finally made it into town after a four-hour drive. Their new home. New life. No reason to be scared anymore.

"Here it is. Not much, but it's exactly what we need." He hasn't spoken for an hour now, and it sounds weird in the quiet of the vehicle.

The car rattles as they drive over wooden palings on the small bridge leading into town; below is a completely dried-up creek bed.

"Is this the creek the town is named after?" Addie scans the baked, cracked land below. "It's dry as a bone."

Toby nods. "Yeah, that's Boney Creek. Not much to look at now, though, with the constant drought and no flowing water."

She glances at her husband, who has been distant the whole trip. No matter what she's tried to do to lighten the mood, he's shot her down. It's not like him. Or maybe it is. After what happened, she can't predict her husband's state of mind like she used to. Maybe he's nervous, too, even if it was his suggestion to move here. Made it happen so fast she hasn't had time to process it all.

Maybe he's having second thoughts like I am. That's all it is, she decides as she catches him chewing the inside of his mouth. His eyes laser focused on the town they will call home, his short black hair sticking up at the back where he's leaned against the seat for so long.

Addie hopes he'll finally validate her own concerns about moving here. Confirm they've made a mistake now that they're driving through the town on its crumbling asphalt road.

"You sure this is it? There's nothing here," she says.

"I told you, most folks live on properties all around. Not in the town itself."

"What town? There is no town," Addie mumbles to herself.

She's seen one house so far since they've passed the sign welcoming them to Boney Creek. *One* house. And it was surrounded by long grass and bad fencing, so it could've been abandoned.

Addie shivers. *These bad feelings were supposed to go once we left the city.*

"You cold? I can turn the air-conditioning down." Toby's hand hovers over the dial that's turned to three. It's a scorcher outside, but in here is like a cool room—and not just because of the blasting frigid air.

"It's okay, thanks. Just someone walking over my grave."

"Speaking of."

Addie follows his head tilt to a dirt road up ahead, lined with parked cars.

She leans forward. "What is it?"

"A funeral, I'm guessing." His voice is matter of fact, almost bored.

They pass the road and the small sign saying it is, in fact, CEMETERY LANE. "How did you know the cemetery was up there?"

"If we're going to run the only operating store in this town, then we should get to know it as well as we can." He shrugs like she should have researched the town as much as he has.

Normally she prides herself on her research, but work hasn't exactly been her thing as of late and moving to this remote town isn't one of her newspaper articles. She hasn't studied anything lately, except the growing worry lines on her forehead. His multiple uses of *we* are also not lost on her, like he's trying to include her in a decision she didn't make.

Addie sits back as more houses appear along the sides of the road. None of them close together. All with acres of dried land between them.

This is a mistake.

There it is again. The voice telling her to turn back. That life in the city was hard, sure, but will this life be any easier? Who's she going to talk to besides sheep?

"Is that a café? I thought we were the only ones selling coffee?" Addie points to a small cottage with picnic tables out front. There's a large area of red dirt for parking cars, which is completely empty. "Maybe we can try a coffee before we grab the keys? Before they know we're competition."

"If you like." Her husband's face is unreadable. It's unnerving. She usually knows what he's thinking after having been together for five years, three of them married. Not anymore, though. Not after that night.

The blinker is on, even though theirs is the only car on the road, and they turn in to the cottage-now-café before Addie's suggestion becomes another reason for him to clam up further. She knows how much running late drives her husband to despair, and they're cutting it fine.

They park, and Addie is out of the car first. The heat blasting her immediately. She squints at the glare of the sun coming from the ground and takes a deep breath. Country air. It's like inhaling the heat from an oven with a whiff of cow shit. Might take some getting used to.

Addie looks around, but they are very much alone. No other cars in sight. She walks up a step onto the wooden veranda and pulls the door. It's locked.

There's a sign taped to the glass inside the door.

CLOSED FOR FUNERAL.

Ah, so he was right. That was a funeral back there. Which means there's been yet another death.

Her husband is still stretching his arms near the car, taking in the nothingness. *He probably loves the smell of baked cow shit,* she thinks.

Stop it. Be nice.

"The café is closed. You were right, a funeral."

He nods. "We should get going anyway. I told Gary we'd be there by one."

She pulls out her phone. They've got a few minutes. The general store can't be far from here.

"It's just there." He points, reading her mind like he always does—even if she's as changed as he is after what they went through. "Spitting distance, as they say."

Addie follows his finger and sees the slightly elevated sign displaying the word **FUEL** through the heat haze.

Under it is the recently purchased store. New business. New home. New life.

Only made possible because Mary, the lady who owned it for God knows how many years, died choking on her cereal just last week. One of seven deaths so far in Boney Creek in the last three months.

CLOSED FOR FUNERAL.

Make that eight.

Chapter Two

"Cutting it close, hey?" Gary glances at a nonexistent watch on his wrist.

Rude, Addie thinks. What happened to a simple hello?

"Nice to meet you. I'm Toby." Her husband, always the diplomat, extends his hand. "This is my wife, Addie."

Gary nods at her and adjusts his aviator glasses. He's pale, but already flushed from the sun, and looks like he's as much a stranger in this town as they are. Sweat has pooled around the armpits of his crisp white polo shirt.

Gary clasps Toby's hand finally and gives it a quick pump up and down. "Japanese, are you?"

"Korean. My mother's side," Toby answers without hesitation or animosity, even if Addie knows he's not a fan of people asking about his background.

There's now an awkwardness in the air to go with the cow shit, mainly coming from Addie. Her husband may be the diplomat, but she's not.

She distracts herself by focusing on their new purchase, taking it all in within seconds. A single-story shop with a two-story apartment attached to the back of it. Dirty windows leading into the store inside. Parking for customers on red dirt in front of a large rusted shed. Two fuel pumps. *Yikes.* She knew there was a coffee machine, supplies, and the post office. But fuel as well? This store is like a one-stop shop.

The tired sign saying **General Store** just adds to her own exhaustion, and she hopes Toby knows how everything works. The whole place also needs a good paint.

Or to be knocked down.

Addie's stomach churns. *This is a mistake.*

"I don't have long. Let's get this over with." Gary doesn't wait for them to follow as he unlocks the front glass door, covered in faded notices selling firewood, grass-slashing services, and sheep poo.

Toby gives Addie's hand a squeeze as he opens the door for her. She smiles at him and hopes he buys it. If he's even remotely nervous about this big change, he's now hiding it.

Gary is already inside, flipping on lights and talking as if they were listening. A single ceiling fan starts up and circulates stale, hot air.

The stench is immediate. *Death,* Addie thinks, covering her nose with her arm. She's familiar with the smell and doesn't like the reminder.

"Yeah, it stinks in here." Gary sniffs the air like he's sampling it. "The heat doesn't help matters. Leave a door open, and it'll be gone in no time."

Addie shakes her head at how much of a dick this guy is, still covering her nose while taking in the store. What there is of it anyway. Two rows of shelved snacks, canned goods, and general supplies. Nothing seems to have an order. Chocolate bars next to car oil next to paprika. It sends her organized journalist brain into a spin.

It's like the room has a washed-out filter over the top of it. Anything with color is subdued, as if she has walked into a museum. She glances at Toby, and he's read her mind again, handing her a jar of fish paste that expired twelve months ago.

"Are you sure this place was still operating?" she asks.

Gary ignores her, already behind the counter. Addie scampers to catch up. Toby does the same.

"You were lucky you got this place—we had another generous offer, but I went with you fine folks." Gary tries at a smile, but it doesn't quite land.

Toby frowns. "I didn't realize there was another offer. Someone local?"

"A guy called Larry. He's a billion years old and acts like this town is a game of Monopoly. Everyone hates him."

There's a story there, Addie notes, then quickly dismisses it. That was her old life.

Gary continues, "Everything is self-explanatory. Lights here, coffee machine here, hot dog warmer there, cash register over there—" Gary stops. "I have no idea how any of this works, so you'll have to figure it out for yourself."

"We'll sort it out," Toby says.

Will we? At least someone isn't shitting their pants at all this.

Gary leans his hand against the counter, then thinks better of it when he sees the obvious grime. "The post office is behind the partition. Just lift that small roller-door window, but only during the operating hours. Someone will come in tomorrow and show you how to do things. Hours are firm—don't let the locals walk all over you and tell you different."

"Wait, *tomorrow*?" She was sure they had a week to get themselves organized.

Gary pulls his sunglasses up and yawns. "The post office is a government business and needs to be run by their rules. So if you're sick, or dying, or dead, too bad. You have to be open."

Addie doesn't mention that the store is closed right now. Given what Gary has been through recently, it'd be tactless to bring it up. She decides now is as good a time as any to say something. "I was sorry to hear about your mom, Mary. She sounded like a wonderful lady."

"My mom was a crotchety old woman who died in the place she loved. Can't ask for more than that, I guess." Gary glances into the back room. "She died in there. I only tell you that because every other half-wit in this town will bleat it openly, just to get a reaction out of you."

"Was there another death? We saw a funeral up the road," Toby asks.

"Nah, that's for Mom. I already paid my respects. Don't want to overstay my welcome." Gary wipes his hands down the side of his pants. "Let's get this tour over and done with. I have a long drive back."

"Of course, we wouldn't want to keep you." Toby is already following behind as Gary walks through the door into the kitchenette.

Addie surveys the store before she goes any farther. A chill crawls up her spine, and the hairs on her arms stand on end. This place gives her the creeps, and she hasn't even stepped into the back room yet.

"Hey, Gary," she calls out. "Didn't you grow up here? Why the rush to get away?"

Gary pokes his head through the door behind the counter and says, "You'll find out soon enough."

Chapter Three

"What's that supposed to mean?" Addie can't believe he would say something so cryptic and just leave them hanging.

Gary waves her response away with a sweep of his hand. Her loathing of him intensifies. She knows if her husband asked, he would've no doubt answered. Yet Toby seems lost in his own thoughts, not giving her anything, which seems to be his specialty of late.

"There's no door here because Mom took it down. She liked always seeing into her beloved store." Gary leads them into the back area as if everything were hunky dory and he didn't just give them some kind of warning about the town seconds before. "This is the kitchen and meal-prep area for anything served outside to the public. Mom baked most mornings, mainly for the locals, as no one really passes through these days. She had a whole *bake it and they'll come* philosophy that bordered on delusion."

Addie steps into the ground level of their apartment, where the smell of bleach mixed with something rotten hits her nostrils like a slap.

Mary died right here, she thinks. Her eyes automatically go to the old mint green linoleum table and matching chairs in the middle of the room.

Gary doesn't seem fazed and continues at a rapid pace. "Stove here, all gas. Need to fill up the tanks yourself. Nothing is plumbed into the town. No water, sewage, or gas. Oven is old but reliable, cooks things quickly from what I remember, so watch anything closely."

Addie knows she'll be cleaning the stovetop as a matter of urgency. It's caked in crusted food and black marks that have been there for who knows how long.

Gary moves over to the wall abutting the storefront and points to an old olive-colored rotary phone stuck to the wall; its chord hangs all the way down to the floor. "The number for this phone is part of your settlement paperwork, and you'll need to maintain the bills. People in this town still call here from time to time, so I wouldn't recommend disconnecting it."

Toby walks over and picks up the phone, listening into the earpiece. "Wow, I can't believe it still works."

"Works just fine," Gary confirms. "Like I said, keep the bills up or you'll have to remove or replace it."

A movement comes from one of the chairs under the table. Addie jumps back.

"What is it?" Toby bends over, then laughs. "Oh, it's a cat."

Gary rolls his eyes. "That's Gravy. He'll come and go as he pleases. Nothing I can do about that."

Addie bends over as well, and the brown cat with the bright-yellow eyes blinks back at her, not understanding the fuss.

Gary keeps going. "Sink here. Use water sparingly, especially now in summer. If the rains don't come, you'll be paying for water, and it really ain't cheap."

Addie sidesteps past Gravy's chair in case the cat decides to strike out. She stands in front of the sink that sits below a double window looking out over dry land that stretches as far as the eye can see.

Gary comes up beside her. "Looks like nothing now, but in the wet season it'll be as green as anything. Most of that's yours, by the way. Watch out for dickheads comin' and stealin' your firewood. Get a gun—shoot 'em if they trespass, like my old man used to do."

The more Gary talks, the more his country accent creeps in, Addie notices.

"We won't be getting a gun," Toby says, opening up the fridge and quickly closing it again when a pungent smell escapes.

"What *do* we do if there's any trouble? How far are the police from here?" Addie eyes her husband as she asks the question. *What have we gotten ourselves into?*

Gary gives a breathy chuckle. "I wouldn't rely on them. A good forty minutes away if they have anyone available. By the time they get here . . . well, you're better off calling on the locals if you need a hand or if anyone causes you any trouble."

He shifts his eyes to the table where his mother died and wipes his hands down his pants again. "Make friends around here as soon as you can is all I'm sayin'."

"That's the plan," Toby says with a smile.

Addie is surprised. Toby isn't exactly the socializing type. *He must mean me,* she thinks. It's usually up to her to manage the small talk.

"If anyone wants to come back here for a look and to get any gossip about Mom, don't let 'em. You allow too many people back here, you'll never get rid of them. Mom was lonely, so she let this town walk all over her." He clears his throat, the first sign of any emotion about losing his mother.

Toby nods. "We appreciate the advice."

"Anyway, that's it." Gary claps his hands together once. "Everything else you need is in the files I left in the spare room upstairs—my childhood room. I know the solicitors still have some paperwork to clear up, given the quick sale, but you agreed to all of that before settlement."

His remark strikes like a dart. The speed at which they got here is something Addie is still coming to terms with. She may have reluctantly agreed with Toby that buying this place was the fresh start they needed after everything they'd suffered, but now that she's standing in the kitchen that smells of death, she's not sure running away from their problems was the answer either.

Gary keeps prattling on. "You'll need to give Mom's room a once-over before you use it tonight, I imagine."

Addie sighs. She knows her first night here will be cleaning and getting everything disinfected. Her resentment at Toby bringing them here festers even further. Granted the store was a steal, but did they really have to come to the ass end of nowhere? She should have pushed back more when he told her he'd made an offer on this place. She should have, but she didn't because all this is her fault.

"I collected all the valuables already, but if you find anything I missed, I trust you'll let me know." Gary addresses this to Toby, like maybe he's the more trustworthy out of the two of them.

Addie jumps in, distancing herself from her thoughts. "Of course, we wouldn't dream of keeping anything that might be sentimental or worth something."

"If it's worth something, I want to know." Gary wipes his brow with the back of his hand, his face growing ever redder from the heat in the kitchen. "If it's sentimental crap, do what you will with it. Mom's hoarding isn't my problem."

Toby brings his head back in from inspecting outside the back door, suddenly interested. "Your mom didn't look like much of a hoarder. Where did she keep most of the things she stored? I'd be interested to see if she has any archives on this town and its history. I love that kind of thing."

Addie chokes on a laugh. Toby has never been interested in anything historical since she's known him. *He's obviously being polite,* she thinks, given Toby is never one to lie.

Toby opens his eyes wide at her.

To not give him away, she guesses.

Gary doesn't seem to notice anyway as he joins Toby at the back door. "There's a big shed beside the shop. Most of it is rusted machinery you can try and sell off for metal. Mom kept boxes of old newspapers and crap from back in the day, but who knows where it all is now."

Addie is sure there's a glint in Toby's eye when he hears about the boxes. *Strange.* Maybe it's part of their new life or wanting to get to know their new home. She'll ask him later.

"And your father? What happened to him?" Toby's question is both tentative and eager.

Addie wonders why he cares.

"My old man was a goddamn hero." Gary spits his words out. It's clear that's the end of that conversation.

Addie moves over to her husband and takes his hand, squeezing it. *Enough with the questions.*

He squeezes back. *Okay.*

"Anyway, this place is all yours now. If you have any trouble, don't bother me with it. I probably won't know anyway." Gary shakes his head. "Haven't lived here for fifteen years. Bloody town and all its bullshit."

Addie suddenly gets the urge to go with him.

"They say home is where the heart is, but that's a bloody lie." Gary eyes the table where his mom choked on her cereal.

Addie shivers again.

Gary notices. "Wouldn't surprise me if Mom decides to haunt this place. Her and all the other ghosts of this town."

Addie's mouth falls open.

He laughs. "Good luck with that is all I'm sayin'."

Chapter Four

Addie texts her mom that they arrived safely and pours her first glass of wine as soon as Gary leaves. *Good riddance.*

The wine is the only thing she's retrieved from the car, along with some kitchen supplies, and it feels justified. Toby doesn't seem bothered by this creepy town or Gary's ominous way of talking about it. Or how the first thing they experienced of the locals was seeing them from afar at a funeral.

Addie strokes the linoleum table that she's already scrubbed down with bleach and disinfectant spray. It's weird that she knows someone died right here. Maybe she's even sitting in the chair Mary was in as she choked to death.

Toby observes Addie taking a long sip of her wine, his hands full with luggage. "Little early, isn't it?"

His voice is light, but she catches the raised inflection at the end. He's judging her. Fair. She's judging herself and all the conflicting thoughts swirling around her head.

"Do you think we made a mistake? I mean, we did buy this place pretty quickly."

His shoulders sag at her question as he places the luggage near the steps leading to the bedrooms. So far she hasn't gone upstairs. Truth is, she's dreading going up there.

He comes over and kisses the top of her head. It's nice. Welcome after the day so far.

"I know it's an adjustment and we talked about how it's going to be hard at first." He rubs her shoulders. Also welcome. "But as long as we're together, we can do anything."

He hasn't said that to her for a long time. It's what he whispered as they took their first dance as a married couple at their wedding reception. He's been saying it ever since. Well, not recently. Recently they've felt more apart than together.

Almost dying will do that to a couple.

She winces as he finds a knot deep under her shoulder blade. "What do you really know about this town? Like really? I'm beginning to see why this place was so cheap."

He pulls his hands away. She's done it again, brought them back to the same conversation they've been having since Toby decided to move them out of the city.

"I know a great deal about this town. I put a lot of time and research into this place before we signed the sales contract. I wish you'd trust me on that."

"I do trust you." Here they go, the same conversation over and over. She needs to reiterate her concern, so he can understand. "I guess I'm nervous about what I'll do here. You know, away from the paper. From my writing."

"Come on, babe." He shakes his head. "We talked about this."

They had, but now she's not so sure. She's only ever gone after other people's truths so she wouldn't have to face up to her own.

Toby says with some trepidation, "I thought you wanted to stop writing about other people's lives and start focusing on your own?"

If I focus on my own, then I'm done for, she thinks.

He's on the move again, the conversation already too much for him. The luggage in his hands as he puts a foot on the first step. Stops. "Maybe if *you* learned a bit about this town and its potential, you'd feel better."

The stairs creak as he climbs them. Addie finishes her wine and thinks about pouring another. She shouldn't. Can't. The van will be here soon with their belongings. Not that there are many. Just boxes of personal items, clothes, and books. Most of the boxes are books. Stories her escape from reality.

Their larger furniture is in storage in the city. That was the compromise. Toby wanted everything sold before they left; Addie said it was a step too far. So they agreed that if they were still in Boney Creek after twelve months, then everything in storage would be sold, but not before.

Now Addie understands why they left most of their household furniture behind. There's no room. The apartment quarters are tiny, well, downstairs at least. She doesn't even know if they have a living space to watch TV.

Addie checks her phone. Nothing back from her mom—not that she expects an immediate reply. After years of estrangement, they are still working out how they fit into each other's lives.

The chair scrapes as she stands. On the floor is a series of black marks where the chair has been moved in and out over time. Addie shivers again, her body's only reaction to Boney Creek, it seems.

She may as well be living in the house of a ghost, only *she's* the ghost, not Gary's mother, as he implied.

Placing the wineglass near the sink, she studies the dry land surrounding them through the window. So much empty space. *If anything bad happens, would anyone hear them scream?*

A face pops up in front of her.

Addie shrieks, staggers backward.

Toby is down the stairs and beside her in an instant.

A girl stares back at them with open-mouthed shock. Her dark hair loose around her light-brown skin and round face.

"There's someone there." Addie's voice shakes. "I'm not imagining it, am I?"

"I see her too." He rubs his wife's shoulders. "Hello! Can I help you?"

Addie's breath comes out staggered. The girl is real.

She's real. No ghosts. Not her nightmares come to life.

The girl hops down off something and skips through the open back door like she's a child, only she's clearly a teenager. She has on a tight pink tank top, black cutoff jeans, and flip-flops.

"Howdy! Didn't mean to scare you. I saw your car out front and thought I'd say hi. I'm Clancy, by the way." She thrusts out her hand.

Toby shakes it. "Toby. This is my wife, Addie."

Clancy steps forward and embraces Addie in a firm hug. It makes Addie gasp.

"We are going to be best friends. I can tell." Clancy steps back and eyes the empty wineglass. "I see someone's having a party without me."

Her smile is broad and seemingly genuine.

"Um, do you want one?" Addie is already moving toward the box of glasses and mugs. She'll have to clean another one, but she has a guest, so it's the polite thing to do.

Clancy's laugh fills the kitchen. "I'm only sixteen. But my mom has totally let me have wine before, so maybe another time."

Addie freezes on the spot. Of course this girl is underage. What's she thinking? She's obviously rattled. Flashbacks of their break-in in the city still too raw.

"You're totally an Aries, aren't you?" Clancy tilts her head at Addie, waiting for an answer.

"Um, like the horoscope?" Addie finds herself tilting her head too.

"I'm really good at guessing them. Go on, tell me I'm right."

"You're right."

She's wrong. Addie's a Taurus.

"Knew it!" Clancy punches the air. "Wait till I tell Mom."

Addie can't help but like the teen's boisterous energy and can feel herself relaxing.

"It's nice to meet you, Clancy. I take it you're a local." Toby is back behind Addie's shoulders, his hands firmly placed on them.

"That I am. I'm not only local, but I work for you. Mary and I were also best friends, but she's in the ground now. I left her funeral early because it was totally depressing." Clancy's smile still hasn't left her face, even if her voice is a little more somber. She pulls at her pink tank top. "I didn't wear this, don't worry. I changed first."

"I'm so sorry. I'm sure that was hard, losing your friend." Addie twists her shoulder away from her husband. The kitchen is closing in on her all of a sudden. Death feels like it's everywhere.

Clancy loses her smile. "This one wasn't the hardest, but there's been so many now, it's hard to keep track." She slaps her hand over her mouth. "Don't tell my mom I said that. She'd kill me."

Addie goes to say something, but Clancy gets in first. "There I go again. I shouldn't joke about being killed. None of us know who's going to be next around here."

Chapter Five

Toby has whisked Clancy outside and left Addie standing in the kitchen, desperately coveting more wine.

None of us know who's going to be next around here.

Surely the teen is just trying to scare them. And she's succeeded. Addie doesn't know how she's going to sleep in this place tonight, let alone for the rest of their lives.

She shakes her head, trying to stop all the intrusive thoughts again, and follows her husband and apparent new best friend outside. The glare is instant, and she has to cover her eyes, blinking until Clancy, standing near the open trunk of the car, comes into focus. Toby is handing her some of their bags.

Addie rushes over. "You don't need to help us with that. I'm sure you have better things to do."

"I don't really." Clancy shrugs. "I much prefer to be getting the gossip from the newest people in town. You're going to be hot property around here, that's for sure. No one interesting has moved into Boney Creek for ages."

Toby passes Addie a box filled with photo albums. It's heavier than she expects, and she has to readjust her grip. "I'm going to go inside with these."

"Awesome. I'll come too." Clancy doesn't wait for a response as she tags behind her.

They enter the kitchen again, and Addie plonks the box straight down on the table. She checks under it, but Gravy has gone.

"Should we take these upstairs?" Clancy lifts up the bags she's holding.

"In a minute. I haven't gone up there yet, and I'm not really keen to see what's waiting for me." Addie walks to the opening where the storefront leads to. "Do you want a bottle of water or a soda or something?"

"For real? Mary never let me have anything for free. Oh, wait. Is it free, or do you want me to pay for it?" Clancy shuffles her feet like she's embarrassed.

"You don't have to pay. I'm offering." Addie heads into the front of the store as a procession of cars passes along the main road outside.

Addie stops and stares as Clancy comes up behind her. "It's weird, her not being here."

"Mary?"

"Yeah. She was like my pretend gran or whatever. Mom is always working so Mary looked after me since I was little. Then she gave me a job here when I was old enough. I just figured she was never going to die, you know?"

"I'm really sorry. You must miss her." Addie grabs two water bottles out of the large commercial fridge.

Clancy takes the water Addie hands her. "Maybe I will, but it hasn't sunk in yet. Truth is, I miss my best friend more. He died last month. He was a Scorpio. Secretive, but loyal as anything."

"Clancy, I'm so sorry. What happened to—" Addie stops herself. "Forgive me, that's none of my business."

Clancy opens her water and takes a small sip. Her hands tremble slightly. "It was an accident with his horse. He was cleaning out its hooves, and I guess it must've gotten spooked or something. Kicked him in the side of the head, and he died in the hospital from a brain bleed."

Addie isn't sure how to respond.

"That's what everyone says, anyway. But I don't believe it." Clancy eyes the last of the passing cars.

Addie waits for more, but Clancy appears to be finished.

"What . . . what do *you* think happened?" Addie can't help herself; it's why she wanted to become a journalist. Always asking questions. Always wanting answers.

"Smoke never spooked. Not ever."

"Smoke?"

"Kip's horse. Kip was my best friend. He'd just turned eighteen, so two years older than me. As soon as I was born, he was latched to my side. He was like my brother, but he wasn't, you know?" She looks down, clearly embarrassed again.

Addie can take a wild guess that they were more than friends but doesn't press.

"When the police said Smoke had kicked him in the head, I didn't believe it for a second. That horse has been around guns, chainsaws, loud teenagers." She takes a sip of her water. "Hell, we were even riding her together one day, bareback, and a big brown snake slithered right in front of us. Smoke didn't even flinch, even though Kip and I were freaking out. That horse just watched the snake go on its way, and then we went on ours. Smoke is smarter than most people in this town."

Addie's interest is well and truly piqued. "So what *do* you think happened?"

Clancy stares her dead in the eye and says, "Someone killed him. He knew too much about something, and they killed him. Used Smoke as a cover."

Addie feels a stirring inside her. One she hasn't felt since their attack that night. It's the desire for answers, to get to the heart of the story. She welcomes the kick of adrenaline she's missed.

"*Who* killed him?" Addie steps closer to the teen, who hasn't lowered her gaze.

"Dunno. Not yet, but I'm going to find out. They say that all these deaths are accidents, but someone's going around killing people and covering it up. I know it." Clancy's eyes go wide as she looks behind Addie.

Addie spins around to where Toby is standing in the doorway to the kitchenette. She wonders how long he's been there and how much he heard. She hopes all of it so maybe they can reconsider this abrupt move to this creepy-ass town.

"I should get going. Thanks for the drink." Clancy tucks the water bottle into the back pocket of her jeans. "I'll be around tomorrow to show you the ropes. That is, if I still have a job?"

She asks this to Toby, who's still standing there not saying a word.

"Absolutely," Addie says before Toby can reply otherwise. "We'll need all the help we can get around here. Right, babe?"

Toby blinks like he's just waking up. "Of course. You are welcome anytime, Clancy. Anytime at all."

Clancy gives Toby a good sizing up, then says, "Capricorn. No, Pisces."

Addie wills him to humor her.

He doesn't. "Close. I'm a Virgo."

"Damn." Clancy snaps her fingers. "I should have known the way your car was packed so well. Losing my touch."

She genuinely looks disappointed.

Addie tries to make her feel better. "He's tough to read. Don't sweat it."

Clancy smiles, takes one giant step, and engulfs Addie in another hug. This time Addie doesn't gasp. She welcomes it, inhaling Clancy's fruity perfume, which brings back her own memories of being a teenager who grew up too quickly.

Clancy leans into her ear and whispers, "You'll help me, won't you? Find who's doing this?"

Addie nods without hesitation. She knows why. This town might not be what she had in mind, but if she's being gifted something so easily, she won't say no.

This could be the story she's been looking for all her life.

Chapter Six

Addie latches on to the idea of doing a story on Boney Creek and all its strange deaths recently. It doesn't leave her no matter how hard she tells herself those days are over.

Not as she's scrubbing the oven, the toilet, wiping surfaces, unpacking boxes, or using bleach on everything in sight. Toby tackles the upstairs as she puts her hand up for the bottom level—including the storefront.

Both think they have the better deal, but after finally going upstairs, Addie knows she won't be spending much time up there until she redoes everything. Opening windows is her first priority, the mustiness clogging up her airways.

There are two bedrooms on the second level. The master, where Mary slept, and Gary's old room, which still contains a single bed with a plain green bedcover and shelves for a few books. She knows this will serve as their library-cum-reading-room.

There's also a tiny living room, which sits between the two bedrooms, with a small fireplace, a worn two-seater couch, and a very dated TV. She'll get Toby to measure the rooms and then order what's needed online ASAP. Especially a new mattress. Sleeping on Mary's old one makes her want to gag.

Sitting on a stool and pulling stock from the lower shelves in the storefront, Addie checks expiration dates as Toby joins her. He has on a pair of yellow dish gloves, and his face is covered in sweat.

She laughs. "Now that's a look."

"I bet." He smiles. "Hopefully the shower works, or we'll be getting to know our neighbors sooner than they'd like."

"Seemed fine when I gave it a scrub. I'm looking forward to jumping in myself." It wasn't meant to be, but it comes out like an invitation.

Toby doesn't miss it either, his eyes still smiling. "It's getting late—we should pack it in anyway. Tomorrow's an early start."

Like she needs reminding. "Do we really have to open tomorrow? Just one more day and I'd feel a lot better about things."

"I hear you, but we have no choice with the post office." He wipes the single strand of hair falling on his face with the back of his glove. "I had a look at some of those files Gary left us, and I guess the town's mail gets delivered here at eight in the morning, and then we have to sort it. The store is usually open at six thirty."

"Six thirty? Every day? For the rest of our lives?" Her laugh isn't as genuine this time. "Sounds fabulous."

Toby looks over her shoulder to the shelf. "What's that?"

"I found it when I was cleaning." Addie picks up a bumblebee necklace that was partially hidden under the oven. "I guess it was Mary's?"

"Maybe. I can ask Gary." Toby inspects it. "It doesn't look too valuable."

Addie takes the necklace back and stares at it. "It creeps me out that she died right in there."

Toby pulls off the cleaning gloves and squats down beside her. "I know you're worried about the move and all the weird shit that's going on around here. I am too."

"You are?" Addie is genuinely shocked. "You seem like this is all totally fine. Just another funeral and some teenager talking about a killer roaming the town. No biggie."

Toby removes the necklace from her hand, puts it back on the shelf, and takes both her hands in his.

"I'm filthy," she murmurs.

"You're perfect." He looks at her like he used to. Deep into her eyes as if he could see right into her soul.

She shivers. A good shiver this time. Thoughts of that shower return. She hasn't been intimate with her husband since . . . she knows when. That horrible night changed everything.

"I know you're scared." He reads her mind again. "I am, too, trust me. But we have to remember why we came here, what we left behind."

Addie squeezes his hands. "I know you heard what Clancy was saying today. About someone killing her friend and it not being an accident."

Toby looks at his feet. "I heard—I just didn't want to interrupt."

"You looked like you'd seen a ghost or were in shock or something. What am I missing? What haven't you told me? The whole trip up you've been acting not yourself . . ." She waits for him to fill in the rest.

He stands and brings her up with him. Her legs stiff from sitting on the stool for so long.

"I was just nervous, got in my head. That's all. I'm sorry if I was being distant. I didn't mean to worry you."

She studies his brown eyes, believing him. "And what about the things Clancy said? About those deaths being covered up to look like accidents?"

"I read everything I could on this town before we bought up here. Do you think I'd really bring us somewhere unsafe after everything we've been through?"

Yet again, he's nailed what has been bothering her.

"Look," he continues. "I knew when Clancy said those things, you'd go into journalist mode and think there was a story here. I know you, Addie."

Yikes. He's reading her like one of their books in the boxes the van delivered earlier.

Addie drops her hands, unsure. "Clancy lost her best friend, and she seems pretty sure that someone killed him. She wants my assistance in finding out what happened, and I think I'm going to help her."

"You—" Toby's mouth falls open. "What do you mean you're going to help her? That makes no sense. One minute you're afraid of this town, and the next you want to act all private detective and immerse yourself with the killer?"

"I never said anything about going full detective. I wouldn't even know where to start. But I *was* a journalist once, and if anyone had actually given me a shot above puff pieces, I would've made a great investigative reporter."

As soon as the words are out, Addie isn't even sure she believes them. Her editor always said her writing was average at best and the bulldog instincts she needed were lacking. When Addie quit after the attack, she was sure her editor had been relieved.

Toby frowns. "So you're going to get a job at a local paper or something? I don't understand."

Addie hadn't really thought it all through until the idea popped into her head. This doesn't have to be like the cutthroat, competitive world she came from, where story is king. She can just dip her toe in. Keep it small, simple. Help Clancy out, just a favor. Nothing more. She won't make the same mistakes again. She's learned her lesson. She's totally got this.

Addie says it out loud before she can change her mind.

"I'm going to go old school and write a blog."

Chapter Seven

Addie crawls into bed in her pajama shorts and T-shirt long after midnight. Her body is bone tired, but her mind is still firing. She knows sleep will be a long time coming.

She showered solo and is now also in bed alone. Toby has been out in the shed since she suggested she might write a blog about the town and its strange deaths. He's probably just worried she'll get sucked into that world again and needed a moment, but it's been hours, and he didn't even come in for dinner.

She's not entirely sure why he is so concerned, his reaction immediate and seemingly out of nowhere. Yet again, her husband is acting not like his calm, levelheaded self. That night, their loss, this move, them both giving up their careers for the whiff of a fresh start, it's all taken a toll on their relationship and how they respond to each other. Toby retreats, deflecting any kind of confrontation, and Addie keeps things light and does jazz hands so she doesn't have to face her own demons and how she got them here.

She checks her phone. Still nothing from Mom. It shouldn't sting, not after a lifetime of being disappointed by her, but it does. It's times like this when she misses her grandmother who raised her. Her gran would have been in Boney Creek with them if she was still alive; a life away from the city was something she often dreamed about. Her companionship and practicality when dealing with tough situations would be welcome right now, setting her granddaughter's mind straight like she always did.

Addie can't go down that path of thinking about the past, not tonight. She should check on Toby. Where is he? It *has* been a long time since he's been gone. He could have been bitten by anything with fangs out there, and she'd be none the wiser.

A chill creeps up her body and ends with her head tingling. What if her husband is out there now, dead or dying? Boney Creek's next victim.

She bolts up, slips on her sneakers, and races to the window. The large roller door leading into the shed is open, and the light is on inside. She listens for any movement. A radio. Any indication that her husband is still alive.

There's none.

She flicks on every light on her way down, still getting used to the house and not taking any chances. She jogs out the back door and into the open shed.

"Toby? Toby, are you okay?"

A groan comes from the back corner of the shed. Addie can't see a thing among the rusted tractor, machinery, tools, and boxes.

"Toby, I'm coming. Just stay where you are." Addie steps into the shed and around the side of the tractor. She looks at her feet, keeping an eye out for snakes and rusted nails. Either, a deadly combination in the middle of nowhere.

A spider's web sticks to her face. She lets out a yelp.

"Addie?" Toby's voice is raspy. He's hurt. She knows he is.

"I'm coming. It was just a silly spider's web. Don't move. If something bit you, it's best to stay still." Addie wipes the rest of the web from her face and hair as she picks her way through the obstacle course that looks like the set of a horror movie. She just misses stepping on a pitchfork.

Toby is in the far corner, surrounded by boxes and loose paperwork everywhere. He's lying on his side, and a pile of papers looks like it's acting as his . . . pillow?

"You were sleeping?" Addie wants to be angry, but she's so relieved she thinks she might cry.

"I'm sorry, babe. I must have nodded off." He sits up and moves his neck from side to side until it cracks. "That's better."

"What're you doing out here? What are all these papers you're looking at?" Addie picks up an old newspaper with the headline Highway of Horror splashed across the top.

"It's nothing." Toby is quick to his feet and grabs the paper from her. "Don't start reading or you'll go down a rabbit hole like I just did. Mary kept some interesting stuff back here."

"Interesting? How so?" Addie can sense her husband keeping something from her.

"Just old articles on this area. Lots of historical stuff." Toby stacks the files and newspapers, putting them back into boxes. "You might even be able to use some of it for your blog."

Addie frowns, sure she misheard. "Did you just say *my blog*? Does that mean you think it's a good idea now?"

"I'm just saying you might be onto something." Toby closes a box and pushes it under a workbench. "Maybe you can do a blog on the town itself and not just the deaths that have been happening. It might be a nice way to get to know some locals while we settle in."

"Maybe." She can't believe he's changed his mind. If he's giving her permission to investigate, then that makes it okay. *Doesn't it?* "I'm not even sure when I'll set it up or start writing. We have a home to establish and a store to run. I don't even know if we have the internet connected yet."

Toby steps toward her with a smirk. "Did you just say what I think you said?"

"Um . . ." Addie has to think. "Internet? I should've known that would get you excited."

He pulls her into him and whispers in her ear. "No, Mrs. Clarkson. You said the *h* word."

She leans into him. The heat no longer just in the air. "Horny?" she whispers back.

"Home. You said *home*."

He leans down and puts his lips on hers. They are soft and taste of sweat and dirt, but mainly of him. Something she's been aching for since the night that everything changed.

Toby is *her* home.

She returns his kiss, and he puts his hand on her bare back under her T-shirt. She gasps in his mouth at the touch she has been craving.

He pulls away and looks her in the eye, his smile playful.

"Did you seriously just say *horny*?"

Addie smiles back, knowing he can read her mind. "Shut up and take me home."

Chapter Eight

DAY TWO

They've only been open for a couple of hours, and it is already chaos.

Toby hasn't figured out how to turn on the fuel pumps, which leads to a line of cars waiting—rush hour for Boney Creek, apparently.

Addie can't connect to the credit card system because their internet isn't set up and has to take an IOU from various townsfolk needing an early coffee.

"And where are the baked goods?" they demand, one after the other as if they were all working from the same script.

Baked goods? Don't you see how clean the shelves are now? she wants to scream. Here she was thinking it would be a lazy day with a couple of drop-ins or the curious few looking to size up the newbies.

Why everyone is awake so early is beyond her. By the time she and Toby finally went to sleep, after their surprise lovemaking, it was well past three in the morning. Their alarm blasted at six, and any romantic glow from the night before has quickly worn off.

Neither of them thought to get Clancy's phone number the day before, and they have no idea when she is supposed to start.

The one thing that *does* seem to be going right is that Addie knows her way around a coffee machine. Having given the machine a good clean the night before, including using the chemical powder that Mary had never opened, seems to be making a difference to the taste of the coffee. Many walk-ins commenting how they like the new beans Addie is using. A new coffee bean supplier is on the list, but for now, she's using Mary's old supply. Not that she tells anyone. Let her earn some brownie points on their first day open.

A big bag of mail and packages get delivered at eight o'clock, and they have no idea what to do with them, so they lie in a heap by the front door. Someone was supposed to come and show them how to run the post office, but they have no idea who or when that is happening. Gary has well and truly thrown them in the deep end. *Asshole.*

By nine o'clock there is a line outside the small shuttered window that houses the post office, but Addie can't find the keys. Things are getting hostile.

Where are all these people coming from, and why aren't they leaving? Addie says with her eyes to Toby, hoping he can read her mind like always. *Fix it. Make them go away.*

It's like the whole town has collectively decided to barrage the general store with their presence today. Or maybe this is Mary playing her first trick on them as a ghost.

Toby comes behind the counter, his face blotched pink from being outside in the sun, or from stress—or both. He blows some of the longer strands of hair off his face. "You don't know where the key is to the ice freezer out front, do you?"

Addie wants to laugh. She doesn't know where anything was, or is, and this has to be some kind of joke. She leans over to his ear and whispers, "Where are they all coming from, and why won't they leave? Surely the whole town is here by now."

He whispers back, "I think there is some kind of prank going on. This doesn't feel normal to me."

"Me neither. You better get back out front before there's a riot. There must be a way to get those fuel pumps working."

Toby leaves her before Addie can also whisper that they should just pack it in for the day and finish the bottle of wine she started instead.

Clancy breezes in through the back door. She's in tight jeans and an even tighter pale-blue Care Bears T-shirt that has sweat patches running down her back; her hair is twisted in two buns on either side of her head.

Addie lets out a huge sigh. "Clancy, thank goodness."

Clancy assesses the chaos, pulls a chair from the kitchen into the middle of the store, and stands on it. "That's enough, you bunch of jerks!" she shouts, the place going instantly quiet and any bystanders outside quickly coming inside an already packed room. "What do you all think you're playing at, being here this early? Whatcha do, call around and organize a party here this morning?"

A few faces look down, and a man coughs. There are whispers. Titters. A giggle.

"I see you, Larry." Clancy wags a finger at an elderly man in work overalls at the back.

Larry. Addie remembers the name. The guy who also put an offer in on the store. His eyes land on hers, and she instantly looks away. He may be in his late seventies or eighties, but he's strangely intimidating.

Clancy still commands the room. "Think I don't know what's going on here? You all decided to make the first day for these nice people a living hell, did you? Well, not on my watch."

Addie wants to go over and kiss her. Whatever they are paying her is not enough.

"This is what's going to happen," Clancy continues. "You are all going to piss off until after lunch, when the mail will be sorted and ready, like it is every other day. Come in before and we won't give you your mail for a week. Yes, that means you too, Mildred."

An elderly woman shuts her mouth before she can get any words out.

Toby comes in from the front, wiping his hands of grease. Clancy nods her head at him, and he returns it with his own nod.

"You all know those fuel pumps aren't working and haven't been for over a year now—so don't make poor Toby try and fix something that's unfixable. You're all a disgrace and should be ashamed of yourselves. This nice couple, Addie and Toby, are here to live, and you treat them like this? Disgraceful." Clancy scoffs, then turns her head to Addie and gives her a quick wink.

Addie loves that Clancy is enjoying this as much as she is.

"Righto. Scram. The lot of you." Clancy steps down from the chair and begins shooing everyone out the door. "And don't come back until you brought your manners with you."

There are a few grumbles and even a few apologies.

The old lady, Mildred, huffs and says in a loud whisper to no one in particular, "The way she's talking, you'd think Mary was back from the dead and taking over that poor child's body. The nerve."

When Mildred and everyone else has left, Clancy closes the door and locks it. "Well, that takes care of that. Don't open those doors until you're good and ready."

Toby claps.

Clancy bows deeply, pretending she's wearing a skirt.

Addie wonders if it's too early for that wine.

Chapter Nine

With Clancy around, things run a little smoother.

They are shown that all the keys live in the same drawer under the oven with the pots and pans. Why? Who knows. Not for long if Addie has anything to do with it, which she does.

Sorting the mail is straightforward and a matter of matching name and address on a wall of slots with the letters and bills to whom they are addressed—she ignores the voice telling her some of the people might now be deceased. The packages are piled in a corner and need to be scanned when they come in and when they go out.

Clancy knows her way around every part of the store and is a godsend. The only thing she doesn't seem to know is how to make coffee.

Addie has just made them all one before they open up the doors again.

"This is delicious!" Clancy says after taking a sip. "It's never tasted so good before. What'd you do?"

Addie laughs. "I cleaned the machine. It seems like that hasn't been done in who knows how long. Look after the machine, and it'll look after you."

"Gotcha! And will do. I always left before the coffee machine got turned off, so no idea when Mary cleaned it. The milk tastes good too. Not scorched within an inch of its life."

It's Toby's turn to laugh. "Addie has had years of practice. Haven't you, babe?"

She has. She was a barista while studying all through university. It's how she and Toby met: he was a new recruit at a local CPA office near the café she worked at. They flirted for weeks before she got tired of waiting and asked him out on a date.

"I'd love for you to show me." Clancy finishes off her hot drink and licks the foam off the sides of the cup. "If you know how to make coffees, you can work anywhere."

"You are not allowed to get a job anywhere else but with us, do you hear me?" Addie smiles to show she's joking, even if she's kind of not. "You saved our asses this morning. We owe you *big* time."

"You don't owe me anything." Clancy wipes her hands on a tea towel. "This town sure does, though. They all owe you a big fat apology for this morning's nonsense. They never would've pulled anything like that with Mary."

Toby finishes his coffee and places the ceramic cup in the small sink behind the machine. "I have a feeling they were testing us. A test we clearly didn't pass."

His tone is light, Addie notices. He seems almost happy. She hopes it's from last night because she's been feeling it too—a shift. Like maybe everything will be okay because *they* are okay.

As long as we're together, we can do anything.

"Of course it was a test. This town loves them with anyone new." Clancy nods. "They probably saw you arrive yesterday while at Mary's funeral and decided everyone coming in at once would be hilarious. You wait, people around here will be talking about it for the next year. It'll never get old."

Addie gives Clancy's arm a pat. "Well, regardless, we are grateful to you. We thought someone was going to show us how to run the post office properly, but they've been a no-show."

"Gale?" Clancy scoffs. "She would've been in on this morning's test for sure. She's a troublemaker, that one. Mom always told me not to trust her. She knows if you don't open the post office Monday to Friday, you'll be fined or whatever, so she'd be rubbing her hands with glee waiting for that to happen. Everyone in this town calls my mom a witch, but Gale's the real wicked witch of Boney Creek."

"Witch?" Addie says, curious. "I have so many questions."

"Lucky we've got all day. I'll fill you in on every local who walks through that door." Clancy glances toward the front glass windows. "Speaking of, this is Mildred."

Addie and Toby move their heads to see through the glass doors at the front of the store. The elderly lady from the morning shuffles toward them, leaning heavily on a three-pronged aluminum cane.

"Watch out for her. She's cunning as a snake and has a bite to go with it." Clancy rushes to the door and unlocks it, opening it before Mildred does. "Well, hello, Ms. Whiteman. Aren't you looking lovely today?"

Toby chuckles beside Addie and leans into her cheek, giving her a light kiss. "I need to go and fix up a few things out front."

"Escaping, in other words?" Addie feels a flutter inside her from the kiss.

"You know me so well. Make Mildred a free coffee as a gesture of goodwill."

"Smart *and* handsome. Lucky me." Addie can't believe she's flirting. It's like she's a new woman. This town is changing her already. Maybe Toby was onto something all along with this move.

Toby blows her a kiss as he steps into the kitchenette to go out the back door. Clancy helps Mildred into the store by taking her arm in her own. It's slow going, but they finally make it to the counter, where Clancy joins Addie behind it.

"I'll check for your mail, Ms. Whiteman." Clancy skips behind the partition to the post office section.

"Ms. Whiteman, hello." Addie clears her throat, nervous all of a sudden and slightly pensive. This old lady reminds her of her grandmother. "I'm Addie. It's so nice to meet you."

Mildred narrows her eyes. "Who said we've met?"

"Oh, well . . ." *Get it together. This old woman can't hurt you.* "So how can I help you today?"

The old lady pulls a handkerchief from her sleeve and wipes her nose. It seems that the conversation is over. Wonderful.

Clancy comes back with two envelopes in her hand. "Here you go, Ms. Whiteman. Looks like bills, unfortunately."

Mildred takes the envelopes without a smile or any acknowledgment. Addie waits for her to shuffle on out of there, but she just stands motionless. Staring straight at her, then glancing back toward the kitchen.

Clancy senses something is up and leans casually over the counter. "Whatever you have brewing in that brain of yours to say out loud should just stay in there, Ms. Whiteman. There's no need to be rude on the first day. Save that up for Addie to enjoy another time."

Addie is sure if she had half the confidence Clancy did at her age, she'd be a much better adult. Instead she keeps her thoughts inside her like a parasitic worm needing to be fed. A side effect of her gran drumming into her that children should be seen but not heard.

"It's okay, Clancy. If Ms. Whiteman has anything to say, she can say it freely."

Addie's phone buzzes in her back pocket, and she takes a quick glance at it. It's her mother finally. The message only five words on the screen: Have fun I'll visit soon.

Like hell she will. Addie knows her mom, along with their friends back in the city, mean well by saying they'll come and visit, but with such a long drive to get here and nothing enticing about where they live, it'll be a while before they host guests.

Not that she has many close friends after what happened; she's pretty much pushed everyone away. Especially after the media hounded her and Toby after the break-in and she was forced to change her cell number. It made having a clean break much easier.

Mildred purses her lips and watches Addie staring at her phone, the older woman's eyes drilling into her.

"Sorry about that," Addie says, putting it away.

Mildred grips her cane and mumbles, "I'm glad that woman's dead. Now I can finally get some peace."

"Who? Mary?" Clancy asks, not really acting shocked at the old lady's statement.

"Of course, Mary." Ms. Whiteman points her cane to the kitchen, her eye twitching. "Mind if I have a look? Want to do a little dance there, even with this busted hip."

Addie decides silence is the best response.

"That husband of yours," Mildred continues. "He seems familiar. He was in Boney Creek years back."

Clancy looks to Addie for confirmation.

"No." Addie shakes her head. "Neither of us have been up this way."

"Piffle," Mildred scoffs. "I never forget a face, and that is the face of someone who has been here before."

Chapter Ten

"Don't mind her," Clancy says after closing the door on Mildred. "She often says things that don't make sense."

"That's good to hear. I was worried for a second there." Addie knows Toby hasn't visited the town or he would have told her. That's just the kind of person he is—never one to lie.

"As you can tell, her and Mary had a hate-hate relationship over the years." Clancy shrugs.

"That's pretty clear." Addie wipes her brow with the sleeve of her T-shirt. They'll have to get air-conditioning, or she'll die. "I didn't think the locals would be so blunt about being happy someone is dead around here."

"Not Mildred." Clancy laughs. "She couldn't care less what people think of her. Never has. That's why her and Mary clashed. They were basically the same person living in a very small town, which only had room for one of them."

"Sounds like there's a story there. I'd be interested to know it." Addie thinks about the blog again, the idea sparking inspiration, which both excites and petrifies her.

"Mom could tell you better than I can. All I know is that Mary and Mildred were in love with the same guy a long time ago. Mary got him, and they've hated each other ever since." Clancy scans the area in front of the store.

"What are you looking for?" Addie comes over, curious as to what, or who, is out there.

Clancy frowns. "Just a tug in my gut telling me something is off about this morning. I've never seen this town rally as a united front like that before. Everyone tries to be amicable, but that controlled chaos was different. Planned almost."

Addie watches the wind pick up a patch of red dirt and turn it into a mini twister. It's like they are all alone here now. As if they could be the only two people left on the planet. Well, three, including Toby.

"So what's your gut telling you?" Addie asks.

"Not sure." Clancy bites her lip. "Just something feels . . . off."

"You know, a few months back, I used to work for a newspaper. I was just writing nonsense, filler pieces, but I was determined to work my way up to the juicier stuff—all I needed was the right story. Speaking to some of those experienced journalists, they all said the same thing."

"Yeah?" Clancy's eyes grow wide, immediately interested. "What'd they say?"

"To trust your gut because most of the time it was right. So whatever you are feeling, let it simmer and see where it leads you."

"Cool." Clancy nods, her eyes still wide. "You'd like my mom. She says shit like that all the time. Follow your light. Trust your judgment. Listen to the signs the universe is sending. She's great. You'd really love her."

Addie's sure she will if she's anything like Clancy, who is just about the friendliest teenager she's ever met. "I'd love to meet your mom. Will she be in later, or is she working?"

"Mom is always working. Mainly up at the hospital in Kerrindale as a nurse. She usually does double shifts so she doesn't have to drive back at night. She also has side hustles as well." Clancy walks away from the door and runs her hands along the shelves. "I like what you've done with everything. I didn't say before."

"Thanks, we were up for most of the night." Addie smiles at the thought of why they were up for some of it. "So how far is Kerrindale from here?"

"Like an hour and a half round trip. Longer if it's night because of all the wildlife on the roads. You gotta take them slow when it's pitch black." Clancy picks up a bottle of shampoo, flips the lid, and smells it.

"Is that where the local police are too?" Addie asked Gary but needs to hear it from Clancy as well.

Clancy straightens some jars of pickles, even though they're already straight. "Kerrindale is where most things are. Big grocery chains, hospital, police, funeral home. You know, all the important stuff."

Addie knows it's a joke but doesn't laugh. Neither does Clancy.

"I wanted to ask you about Kip again if that's okay?" Addie heads back behind the counter to busy herself, wanting to keep the conversation light. Like it's no big deal. Even if she does have a hidden agenda.

She can feel it coming back, that drive, the desire to get to the truth. Journalism is about playing a part, and she's slipped that costume back on—or maybe she never actually took it off. Where she would exploit her subjects and do anything for a story. She could feel the old her stirring and with it the reminder that stories can ruin lives.

Now that she'd had a taste of what it felt like to *be* the story, Addie wasn't as keen as she once had been to splash people's trauma around for entertainment. She hated journalists after the attack. Their home invasion quickly turning into a media invasion.

"Sure, I'm always happy to talk about Kip." Clancy stands beside her. "People get weird when I bring up his name now."

Addie takes her time, choosing her words carefully. "I was thinking about what you said yesterday, about Kip's death not being an accident."

Clancy's shoulders slump, and Addie kicks herself. "Clancy, I'm sorry. I didn't—"

"No, it's okay." Clancy goes back to the front door and picks up two empty milk crates from the morning's delivery that they'd organized the day before. "I brought up needing your help first. You can ask me whatever you like."

Addie takes a breath, reminding herself that Toby gave her permission to dig around and get answers. This time she will go slow, do it right. No more ruining lives. "Listen, this may sound weird, but I was thinking of writing a story on what has been happening here in Boney Creek. Not just the deaths but the people *behind* the deaths."

Clancy walks to the counter and stacks the milk crates on the ground. "What, like go to the big national papers? That sounds awesome. We can tell people what happened to Kip. That someone killed him."

Her eyes glisten, and Addie can't tell if it's from excitement or because of her grief. Maybe both.

Addie inhales, taking her time with her answer. "Well, not exactly. I was thinking of doing something a little more personal, something that anyone in the world can read if they want to."

Clancy looks suspicious. "I don't know what you mean."

"I'm thinking of writing a blog. Maybe give my own personal commentary on what has been happening around here, but also talk about who each of these people are—were."

Addie waits. Expecting the worse.

Instead Clancy says, "A blog? I think you mean a podcast."

"No, I mean a blog." Addie laughs with relief. "I prefer the written word and highly doubt anyone would want to listen to my voice. Besides, a blog is easy to set up and doesn't require a bunch of gatekeepers."

Gatekeepers like her old editor, who constantly told Addie she didn't have what it took to be a journalist. That there was always someone better than her, hungrier than her. She always questioned Addie's "killer instinct" and if she actually had one.

Screw her. If only she knew how wrong she was.

"Addie?" Clancy looks concerned. "I asked what if no one reads it?"

"Right, um." Addie centers herself. "Maybe no one will. But we have to start somewhere. I think let's kick off small, and if there's something there, I can pitch it to one of the national papers. What do you think? Want to help me?"

"Of course I want to help." Clancy doesn't hesitate. "But, Addie . . ."

"Yes, Clancy."

"What if the killer reads it and knows we are looking for them?"

Addie's already thought about this. "Then we smoke them out. Make them show themselves."

"Just like Kip's horse. Smoke."

"I guess so."

Clancy tugs at her lip, thinking. "You know, before Kip died, he also said some phrase with the word *smoke* in it."

"Oh yeah?" Addie studies Clancy's face.

"Yep, he said it on one of his videos he posted. Where there's smoke, there's fire, or something like that. It was hard to hear him, but everyone around here knew immediately what he was saying." Clancy tugs at her lip again.

"That's interesting. Do you know why he would use that phrase?"

"I don't. I'd never heard him say it before. Some people around here have said they're pretty sure it had to do with the Donolly family and how they all died in that house fire. That Kip was admitting to something."

"Admitting to what?"

"That he set the fire that killed the Donolly family that night. There were whispers Kip was galloping away on Smoke around the same time. Everyone had their suspicions."

"What do you think?"

Clancy chews her lip. "I think someone found out what Kip knew, and he died because of it."

Addie's brain is sparking with curiosity now.

Clancy adds, "Kip made videos for his socials, which his dad has taken down. I still have a couple, though, if you want to see for yourself. Maybe you can find some clues or something?"

"Maybe." Addie doesn't want to get Clancy's hopes up.

"Let's do it." Clancy leans forward, her face serious. "Let's smoke out the asshole who killed Kip."

Chapter Eleven

Only three more locals come in for the rest of the day.

Mildred visits again later in the afternoon, begging to see the kitchen. Addie knows she'll have to keep an eye on her and plans to make Mildred an ally if she's going to get any intel for her blog. The first free coffee may have just done the trick, as Mildred gives her a satisfactory thumbs-up.

A lady in her forties or so comes in to pick up mail and some milk. Sharmi Wilmer is her name, and she wears a flannel shirt tucked into cream riding pants and long black boots. Her eyes are a striking brown, and she seems warm and genuine, if a little shy, when she introduces herself. She doesn't stay long, claiming she's in a hurry.

The sun is slowly setting. Clancy's gone for the day, and Toby is at the table in the kitchen doing paperwork and organizing suppliers and deliveries when their last customer walks in the door.

He's tall, slim. Possibly in his late sixties, early seventies, but there's something youthful about him. Maybe because he's wearing faded jeans and a T-shirt with *Who you gonna call?* on it. The word *you* has the *Ghostbusters* logo in place of the *o*.

"Hey there. I thought I'd come and introduce myself." His smile and the rich timbre of his voice instantly make Addie feel at ease. "I'm Walter. Walter Brooks."

Addie can't help but smile back. "I'm Addie. Addie Clarkson. Nice to meet you."

He does a small spin, taking in the store. "You've cleaned. Looks good. Smells even better."

She definitely likes this guy. "Thanks for noticing. Can I get you anything?"

"Is it still on?" He gestures to the coffee machine. "I'd love a coffee. I heard you make quite the brew."

"Of course." Addie is glad she hasn't cleaned it already, although she'd make him a coffee even if she had. "How do you have it?"

"How about you surprise me." He gives a quick nod of his head like it's his version of a wink.

"I can do that." She knows right away she'll make him a mocha. It's one of her specialties.

He wanders around the store as she preps his order, picking up jars and boxed goods. "I see you've culled everything that belonged in the Dark Ages."

Addie laughs. Her first genuine one of the day. It feels good. Welcome, finally. "Again, thanks for noticing. Still a long way to go, but this place definitely has potential."

"That it does, and it's nice to see someone so young and eager running it." He does four points of the cross. "We'll miss our Mary, though. Good woman."

Addie has nothing to add given she never knew her. "I'm running the store with my husband. Toby. He's just out here. I'll get him as I'm sure he'd love to say hi."

Addie puts down the jug she's filled with milk and sticks her head in back. The table is covered in bills, paperwork, receipts, and an open laptop—but he's not there.

"Toby?" She yells up the stairs. "Come down for a minute. There's someone here who you should meet."

Addie isn't quite sure why Toby should meet Walter. Just her gut saying he should. She listens for his reply or any sounds that he's upstairs, but she hears nothing.

"Strange. He must be out back somewhere." Addie returns to the jug and scoops some chocolate powder into the milk.

"That's okay, plenty of time to get to know you fine folk." He dips an imaginary hat.

Addie smiles at him as she froths the milk. If all the locals were as easygoing as this guy, she'd be happy to stay forever.

"So I take it everyone in Boney Creek has been coming in for a look-see today? Me included, if I'm going to be honest. I hope you're settling in okay." His voice has a singsong way about it. It's soothing yet demands to be listened to. *His voice would be perfect for a podcast,* she thinks.

"It's been an . . . interesting opening. But everyone has been nice. It's only our first day, so a few teething problems. But otherwise, yes, settling in just fine." It's a lie, and she knows he can probably see through her just by the way he observes her.

"Give it some time. This town can be prickly with outsiders, but if they know you're here to stay, they'll be like family before you know it." He stands in front of the coffee machine so she can just see above his eyes.

"Here's hoping, hey?" Addie pours the chocolate milk over the espresso shot, then sprinkles it with chocolate. "Did you want a lid?"

"I don't. I might just drink it while I'm here, if that's okay with you?" He checks his watch, and Addie glances at the clock on the wall. It's past seven. They should be closed by now.

She flicks her eyes toward the kitchen but already knows Toby isn't there; she would've heard him otherwise. "If you don't mind watching me clean this beast, then of course. I'd like the company."

"Good. Very good." He takes a sip of his mocha, and his eyes light up. "What on God's earth have you made me?"

Addie laughs as she lets out a burst of steam to clean out the end of the wand. "It's a mocha. Coffee and chocolate combined. Hopefully it won't keep you up all night."

"Smart." He blows into the cup and takes another sip. "Wowee. A man could get used to this."

"Happy to oblige. So tell me about yourself, Walter. What do you do around town?"

"I'm only part time now, but I'm the pastor of the local church."

"There's a church?" Addie really needs to get out and explore this new town she calls home.

"There's always a church, my dear," Walter says lightheartedly.

Addie now knows why he's here. To ask her to join said church.

"It's also why I'm here. I'm afraid I've come on false pretenses, and I hope you will forgive me."

Yep, there it is.

Chapter Twelve

She should've known this was too good to be true.

Addie stops wiping the coffee machine down and steps out from behind it. "Go on then. Tell me why you're really here."

"Whoa there." Walter puts up the hand that isn't holding the coffee. "It's nothing bad or untoward. I only wanted to be honest that I had a true purpose for coming to see you at closing time—and it wasn't just to introduce myself."

Addie looks at him warily. "Maybe it's best I give you a lid for that and you come back another time. I should check on my husband."

"If you'll allow me, I'll be brief. You see, I have a deadline for getting all the donations in for the fair by tomorrow and . . ." He pauses. "This is rather awkward."

"Spit it out." Whatever it is, it can't be good. She's sure of it. If this whole day has been anything to go by.

He starts slowly, taking his time with his words. "Every year Boney Creek holds an annual fair. It's good for the town. Brings in much-needed traffic, and locals can sell their wares to passersby. There's a famous wood-chopping event too. The kids love the ice cream and the horse rides. It's a lot of fun." He looks at her hopefully, seeing if he's selling her.

On what exactly, she's not sure.

"I don't understand. What's this got to do with us?" Addie glances at the clock again. It's now almost seven thirty. *Where is Toby?*

"Every year Mary gives . . . gave us a sizable donation to sponsor the fair for all the marketing expenses we have. And, well, she passed before we could collect that donation." He does the four signs of the cross again.

It annoys Addie for some reason. *Okay, we get it. She's dead.*

"So now you expect us to pay this donation." Addie doesn't want to tell Toby. He already hit the fan earlier when he saw how many unpaid bills and expenses were left on the store. It was like Mary had been living off credit. Something Gary hadn't disclosed with the sale and Toby would be following up on. Normally she'd sympathize with her husband, but it's just another example of how quickly he'd gone through with this purchase without too much thought. A surprising oversight on his normally meticulous planning before making any kind of decision—big or small.

Walter sips his mocha, clearly uncomfortable. The easy, charming swagger he had before, now gone. He clears his throat. "I really hate to ask, but if I don't pay for all the ads and printed materials tomorrow, then there'll be no fair."

"How much is it?" Addie knows they'll pay. Like they can say no.

"It's a few hundred dollars. All in. That includes hiring banners and flags for the day for traffic."

"For traffic? What traffic?" The words come out before Addie can stop them. "Forgive me, that was rude."

Walter doesn't seem too fazed and waits silently for her decision.

Addie figures a few hundred dollars is a wise investment for the sake of making a good first impression on the town. "Of course we'll give you the money. It'll have to be a bank transfer, as we don't have that kind of cash lying around. I presume we get some kind of endorsement on any publicity or marketing?"

"Yes, of course. The Boney Creek General Store is always the one and only sponsor." He sighs with relief. "And thank you so much, Addie. You have no idea how important this fair is to the town, and I appreciate your understanding."

"It's okay. Happy to help, honestly. We can't see the famous fair being canceled." Sarcasm edges into her voice.

"It'll be a lucrative day for you too. You wait. Mary said she could keep this place open just from the takings on the fair day alone."

Addie doesn't want to tell him that if he could see their books, he would know that Mary was a liar. "I'll be sure to tell Toby. He'll be thrilled." He probably *would* be thrilled if the profit was real. "When is it? The fair?"

"Two weeks. On the Saturday. It's a jolly good time. You'll love it." His ease of talking is coming back, even if Addie can still sense his embarrassment from before.

Addie hands him a piece of scrap paper and a pen. "Write down the bank details, and I'll organize payment tonight. If you don't know them, just send me a text." Addie writes down her cell number and rips off the paper for him.

He takes it from her. "Thank you. I will be sure to text you when I get back home."

"Do you live at the church?" Addie's stomach rumbles. It's time for dinner.

"I live behind the church, yes. You are welcome anytime. I open the doors on Sunday for anyone who wants to pop in. No set hours, just come and go as you please. If you need me any other time, just knock on the door of the cottage in back. I'm always available for a chat."

"I'm not really religious, though, and neither is my husband."

"God won't hold that against you, and neither will I." He does his head bob again. It's definitely his version of a wink, Addie decides. "I best get on and leave you to it."

He glances outside. "Look at that. Got dark quickly tonight." There's an edge to his voice.

"Will you be okay getting home?" Addie doesn't see a vehicle out front, so he must've walked.

"I'll be right as rain. Don't you worry." He strides up to her and puts his hand out. "I want to thank you again, Addie. You and your husband. Boney Creek is lucky to have you both."

Addie takes his hand, which has a slight tremble she didn't notice before. "We'll see you around, I guess."

He doesn't release her hand and instead grips it harder. "You come see me, Addie. Anytime. For anything at all. You hear me."

"Okay, sure." Addie winces as he pulls his hand away.

He leaves, and Addie locks the door, watching him walking down the completely quiet main street of town. She waves when he turns around, but he doesn't wave back, like he's looking at something other than her.

Her hand hangs in the air, and it's red from where he gripped it.

Chapter Thirteen

Addie finds Toby in the back of the shed again.

"I closed up the store. Are you ready for dinner?" she asks.

He has pulled all the same documents and articles out of the boxes as he did last night and sits among them. This time he doesn't act strange or try to hide anything from her.

He looks exhausted, defeated. Not surprising after the day they've had.

"Sorry, babe, I lost track of time. I should've made us something while you were closing up." He gives her a halfhearted smile, dark circles under his eyes.

She agrees but doesn't say anything, instead telling him about Walter and the sponsorship money, waiting for him to be excited about the potential profit and comment on how well she's doing at playing nice with the locals. Instead he just mumbles like he's not listening.

"What's going on here? I've clearly caught you in the middle of something." She kneels down beside him, conscious of keeping the edge out of her voice. "Can I help with anything so we can go back inside?"

Toby takes a deep breath, and . . . *Are those tears in his eyes?* Something must have happened.

"Babe, what is it? Was it one of the locals? Were they awful? Is it the accounting books? Are they worse than we thought?" The questions spill out of her as she waits for him to give her any indication that she's confirmed why he's upset. "I can go back to that pastor right now and tell him to shove the sponsorship money where the sun don't shine."

She waits for Toby to laugh. To react in any way that is his normal charming, easygoing self. He always has it together. He always knows what to do, what is right for *both* of them. Not like her. Always impulsive, chasing after the wrong things, barely masking her trauma anymore. If her husband is starting to lose it, then what hope has she got?

Toby doesn't laugh, his lips quivering instead. Her stomach sinks, and her heart sounds loud in her ears. *This can't be good. He must know.*

"Tobe, you need to tell me what's going on. You're distancing yourself from me, and it's scaring me." Her voice is firm, even if she's afraid of what he will say.

Toby's chest rises as he takes in a deep breath. She knows he can't hold in what's been consuming him anymore, and she's pretty sure this is where it all ends for them. Blood rushes to her head, and all she can think is *It's happening again.* Something bad. Something from that night.

"I need you to sit down. There's something I have to tell you." He pulls over a folded newspaper next to him and pats the top of it for her to sit on. "Here."

"Is it about the break-in?" Addie doesn't move. Her head spins. *That's it.* She knew it would all come back to haunt her. To haunt them.

Toby puts out a hand. "Please, just come sit down. I'll tell you everything."

Now she wants to cry. This was supposed to have gone away. They moved all this way for a reason. A new life. A new home. *Home.* Maybe Gary was right about home just being bullshit.

Addie takes Toby's hand. It's warm, clammy. He's nervous. This makes her nervous. She bends her knees and finally tells her body to sit before she faints.

He looks down at his hand in hers. She waits. Not wanting to hear whatever it is. *No more bad news. No more.*

A loud bang sounds on the tin roof of the shed. The metal moving after being in the sun all day. Still, it sends a chill right through her. "Whatever it is, just tell me. We'll work it out. We'll get through this together." Addie's voice gives her away. She's full of shit, and Toby probably knows it too.

He pulls his hand aside and wipes it on his shorts. They are filthy. Covered in dirt and oil. *I'll have to wash those later.* Addie can't believe she is even thinking of cleaning right now.

Enough of this. She can't wait any longer. "Toby, tell me. What is it?"

"If I tell you, you'll never forgive me. But I know if I don't tell you and you find out another way, I'll never forgive myself." He looks up at her. His face ashen. Tears still swimming in his eyes, threatening to spill over. "How I thought I could keep this from you is beyond me. I'm such a fool."

Bile rises into her mouth. It's like all her paranoid fears coming true. "You're having an affair. No, you had an affair, but it's not over. Coming to Boney Creek was a mistake. You want to go back, to be with her. Who is it? Have I met her?"

His eyes scan her whole face. It's like he's taking her all in. Like she has just exposed herself and now he knows what keeps her up at night. Well, one of many things that keep her up at night.

"I love you. You know that, right?" There's no emotion in his voice. She's never seen him like this before. Is he in shock, or is he worried she'll lash out if he doesn't keep everything calm?

She rubs the tip of her tongue over the roof of her mouth. *Don't cry. Don't cry. Don't cry.* She waits for the inevitable. For there to be nowhere she can call home. For everything to finally be over. Something sparks in her brain as he continues to study her. Working out what to say next, she supposes.

He knows.

It's loud. So clear. She kicks herself for not getting there sooner. Of course. He found out her secret instead. It was always bound to happen. Secrets never stay hidden, and cavernous truths once revealed can change the trajectory of a life. She's about to become one of her stories.

All she can do is wait for him to say he knows the truth of that night. That she almost ruined everything because of her own selfish desire. *I owe him the truth,* she thinks. That she is a vile and horrible person.

A sob escapes her. She has no right to be upset. *This is* his *right, not mine.*

Toby grabs both her hands and leans closer to her face. His eyes are wild and filled with . . . fear? Pain? She can't tell anymore.

"I don't even know where to start." He licks his lips, and she wants to kiss them. Take everything back. "I'm sorry."

"Wait." She blinks. "*You're* sorry?" Her brain is swirling and not keeping up. *Maybe it is just an affair? If it's an affair, I can live with that. Yes. Yes, I can live with that—*

"Addie? Did you hear me?" Toby's voice and face come back into focus.

Oh shit. What did he say?

"No. I didn't. I'm sorry. Can you repeat it?" She holds her breath.

Toby releases one. "I said that I'm really sorry for bringing you to Boney Creek. I should've told you before, but I have an ulterior motive for moving us here."

Huh? Her breath comes out fast. "What do you mean *ulterior motive*?"

Toby closes his eyes and grips her hands like Walter just did in the store. She waits.

"I'm here to find the man who killed my father."

Chapter Fourteen

Addie frowns, has to take a moment to make sure she heard right.

"Toby, what are you talking about? Your father took his own life. I don't understand."

"Yes, he did. I mean . . ." He pulls away his hands from hers and runs one of them through his hair. "I knew I'd say it all wrong. Let me start at the beginning."

Addie nods. *Yeah, an affair would've been easier than this.* "That might be best, because right now you've lost me."

Toby gets up. He thumps one of his boots on the dusty shed floor.

"Pins and needles?"

"Yeah."

Toby looks at her, and they both smile, the solemn mood broken for the moment. He punches his leg a couple of times and then begins to pace, sidestepping the newspapers scattered everywhere.

"Just let me get this out, okay? I promise I'll answer any questions you have, but if I don't explain this properly, I'll explode." He gives her a pained look.

"Just tell me. I won't interrupt." She shakes her head. "Okay, I'll *try* and not interrupt."

"Good enough. And thank you. You're going to hate me after I tell you, just a heads-up." It's an attempt at humor, but she knows he also means it.

"How about you just spill it first and I'll decide who's hating who." She thinks about her secret and how he would do more than hate her if she was spilling her own guts right now.

"So back in the late seventies and eighties, Boney Creek used to be a major thoroughfare town. It was the last stop for hours before going on to the poor excuse of a highway they had back then. Today, of course, they've built a real honest-to-goodness highway and Boney Creek got sidelined to just being an exit on that highway—which now no one has any reason to get off for."

Addie nods. Knowing he has to have a point in telling her this.

"With Boney Creek being a hot spot back in the day, there was a lot of traffic, a lot of work in the town, and because it was all the rage back then: hitchhikers." He stops pacing and asks, "You see where I'm going with this?"

Addie runs through the archives in her brain. She feels like she knows this story but can't quite get there. "No. Not yet. Keep going."

"For about a decade or so, there were a number of disappearances and strange deaths that occurred around this town."

Addie gasps. "Just like now."

"Maybe. Probably." Toby keeps pacing. "It was different back then, though. Back then everyone knew there was a killer among them. A predator who was picking up drifters or overseas backpackers who wouldn't have anyone looking for them in a hurry. I think it took around seven missing or dead for it to even make it to the mainstream media."

"Seven? Just like now," she says again. "A serial killer?"

Toby stops and wags his finger by his ear. "That's the theory, yes."

"So did they catch him?"

"No. There were some suspects and an investigation, but no one was arrested. Then, in the nineties, the new highway was built, and the old highway—the 'Highway of Horror' as it was called—stopped being a predator's playground. And Boney Creek became a victim instead, slowly dying. Becoming a ghost town. A shell of its former glory."

Addie finds the right file in her archive all of a sudden. "The Highway Reaper. That's what they called him. I remember this now."

"That's him," Toby spits out.

Addie tries to connect the puzzle pieces but still struggles. "I don't understand—what has this got to do with your father? He died before I met you."

A sadness washes over his face. "Yeah, I was twelve."

"So are you saying this reaper serial-killer guy murdered your dad? Toby, that's awful." Addie goes to stand, but he waves her back down.

"No, don't get up. Not yet. I need to finish. Tell you everything."

She nods and sits back down. Her hunger long gone.

"It wasn't my dad but my uncle. This reaper dickhead killed my uncle. His name's Steve. Steven Clarkson."

"You've never mentioned him before. Why didn't you tell me this?"

Toby looks down at the newspapers. Addie follows Toby's eyes to the articles beside her. She knows why. And he's not wrong.

"You think I would've done a story on it."

Toby looks at her like *come on, babe.*

"You're right. I might have." She sees him wait for more. "I definitely would have."

"You were like a dog trying to find a bone back in the city. We both know you would've done anything to get that byline. With this story, you had exactly what every journalist covets."

"Access," she whispers. She wishes it weren't true, but he's right. She would've jumped on this story and not looked back. Even now her mind is trying to work the angle, connect the past and the present into a major scoop.

"You're doing it now, aren't you? I can see it in your eyes. That twinkle you get. It's like someone about to become possessed." He rubs the bridge of his nose. "This isn't a story, Addie. It's my life."

Addie is about to apologize but stops. "I see what you're doing. You're twisting this and getting ahead of it before I blame you and realize why you've brought me here. To this creepy town and all its bizarre deaths. I still don't understand what the hell we are doing here and what this has to do with your father."

"My father *and* my mother, actually." He's pensive again. "When my uncle was killed, it ruined my dad. He came up here to Boney Creek often. *Hunting*, he called it. Did it for years, I even came with him a couple of times—although I just thought it was a father-and-son road trip."

"You've been here before? No wonder you seemed to know so much. What the hell, Toby?"

"I know. I know. I should've said something before now." He looks like he might be sick. "I thought I could do this without telling you. You'd already been through enough."

Addie doesn't want to have *that* discussion right now. Not with this new bombshell.

"You mentioned this reaper guy was never caught . . ." Addie keeps her tone neutral even if she's filing everything away in the archive in her brain. She knows she is. She can't help it.

"That's right, no one was even charged. But it didn't stop Dad from looking. Doing his own investigation. He said the best way to get information was to be one of them. Infiltrate the town and not be looked at like a stranger."

"How'd he do that?"

"He was the general store's accountant back then. Mary and her husband, Frank, hired him."

Chapter Fifteen

Addie's mental filing cabinet threatens to burst with all this new information.

"So what you're telling me is you've been to this town before, and not only that, your father did *business* here? I can't believe you didn't tell me any of this."

No wonder Mildred recognized him.

Toby squats down in front of her. "I should've told you. I've wanted to so many times and just didn't know where to start. If I told you, you wouldn't have come. You wouldn't have let me buy this place."

"Let *us* buy this place! Toby, you had no right to keep this from me. I thought we were coming here because of the break-in, because of everything we lost and how we couldn't live in that house anymore—that horrible city anymore. And instead you've brought me to where a serial killer has decided to resurface?" She pants, the heat and lack of water now catching up with her.

"That's my thinking, yes. It can't be a coincidence, babe—"

"Don't you *babe* me." Her tone is light, almost joking when it was supposed to come out angry. *I must be in shock,* she thinks.

He moves on quickly, clearly wanting to get it all out. "It can't be a coincidence, Addie. Those disappearances and people dying around here all those decades ago, including my uncle, and now seven people dead within three months. He's back. I know he is."

Addie rubs her temples. It usually helps her think, but right now her mind is a jumble of too much information. "Come on, Toby. How old would this guy be? In his seventies? Eighties? And why now? Why the break in between?"

"See? You're already asking the right questions." Toby smiles. It's slow, considered.

Addie isn't going to fall for that. "Don't pretend like you meant to get my help all along with this. You kept this from me. You bought this place, why? To go 'hunting'"—she does quotation marks with her fingers—"like your dad tried to? Seriously?" The anger finally brews inside her.

"I don't know what I was thinking. I guess I wasn't. I knew we had to get out of the city, especially after everything with your job and the paper . . . and the baby."

Addie gulps. There it is. The real reason they are such a mess. The one thing they never talk about.

"I knew we needed a fresh start after that night . . . what we lost. You were a wreck, Addie, and I just wanted to make you happy again."

Addie frowns. "What am I missing? How on earth would coming here make me happy?"

"I knew how much your job meant to you, how getting your first big story was something you were always looking for. We couldn't have known that *we* would become that story. Look, it wasn't just a fresh start but a way to get you excited again about what you loved. When I saw what was happening up here, I guess I saw it as a sign." He falls from the squat to his knees. "I fucked up, didn't I?"

"This is beyond fucked up. None of this is okay." Addie picks up some of the old newspaper articles around her. "Is this why you've been out here, looking for clues as to what happened back then?"

Toby nods, sheepish in his body language. "I knew Mary kept articles from that time. Dad had seen them back when we visited. He had access to anything in a box. It was a different time back then, no emails or spreadsheets. Accounting had to be done manually—which gave him an excuse to come and pick up all their receipts and files in person. You know how it is."

"Do I? Why was Mary collecting all of this anyway?" Addie surveys the many boxes that are still to be opened.

"She was as obsessed as Dad. They would sit and gossip about what had happened in the town for hours while I played outside. I figured all this stuff would still be on-site somewhere." Toby looks around at the boxes. "Dad was right, the only way to really find out what's going on up here is to be one of the locals. I'm not good at this stuff, but you are. You know how to read people, ask the right questions."

Addie isn't sure whether to laugh or cry. If this were six months ago, she would have been here in a heartbeat, tracking down the story alongside her husband. But coming here, after what happened to them that night, is just cruel. Like a well-deserved slap in the face.

Only . . . he is right. Like always. As soon as she heard Clancy talking about those accidents possibly being connected, the first thing she wanted to do was write about it. It was one of the few times she has been excited since that horrible night.

Addie scans one of the articles, with the headline: Reaper Strikes Again. "I still don't understand. Your father killed himself."

"He did. That's true. But he left a note. Did I ever tell you that?" His sheepish look is back. He knows full well he's never mentioned a note. "He said he couldn't live with himself for not protecting his brother, for not bringing his killer to justice. For never finding his brother's body."

Addie looks up from the article. "They never found your uncle's body? So how do you know he's dead?"

"He was supposed to meet my dad at a country music festival the weekend he went missing. He called from here. From Boney Creek. Said he'd stay the night at the pub and hitch in the morning until he made it to the festival. Apparently no one saw or spoke to him again. His bank accounts were never touched after his last withdrawal from Boney Creek. He just vanished. And given there'd been other disappearances and two confirmed murders up here, it was a fair bet he'd been taken by that sick son of a bitch."

Addie's stomach rumbles. She looks down at it, almost surprised. *How can you be hungry at a time like this?*

Toby gets up and puts his hand out to her. "Maybe we should go in and make some dinner. I still need to finish off all that paperwork and get ready for tomorrow. Hopefully, we will have a smoother day."

She looks at his outstretched hand, confused. "So that's it? You dump all of that on me, and we just go on like everything is perfectly fine and you didn't just act like a total twat. One who forgot he has a wife who might need to be told about all of this."

Toby brings his hand to his side. "Look, I know I went about this all the wrong way, and I should've told you from the beginning, but I didn't. I can't change that now. Once I explain everything properly, you'll understand. You can even tell my family's story if we find out what happened to my uncle, do that blog thing you were talking about."

"Blog thing?" Addie places the article at her feet and stands in front of her husband. "I knew I had a bad feeling about this move, and now I know why."

He wraps his hand lightly around her wrist. "What can I say to make this up to you, to make this okay?"

She stares him straight in the eye. "That we are leaving and never coming back here."

Toby flinches like she's struck him. "I-I can't do that. You don't understand."

She pulls her wrist away. "Stop saying that I don't understand. The only reason I don't understand is because you haven't given me a chance to. There's a big difference. I am not here to chase ghosts. I left those behind in . . ." A sob escapes her. "In the city."

Toby dips his head. It's hard for him too. She knows that.

Still, there's no excuse. "Why did you bring us here after everything that's happened? After everything we went through? We came here to be safe. To start a new life—"

"A family," he murmurs.

Her stomach clenches. "You've screwed that up now. I can't trust you after this. It's too big for me to let slide."

Hypocrite.

Toby says something under his breath she doesn't quite catch.

"What did you say?"

He looks at her. His eyes red with tears. "I said, I promised."

Addie's heart drums hard in her ears. She doesn't like this. "Promised what? Promised *who*?"

"I promised my mom, before she died. I said I would find the man who killed my uncle, took my father's will to live, and broke her heart. That I would find the man who stole my family from me, and I would kill him."

Chapter Sixteen

Addie sits in the kitchen in the dark.

It's two in the morning, and Toby is asleep upstairs. Being able to sleep like the dead is his superpower. If only she could be so lucky. She tossed and turned next to him before finally giving in and making herself a cup of peppermint tea.

Gravy sits on a chair beside her. His paws tucked into the front of his body, his purrs soft as he sits and stares at her.

I know. I'd be staring at me too. I'm a hot mess.

Her brain won't be quiet. It's tugging her left and right, back and forth.

She was shocked when Toby said he would kill the man who destroyed his family, but he hadn't meant it. Not really. Toby wouldn't hurt anyone, even under duress. She knows that firsthand.

Her anger and shock still simmer, but she has no right to be upset at him. At least he was brave enough to tell her the truth of what has been consuming him. If only she could follow suit. It would free her just like it had seemingly freed Toby, his mood instantly light after he'd told her and his sleep currently without burden. Not like hers.

A pad and pen sit beside her. She has already made herself a list for the morning. Anything to feel like she is in control. Priority is getting the internet connected. So much of her list relies on it, and the data on her phone isn't sufficient. She has so many things to research, to investigate.

If she dives into that, then maybe she can feel at peace as well. Doubtful, but better than the alternative of telling Toby what she did.

Addie knows how to pull a story together, and if she just makes this feel like "work," then she can distract the voices in her head telling her to find somewhere else to live.

Get the hell out of here.

It's incessant and totally valid. Yet the journalist side of her wants to stay. Of course it does. Not only does she have the current deaths in Boney Creek to write about but the past ones too—one that includes her husband's family.

Like Toby said, access is everything in her world. You have the access, you have the superior story. It's like winning the lottery for her.

Get the hell out of here.

How can she? Toby won't leave, not now that he has set them up here. Not when everything back in the city is filled with hurt and shame. There is nothing back there for them, and she knows it.

Her husband uprooted their whole lives for a promise. A promise he was close to fulfilling, that he'd made his mother on her deathbed. He wasn't wrong; his mom did slowly die of a broken heart after the loss of her husband. Even her son couldn't save her from becoming a shell of herself before her heart finally gave out. That was a year ago, his mother only fifty-eight.

Addie sips her tea.

She flips the page on her pad and starts another list. This time a series of questions:

Are we in danger? *Unclear.*

Has the serial killer come back? If so, what triggered him? *Priority is finding out if the present deaths are accidents or murders. Then this will become clear.*

What is the connection between the past murders and the present deaths? *This is key. Establish if anything binds the two.*

What happened to Toby's uncle Steve? *Establish timeline and go through old articles.*

The past serial killer had opportunity and targeted strangers. But what's happening now feels personal. Why? *Start with present-day deaths. If they are all accidents, then this could be a coincidence. If they aren't, then the serial killer is back.*

Then we are in danger.

It's not a question.

She finishes her peppermint tea. The voices now quiet. Opening her laptop still on the table from when Toby was working on it, she clicks on a blank Word document.

Addie won't be going back to bed, because she knows now what she needs to do. And it all starts with the blog. Go slowly, learn what it takes to be a crime reporter, and prove her old editor wrong.

She'll do whatever it takes to get the story—she's done it before—and if that means supporting Toby and staying in this creepy-ass town, then that's the easy part. Because one day soon she'll be on the stand under oath, telling everyone what happened that night in their home. Toby will never forgive her unless she forgives him for what he did first. A welcome trump card.

Gravy's purring thrums in the otherwise quiet kitchen as she strokes him along his body.

"I guess we're staying then."

It's also not a question.

A TOWN CURSED?

First blog.

Posted by Addie Clarkson.

Boney Creek. Population 217. A last stop on the road to nowhere. Life is quiet here. Simple. Nothing ever happens, and that's just how folks like it. Well, that is until all those strange deaths started happening. Seven bodies in a matter of months. All accidents. No connection. Coincidences, surely.

One suicide, a gas-leak-turned-house-fire killing a family of four, an incident involving a horse, and a food choking.

A lot of deaths for a small town. A town without any lawmakers. Or a coroner. Not even a funeral home. There is a little cemetery, but it's getting a tad full. It's not time to panic. Not yet, anyway. But people sure are nervous. Edgy. Wondering who might be next.

I know all of this because I recently moved to Boney Creek, and these mysterious 'accidents' are not adding up.

Is this merely a town cursed, or is something else sinister going on?

In this blog, *A Town Cursed?*, I will set about to answer these very questions.

Stay tuned.

Addie Clarkson has a degree in journalism and now runs the general store in Boney Creek with her husband and an immovable cat called Gravy.

If you are passing through, mention this blog to get a two-for-one coffee deal.

Chapter Seventeen

DAY THREE

Addie calls about the internet as soon as their provider opens in the morning, and because everything is already on-site, the setup is straightforward and immediate.

She opens an account on a free blogging website and uploads the first blog she drafted the night before. Addie knows it's not her finest work and she still needs to figure out her voice for the blog, but for now, it's perfectly fine. Main thing is it's live and she's committed.

There's no turning back now.

Toby is skittish, waiting for more questions from her or for Addie to demand they leave—which never comes. She's lighter this morning, having made her decision to stay. To discover the truth and help her husband find his in the process. She is now knowingly banking her goodwill toward Toby for her literal day in court, and for the first time in a long time, the weight pressing down on her is slowly dissipating.

The fact that this story fell into her lap is not lost on her either. The old Addie would have gone to great lengths to get a scoop like this. No way was she losing the opportunity again.

Their second day of opening has gone smoother. No influx of locals demanding to be served. Just the two or three deliveries, including the mail. Addie already feels more confident in the running of the place now that Clancy has done such a good job of training them both.

Still no word from the post office representative, Gale, who was supposed to turn up and show them the ropes. Addie's doubtful she was ever coming after Clancy's warning.

Her first customer is Mildred. It's only seven thirty in the morning when she hobbles in on her cane. Her tight smile not giving much away. She asks for "that delicious coffee like yesterday," so Addie knows she's already breaking through her tough exterior.

She'll be calling her Mildred and not Ms. Whiteman in no time.

Toby is in front of the store with a guy from their fuel supplier and the local fix-it man, George, who also happens to be Clancy's father. They are making a plan on how to get the fuel lines back up and running.

Toby waves at her as she makes Mildred's coffee, the glass now clean so they can actually see clearly out of it. Addie waves back, feeling a sudden sense of calm and peace that she hasn't in some time.

"Have you been married long?"

Mildred's crackly voice breaks through Addie's reverie. She was sure she was in for the silent treatment again. "Just over three years now," Addie replies.

She pours the milk over Mildred's espresso shot, which already has two sugars mixed in. She makes sure there's the perfect amount of foam and then sprinkles chocolate powder on the top.

"What about you? Ever been married?" Addie knows Mildred isn't and hasn't been because Clancy already told her but doesn't want their nosy customer probing further into how she recognizes Toby.

"Good heavens, no. Thought about it for a blink of an eye, but that was a long time ago." Mildred has a hand on the counter to support herself, along with the cane.

"You know, I saw a small table and chair set in the shed and was thinking about placing them by the front windows. If I did, would you use them?" Addie hopes she isn't coming on too strong, but she has a feeling Mildred is lonely and that's why she keeps coming in.

And if Addie's going to get any intel on this town, past and present, Ms. Whiteman will be her best bet.

Mildred cocks her head a little, thinks about it, then says, "I think that's a lovely idea. It's a bit of a hike for me to walk here now with my bung hip, so a tiny reprieve would go down nicely."

Addie smiles to herself about the small win. She puts a lid on Mildred's cappuccino and hands it to her. "As soon as Toby is done with the fuel people, I'll get him to pull them out. Will you be back later? I take it you're not far from here."

"I'm your immediate neighbor on that side." Mildred points to the left of the shop and then hands over some coins for the purchase. "I'll be back if this coffee is still going."

Addie recognizes Mildred is using the coffee as an excuse for her company. She doesn't blame her; she would, too, if she had no one to talk to. "I made Walter a mocha last night, and he seemed to like it. Maybe I can make one for you when you come back this afternoon?"

Mildred frowns. "What was *he* doing here?"

Addie banks the inflection on *he*. There's a history there, and she'll draw it out of Mildred soon enough. Not yet, though. Too soon.

"Walter was here for the sponsorship money. For the fair," she adds, in case it's not common knowledge.

"That bloody fair," Mildred spits out. "Can't believe we are still running it after everything this town has lost these past few months."

Go slow, Addie thinks. Not wanting to spook the old woman with too many questions. "Yes, it does seem like the timing is a little off. What does the rest of the town think? About having the fair this year, I mean."

Ms. Whiteman blows into the hole in her lid. "No idea. I couldn't give a hoot about that blasted event. That was Mary's thing. I stayed clear away."

Addie finds that hard to believe somehow. Mildred seems like the kind of person who would be at the center of an event, not hibernating at home. "Forgive me. The way Walter was talking, he made it seem like a town affair. That everyone would be there and some even selling their goods."

Mildred looks behind her like someone's listening in, even though the shop is clearly empty. She leans in closer to Addie at the counter. "You know, I used to run the baked goods stall way back when. My pies were relished for miles around. Mary didn't hold a candle to my baking, even if she tried."

Another story there, Addie thinks. "So you don't bake for the fair anymore? I mean, without being disrespectful, Mary's not here anymore if it's something you'd consider doing again."

"That's true." Something passes over Mildred's face. Fatigue? Sadness? It's hard to tell. "You've given me something to think about, young lady."

Addie wants to laugh at being called young lady. She's twenty-nine, but it still sounds odd. Growing up without a mother and having to fend for yourself while living with your gran will do that.

"If you ever want someone to bake for the store, I'd be happy to. You've got to watch that oven, as it can burn the bottoms." Mildred glances into the back kitchen like she's sizing it up. "Money is always tight on the pension, especially when you have a little one to feed."

"Little one?"

"My dog, Betsy. Cute thing when he's not barking up a storm at anything that moves." Mildred places her purse under her arm and adjusts her coffee. "I best get back to him. He's getting cranky in his old age."

Sounds familiar.

"Are you going to be okay getting home? I can ask Toby if he's almost done or"—Addie glances at the clock—"Clancy will be here shortly."

"Ha! No thanks." Mildred scoffs. "That girl will talk my ear off if she walks me home."

Addie is surprised. How could anyone not like Clancy's company?

"Clancy seems like a good kid. She's been a godsend since we got here."

Addie kicks herself when she sees Mildred's open face close down into a scowl.

"It's not that girl who's the problem—it's her mother." Mildred clears her throat. "Everyone knows that woman is a witch. Some of it is bound to rub off on that girl, and when it does, I don't want to be the one having a nasty spell put on me."

Another throat clears behind Addie; this one sounds deliberate.

She spins around to Clancy standing in the door leading into the kitchenette. Addie didn't even hear her come in. Clearly neither did Mildred, or maybe she wanted to be overheard.

Clancy steps beside Addie. "I'll have you know, Ms. Whiteman, that the only spell I would cast on you is a love spell because we all deserve some of that in our lives."

Mildred huffs off without saying anything more, and Addie can't help but be impressed by Clancy's tact.

"Nicely played," she says. "I wouldn't have been so kind if someone called my mom a witch."

"That's okay. My mom *is* a kind of witch, to be honest—a good witch. So Ms. Whiteman isn't wrong." Clancy picks at something between her teeth. "Oh, and Mom asked if you could pop over later today when you can. She has something she wants to talk to you about."

Chapter Eighteen

The store has just closed for the night, and Addie takes the opportunity to walk to Clancy's house to visit her mother, wanting to get a sense of the town and its surroundings to their store. She carries a bottle of wine, which she can't wait to open. It's a good fifteen minutes to get there, but it's a straight hike along the main street, which used to be the old thoroughfare back when the Highway Reaper stalked the town.

Addie has yet to do a deep dive on all Mary's boxes, which Toby has been so immersed in, but she'll get there. Her priority is seeking the truth about what has been happening in the previous three months in Boney Creek, to see if there is a connection between past and present events.

What she is finding is that the locals love a good chat when they come into the store, especially about its previous owner, Mary, and the day she died. Like how Clancy's mom, a nurse, had tried to resuscitate the old lady to no avail. Or how Mary had been eating a bowl of bran swimming in milk that morning—Mildred offering up that tidbit.

There's almost a morbid fascination with everything that has been happening around town. Addie is banking it all and plans to write a blog post on Mary Peterson next.

The setting sun is still warm on her face as she walks along a footpath that has seen better days. A small dog yaps as she passes Mildred's place directly beside the store. Otherwise the old weatherboard house is quiet.

She crosses the road completely barren of any people or traffic. Anyone passing through would think the town was uninhabited. Toby was right about very few houses actually being in the center of town. Apart from the closed coffee shop, the general store, and Mildred's place, Addie can't see much ahead of her, except for the top of the church steeple peeping through some trees. Clancy told her their house is just next door to the church, so at least Addie has a destination point.

She's curious about the woman who raised Clancy, and even more so about Mildred calling her a witch. She has a vision in her mind of what a good witch looks like, and it's a combination of Glinda from *Wicked* and Sandra Bullock from *Practical Magic*.

Addie had never thought much about supernatural stuff before her grandmother died, but now she's more open to it, often feeling like her gran's presence still lingers—or maybe hoping it does.

As Addie reaches Clancy's place, her back is sticky with sweat and her face surely flushed pink. She walks up the stone path, admiring all the flowers and colors in the front yard. How it's possible to have such a beautiful garden in this heat is beyond her.

Witchcraft? Doubtful but impressive, nonetheless.

The tinkling of the wind chime is calming, though, and the yellow chairs and small table on the veranda are inviting.

The cottage is quaint and painted a navy blue that has faded with time. The door is bloodred and has a yellow star-shaped knocker on it, matching the table and chairs. Addie shifts the wine in her arms and goes to use the handle of the knocker when the door opens.

A woman with pale skin, long brown hair flecked with grey, and a blue flowing dress gives her a big smile. It's the spitting image of Clancy's. She's more Stockard Channing in *Practical Magic* than Sandra Bullock, but Addie isn't far off in her visualization.

"Hello," Addie says. "You must be Clancy's mom."

She nods. "Beatrix. It's nice to meet you finally. Clancy hasn't stopped talking about you since you arrived. I hope she hasn't been a bother."

"Bother? No. Lifesaver more like."

"That's my girl." Beatrix waves Addie in. "I was told when she hit puberty to expect a moody teen who would live in her room and hate me, but Clancy didn't get that memo."

They walk up a narrow hall with wooden floorboards and walls covered in bright paintings and framed photos. It's a lot to take in, and Addie's not sure where to look.

They pass various rooms until entering a sunlit kitchen area filled with plants in bright painted pots. Addie instantly feels at home here.

"This is for you." She hands Beatrix the wine. "Just a little thank-you for loaning me your daughter so much. She really has been a godsend. I don't know what I'll do when she goes back to school."

Beatrix takes the wine and places it on a round wooden table with four chairs in the center of the room. "I made us tea. But we can open this if you prefer."

"No, tea is great." She'd prefer the wine. "Your house is lovely."

"Thank you. It's home, and everything I love lives within these walls." Beatrix moves to the counter where she has a tray with a teapot and two mugs set up and brings it back to the round table.

Addie sits down as Beatrix pours the tea. She must've seen her walking up the road because the tea is brewed but still hot.

Addie takes a sip, and a burst of mint fills her mouth. "Oh, wow. This is delicious." She doesn't mean to act so surprised, but she is. Tea is not usually her go-to drink at this time of the evening.

"It's mint from my garden. Spearmint as well. A touch of lavender for relaxation and honey because we could all be a little sweeter."

Addie nods and takes another sip. "I'd happily buy this if you make more."

Beatrix sits across from Addie. "I actually will be selling some of this at Boney Creek's fair. I make soaps and lotions as well. You are welcome to anything whenever you like. No charge."

Beatrix's voice is as soothing as her tea, and Addie could listen to it all day. Her face is open and inviting. Small laugh lines are visible as Beatrix talks and smiles, but otherwise Addie couldn't guess the age of Clancy's mother.

"You should sell your stuff at the store. It'd be nice to have some locally made items. And anything that helped the store smell nicer, I wouldn't say no to." Addie knows she's rambling, not sure why she's so keen to make a good impression.

Beatrix smiles briefly and sips her own tea. Addie thought she'd jump at the chance to sell her goods but can see there's something there.

Hurried footsteps crunch along the rear of the house, and a shadow passes by the window before coming through the open back door.

Clancy huffs and bends over, her hands on her knees. "You beat me! Damn. How long have you been here? What have I missed?"

"Take a breath, my love. Addie only just got here." Beatrix stands to get another mug. "I'll pour you some tea."

Clancy smells her mom's mug with the tea in it. She wrinkles her nose. "Gross. You know I can't stand the one with lavender in it. I'll just have some water. Or we could open this wine."

Clancy picks up the bottle Addie brought and holds it up questioningly at her mother.

"You know my answer to that without even being a psychic," Beatrix says good humoredly.

Clancy snaps her fingers. "Did you work out Addie's star sign yet? I guessed it right out of the gate, not even a couple of minutes from meeting her."

Oh shit, Addie thinks.

Beatrix takes her time, reading the room, it seems. "I can't say I have worked that out yet. Addie hasn't been here for long enough."

"Ha!" Clancy is excited. "I can't believe you didn't get it, Mom. You must be slipping. She's obviously an Aries."

"Obviously." Beatrix glances at Addie, her face unreadable.

"Are you going to do a reading for her? I bet she'd love it." Clancy joins them at the table, waiting for her mother's response.

Beatrix pours Clancy a glass of water and places it in front of her. Her movements controlled, steady. Not matching her daughter's energy in the slightest. "Don't you have somewhere to be, my love. I'm sure Addie would like to enjoy her tea in peace."

"You *know* I have nowhere to be. I promise I'll be quiet if you let me hang with you both." Clancy mimes zipping her mouth shut.

"Don't promise something you have no intention of keeping." Beatrix sips her tea, a slightly impatient tone to her voice now.

Addie changes the subject. "I was just telling your mom how amazing you've been at the store since we arrived. I don't think we've seen you in there since we opened, have we?"

Beatrix blinks furiously at the question addressed to her.

Clancy answers for her, "She doesn't like coming up there anymore. Do you, Mom?"

"True." Beatrix nods, tugging at the skin on the base of her throat. "Mary was a friend, and it is a little painful for me, if I'm honest."

Addie shifts in her chair, deciding for another subject change. "Clancy, what did you mean before by *doing a reading for me*?"

"OMG!" The letters practically burst out of Clancy. "Mom does tarot readings. She also has angel cards, but I like tarot the best. Have you never had a reading? You have to have one—they're the best. Mom will be able to predict your future and can even tell you what happened in the past. I'll go get them—"

Beatrix puts her hand on Clancy's arm before she can get up. "That's enough. I have not prepared for any readings today. Besides, look at our poor guest—you are overwhelming her."

Addie obviously isn't hiding her thoughts very well. The idea of Beatrix knowing both her past *and* her future scares the shit out of her.

"Wait." Clancy stands, then rushes down the hall as she calls out, "I totally know what we'll do instead. But you're going to need the wine for this."

"Forgive my daughter," Beatrix says warmly. "She can get hyperactive around company sometimes. She also doesn't have the patience of a Taurus—not like you."

Addie gasps as Beatrix smiles.

Chapter Nineteen

Clancy is back before Addie can ask how Beatrix knew her star sign was Taurus. In her hands is a game of some kind. Clancy shifts their mugs out of the way and places it onto the table.

It's a Ouija board.

"Clancy, no. I told you to put that thing back in the shed." Beatrix is clearly upset, as her voice is now firm and direct.

"Mom, don't stress. It never works anyway. I thought it'd be fun while Addie was here. We're trying to find out what happened to everyone who died recently in this town, and for once maybe it'll give us some answers." Clancy pulls out a flat piece of wood shaped like a triangle with a hole in it and places it on the board. Addie knows it has a name but can't remember what it is.

Beatrix picks it straight back up. "I said no. This isn't a plaything you bring out like show-and-tell. I asked you to put this in the shed. Why is it still in the house?"

"I—" Clancy scratches her head, suddenly awkward. "I wanted to talk with Kip. I miss him."

Addie feels a tug at her heart, and Beatrix must, too, because she softens her tone. "My love, I know you miss him, but this isn't the way. No good comes from things you don't understand. I thought I taught you that."

"You did," Clancy mumbles. "Sorry."

"It's okay, but I need you to put this in the shed like I asked you. If I see it again, I'll have to burn it." Beatrix gently places the piece of wood on top of the board. "Understand?"

"I understand." Clancy puts the wood back in her pocket. "I don't get what the big deal is. It never does anything anyway. Kip hasn't talked to me once."

"Kip is here all the time. You just need to listen—only not with this. If you really want to talk to him, we'll do it the right way."

"For real? That'd be awesome." Clancy hugs her mom from behind.

Addie can't control the visible shiver she has. *What do they mean they'll talk to Kip? What right way?* Suddenly the tea isn't strong enough.

"Now go and put that in the shed. Lock it in the old chest." Beatrix puts her hand down the front of her dress and pulls up a long chain with a key on the end. "Use this, then bring it right back."

Clancy grabs the key like a child being handed an ice cream and runs out the back door, carrying the Ouija board under one arm.

"Forgive me. That was a lot to take in. I hope we haven't scared you off." Beatrix moves to fill up the kettle. "I'll make us some fresh tea."

"No need to apologize. I miss having Clancy's energy. Life seems to sap it out of you." Addie finishes off the remainder of what she has in her mug. Normally she'd be craving the wine, but the tea seems to be exactly what she needs.

Beatrix lights the gas stove and returns to the table. "I worry for her sometimes, especially now Kip has gone. She needs to hang out more with kids her own age, but it's hard when you live in a small town."

"I didn't have a lot of friends, either, when I was growing up," Addie says. "My gran raised me after my mom abandoned me, and I was so petrified she was going to leave, too, that I made myself useful. Instead of inviting friends over, I'd do chores, run errands, anything to feel wanted. Maturity can be overrated when it's required of you too early."

Beatrix studies Addie as if she's searching for something, then says, "You know, Clancy hasn't been doing so well since Kip's death. That was, until you got here. I've noticed a big change in her, and I wanted to thank you for that. It's why I asked you over today."

Addie shifts in her seat again. She knows there's a *but* coming.

"She's been through a lot, and there's been times I was worried she wouldn't get through this . . ." Beatrix now stares at her hands, which are clenched together.

But.

"But . . ."

There it is. The real reason Addie's been invited today soon to be revealed.

"Clancy is impressionable, and this new blog you've started has gotten her thinking things that are not true." Beatrix looks Addie in the eye.

"She showed you the blog already?" Addie hasn't checked the views yet, but she did let Clancy know she had posted something.

"We have no secrets in this house." There's a visible shift in Beatrix's eyes, and Addie knows she's lying.

Everyone has secrets, she thinks.

"Go on." Addie returns Beatrix's gaze. "You'll need to be a bit more specific on why Clancy is thinking things that are not true."

"For one, you've got my daughter saying there's a killer in this town, and it's an unhealthy obsession to have. I appreciate it is a welcome distraction after Kip's passing, and I *am* happy for the change in her, but I'd prefer this wasn't her new preoccupation."

The kettle boils, sending a shrill whistle through the kitchen. Beatrix sighs and gets up to turn it off.

Addie takes her time with her words, not wanting to say the wrong thing. Beatrix could be her ally if she doesn't mess this up. And an ally is exactly what she needs in this small community of souls.

"Beatrix, I appreciate what you're saying, and the last thing I want to do is cause any more harm to Clancy's well-being. I think it's important for you to know it was Clancy who first expressed the idea of the deaths around here being more than accidents. She is sure that Kip's death was deliberate."

She holds her breath and waits for Beatrix to respond. Any initial reaction is lost, given her back is to Addie as she fills up the teapot with fresh tea leaves and boiling water.

Beatrix takes her time. Maybe composing her words as she sits back at the table sans teapot.

Addie tries again. "I followed up—"

"It's okay. You don't need to explain." Beatrix puts out her hand and places it softly on top of Addie's. "I already know what Clancy thinks about Kip's death, and she would be wise to keep that mouth of hers shut from time to time. It'll get her in trouble one day."

The weight of Beatrix's hand is heavy and hot on top of her own. "Are you saying you don't believe her? That you think everything going on around here is just one big coincidence? A series of unfortunate accidents?"

Beatrix pulls away her hand and rubs the corner of her eye. "I'm going to tell you something now, and I want you to keep an open mind. Can you do that?"

Addie swallows.

Then nods.

Chapter Twenty

Beatrix gets up and brings the teapot back to the table. Addie waits silently, patiently as her host pours fresh tea into their mugs. Her heart races at whatever Beatrix is going to say. This might be the lead she's looking for, and she hasn't even done anything to earn it.

Beatrix watches her carefully as she seemingly chooses her words. "I read some of your old newspaper articles."

Addie almost spits out her tea. That wasn't what she was expecting. "Um, okay. What made you do that?"

"I needed to know a little bit more on who my daughter was spending her time with and who she seems . . . so taken by." Beatrix's voice is calm and steady, but Addie can sense there's something more.

She doesn't blame Clancy's mom. Addie is a stranger. She'd be cautious too.

"Your writing is good. The subject matter was average, but I imagine with the right piece, you have a real gift waiting to be discovered." Beatrix's eyes never leave Addie's face, even when she sips her hot tea.

It's unsettling, and she isn't sure why. "Thanks, I guess. I'm not really sure I understand where you are going with this."

"I was trying to work out why you're here in Boney Creek. Right now." She tugs at the base of her throat again, like it's a nervous tic. "Then Clancy showed me the blog you plan to write, and I understood. We are a story to you. This town has always intrigued the media, and why would you be any different."

Beatrix would make a good journalist of her own, the way she's drilling down on her. Addie contemplates sidestepping the conversation but thinks better of it. She's sure Beatrix would see through her.

"I didn't plan on starting a blog until I got here, actually, and it was my husband's idea for us to come to Boney Creek. We'd had a bad experience back in the city, and well, it led us here." Addie isn't planning on giving away Toby's real reason for being here.

Beatrix nods. "I read the articles on what happened to you and your husband, and I'm sorry. I really can't imagine; it must have been terrifying. To have them target you like that and in your own home."

Addie is uneasy; there's something in Beatrix's unwavering gaze and direct tone she doesn't like.

"This is where I need you to keep an open mind," Beatrix continues. "Is it okay if I hold your wedding ring?"

Again, Addie is taken aback. Beatrix doesn't give anything away and is impossible to read, so she has to presume it's a serious question. "Can I ask why?"

Beatrix smiles, her face softening. "How about you humor me."

It's not a question.

Addie flicks her eyes to the wine on the bench and wonders if it would be impolite to open it after all. Things are starting to get weird. Like they weren't already weird enough in this town. She has nothing to lose and is genuinely curious.

"Sure, why the hell not." Addie pulls off her ring and says, "You've got my interest well and truly piqued."

Beatrix takes her ring and places it in the palm of her right hand, then places the palm of her left hand on top. She closes her eyes.

Addie wants to laugh. Open the wine or laugh. She can't decide.

Keeping her eyes closed, Beatrix monotones, "This wasn't your ring originally. It was given to you as . . . hmm. I want to say a hand-me-down, but that would be slightly odd for a wedding ring to be given while the wearer was still alive."

Addie almost falls off her chair. *How could Beatrix know that?* Toby's mother gave him the ring before they got married, saying she wanted a piece of her own marriage to live on, given her husband wasn't alive anymore.

Beatrix is staring at her, the ring still covered in her hands. "You don't have to tell me, as long as you understand its meaning and what I am picking up."

"Picking up?" Addie's stomach drops. *What is going on here?*

Beatrix closes her eyes again and frowns. "I can see why you do not want to be in that house anymore. It has a blackness over it. There's something red. A red handle of some kind?" It is like she is asking herself the questions and not Addie.

Addie wants to scream. There's no way she could know about the weapon with the red handle the intruders used. No way. There's nothing online about that crucial piece of evidence. The police never gave that out publicly.

"Can you tell me the importance of the red handle, Addie?" Beatrix blinks at her.

"I-I . . . how do you know about that?" Addie can barely breathe.

"I don't understand what its meaning is, just that it's important. All I can see is: red handle, red handle, red handle. Wait, there's something else that's red. Blood?" Beatrix opens her eyes like she knows she's right. "I'm so sorry, Addie. That must have been so hard to lose your unborn child."

A tear falls down Addie's face without her consent. She brushes it away with the back of her hand. "You can't know that. It's impossible."

Only Addie knew she was pregnant that night. Toby didn't know until she'd lost it; she'd been planning to tell him, but the break-in came first. Maybe Mildred saying Beatrix is a witch is true.

No. It's impossible. *Yet . . .*

"It's okay, Addie. Let it out. You're in a safe place here." Beatrix's voice is calm, inviting her to be free of this secret. Then she frowns again. Gasps. "Oh—oh, I see. You knew—"

Addie cuts her off. "Can I have my ring, please? I don't know what this is, but I'm not into it."

Beatrix hands the ring back without hesitation. "I had to be sure."

"Sure about what?" Addie slides the ring onto her finger, but it doesn't bring her comfort, more like it's betrayed her.

"I had to be sure your intentions for coming to this town were real." Beatrix shakes her hands loose.

"Why wouldn't they be real?" Addie knows she should leave before exposing herself and Toby any further, but her curiosity for the truth is always stronger.

"People do strange things when they are given no other choice." Beatrix's calm resolve is getting under Addie's skin. "It doesn't always have to make sense."

She sighs. Going all in. She'll need Beatrix's information about this town soon enough, and the trading of information is important in building up trust. "Three youths broke into our house while we should have been sleeping. Only I was awake and disturbed them. I was pushed into a wall, and it woke Toby up. He came downstairs and was attacked. A cut to his upper arm and leg. Nothing serious, but there was a lot of blood. They stole our wallets, a computer, and our car. They were drunk, it seems, and ended up driving into a pole. Two died, and one escaped and was hospitalized. The whole car went up in flames."

Beatrix nods like she already knows this.

"There had been a few other break-ins to steal cars in other neighborhoods, which my paper had started reporting on, but I never thought it would happen to us. It was my fault for getting up and seeing what the noise was. If I'd just stayed upstairs and left them to it, it would've been a simple insurance claim and a bit of a scare. Nothing more."

Addie's phone sounds with a text message. It's Toby asking if she's coming back for dinner.

"And you blame yourself." Again, it's not a question. Beatrix reaches out her hand, but Addie pulls hers away. She doesn't need any more of this psychic bullshit.

"You blame yourself," Beatrix repeats, this time bringing home it is definitely not a question.

Addie decides to give Beatrix part of the truth to stop this nonsense. "Of course I blame myself. I was the one who came downstairs to investigate like some bloody hero. I caused them to attack me, then Toby when he came down soon after. They could've killed us, nearly did. Why wouldn't I blame myself?" Addie twists on her chair and parts the back of her hair, showing Beatrix a fresh scar.

"I'm sorry. That must've been very traumatic. I can see why you would want to escape the city after everything that happened." Beatrix's face is soft, but her eyes bore into Addie's like there's something she isn't saying. "Sometimes we have to live with the things we've done, even if we try and run from them."

She knows.

"I should go. Thank you for the tea." Addie picks up her phone and stands, her stomach queasy. "It was really nice to meet you, Beatrix."

"You too." Beatrix also stands and looks into her eyes, then down at Addie's trembling hands.

Yep, she knows. That bloody ring.

A TOWN CURSED?

The Death of Mary Peterson
Second blog.

Posted by Addie Clarkson.

It's around four thirty in the morning. The sun is sleeping, and the birds are stirring.

The town of Boney Creek is quiet, still. Save for one bustling kitchen filled with sixties tunes and a warming oven.

Mary Peterson (81) has already had her morning cup of tea and is preparing a batch of brownies for her customers that day. Mary owns and operates the town's general store and has done so for forty-five years.

It's her favorite time of day, according to locals. When she feels most alive.

Except today will be different.

Today is when she will meet her untimely death.

It will involve a bowl of bran swimming in milk. One spoonful is all it took for Mary's life to end. With no one there to save her, she choked on the tasteless mass that clogged her throat and, with it, her last breath.

If the store had been open, someone may have been quick enough to help her. Most people know about the Heimlich maneuver from watching TV or social media—even if they've never had to use it before.

But Mary's fate was sealed that day when her spoonful of bran went down the wrong way and stopped her breathing forever.

Mary hadn't given up without a fight though, attempting to dislodge the food from her throat by driving her stomach into objects around her kitchen—the bruises telling the story of her desperate effort to save her own life by performing the self-Heimlich techniques.

She was found on the floor and was unable to be resuscitated by a town resident, who happened to be a nurse. Her cat, Gravy, was sitting nearby, Mary's last ever batch of brownies never making it into the oven.

While there is nothing strange or unusual about Mary's final minutes—an accident, obviously. It *is* curious that Mary is (hopefully) the last in a line of seven mysterious deaths in the small town of Boney Creek.

In isolation no one would think anything of an old woman's passing. Yet when it's combined with several other "accidents," it does seem odd.

Especially because the town of Boney Creek doesn't have a lot of residents to begin with. 217 to be exact. No, make that 210. No, make that 212. The town lost seven and gained two. My husband and me. We bought Mary's store soon after she passed.

Some of the locals miss Mary deeply. Some are quick to tell me of her sharp tongue and the long line of townsfolk with a grudge to bear against her.

She could be someone's biggest ally, standing up for anyone who needed it. But in the same breath, she could also be their greatest enemy—making sure to bring everyone over to her side.

Regardless, Mary was a pillar of this town. One of its oldest residents, who had surely earned whatever judgment came her way. She got up early to bake for this town and seemed to love doing so, having a *bake it and they'll come* philosophy, according to her only son, Gary.

I wake up early every day now too. Not to bake but because my sleep is scattered and sparse. It's like someone or something is keeping me awake since our move. A heaviness that presses on my body or a silent breath that makes me wonder what is there beyond my husband, who lies beside me.

No longer do I sleep like the dead. Now, instead, I listen for them. Waiting for them to tell me their secrets. The town's secrets. Because surely seven deaths in a matter of months is no coincidence.

And maybe, if I listen long enough, I will hear what they have to say. Maybe they will tell me my lack of sleep is for nothing. A grasping at straws if you will. Looking for something that is not there.

Or maybe these are not all accidents but something dark and evil that has settled over this town. A curse? Or something more simply explained—like evil in human form.

What's worse? I wonder.

Either way, I have no idea if I am in any danger or if the danger lies in my consuming thoughts and ridiculous presumptions. Or maybe it will be Mary who comes to me early one morning as I sit at the same table where she died. Her house is now my house. Her life is now slowly becoming my own.

My morning cup of coffee warming my hands as the sun slowly wakes, along with it the birds and their chatter. I keep the kitchen quiet. No sixties tunes for me. Because I am waiting. Listening. Sure that if I am patient, Mary will come to me and whisper, "I know what you seek, and if you listen, I will tell you."

So far she has not come to tell me her and the town's secrets.

Maybe I need to discover them for myself. The question is: What will I find when I do?

Because while there hasn't been a death since Mary's, the town is on high alert. No one knowing if the curse has passed or if a killer is still unsatisfied and walks among them.

Us.

Addie Clarkson has a degree in journalism and now runs the general store in Boney Creek with her husband and a wandering cat called Gravy.

If you are passing through, mention this blog to get a two-for-one coffee deal.

COMMENTS:

UserBC217: If you are really interested in the truth, maybe you should look at all the deaths that happened around here in the eighties. There's your coincidence. It sure looks like our resident serial killer is back.

Chapter Twenty-One

It's on the sideboard in the entry hall.

The red handle is as clear as day. It's like a beacon begging for someone to pick it up and use it.

You? No.

Them? Yes.

There's that smell. *Death.*

It's been days now. Days of decay.

One foot in front of another. Deep breaths.

No, not deep breaths, the smell is too much.

Too much.

The bedroom is three steps away. Just push the door open. Look inside. Be sure.

The doorknob is old. Brass. There's a discolored spot where it's been worn away with time. Turn it. Twist it.

Take a look.

Be quick. Be sure.

The smell. It's corroding everything. Everything.

Turn it. Twist it. The door opens. Eyes water. Vomit flies.

She's dead.

Dead.

The phone's ringing. Trilling. Screaming?

Ringing.

The phone's ringing.

The phone's ringing.

Addie forces her eyes open. Her brain still part in dream, part in reality. The phone rings below them.

She shakes Toby, but he is sleeping like the dead. There is no waking him.

Addie swings out of bed, a heaviness on her as she tries to remember what she was dreaming about. Whatever it was, her heart is still booming deep inside her.

Or maybe it's because of the phone drilling into her brain with how loud it is.

"Okay, okay. I'm coming," she grumbles, using her phone flashlight as she heads downstairs.

She rubs the sleep out of her eyes as she picks up the old phone on the wall. "Yes, hello?"

She waits, but there's no answer.

"Hello? Is anyone there? I can't hear you." She stares at the earpiece, wondering if maybe it's not working properly. How old is this phone anyway?

She frowns and presses her finger to cover the other ear from external noise. There's something on the other end.

Wind? Breathing?

"Listen, if this is your idea of a joke, it's not funny. It's"—Addie looks at her cell phone screen—"it's three o'clock in the morning, for crying out loud."

The line goes dead, and she's left with the pounding of her heart in her ears.

"Fuckers," she whispers as she hangs up.

There's enough illumination in the kitchen without her phone light, so she gets herself a glass of water. Her hand trembles as she turns on the tap and puts a glass underneath it.

Mildred's dog is barking next door. Betsy. He barks at anything that moves, the old lady said. There must be someone close by.

Is it them? No. Two are dead and one in the hospital.

Has he been released? She doesn't know.

Does he know where they are? No.

Yes. The blog is now like a pin on a map. A welcome mat saying **IMPULSIVE JOURNALIST LIVES HERE.**

When will I learn? Never.

The tap runs. The glass overflows with water in her hands. Addie stands frozen.

It's pitch black outside through the window. She couldn't see anyone even if they were standing right there. Watching her.

She looks toward the back door. Knows it's secure. They don't go to bed without locking everything up. Not after what happened.

Only . . .

It's ajar.

The door is open.

She screams.

Chapter Twenty-Two

DAY FOUR

Addie sits with a cold cup of coffee in front of her, leaning her elbows on the table, her hands in her hair. She feels like she's been hit by a shovel. Multiple times. All over her body.

Toby hovers, checking in every five minutes, asking if she's okay. Of course she's not okay. A strange phone call at three o'clock in the morning and then seeing the back door ajar. It was like reliving their trauma all over again.

Toby has apologized multiple times for not locking the door properly after letting the cat out before he went to bed. She wants to believe him, but part of her wonders if he's lying to make her feel better. Toby would never leave the back door open, even if they now live in the middle of nowhere.

She's checked the lock herself, and nothing seems to have been tampered with or obviously damaged. Still, it's a reminder to get the locks changed, given they have no idea who has, or has had, keys to the store.

She opens up her phone to look for a local locksmith and sees there's a notification for a new comment on the blog she posted after returning from Beatrix's last night. At least she won't have to worry about Beatrix coming into the store and having those piercing eyes looking right through her. One small mercy.

"Check out this comment someone posted on my blog last night." Addie points at the phone screen. The blog has already had twenty views. Not great, but a start.

Coffee in hand, Toby reads over her shoulder. "Interesting. So it looks like I'm not the only one around here making that connection between the past and the present. Any idea on who made the comment?"

"BC217 could be anyone. But it looks like it might be a local," Addie muses, taking a bite out of the toast Toby made her earlier.

"How so?"

"*BC* might stand for *Boney Creek*. And *217* is the population before the deaths started happening. Although, it could be someone throwing me off and making me think it's a local." Addie gets up, puts her plate in the sink, and forces the last of her toast down.

Toby takes her place in the seat, studying the phone with the blog post on it. "Still, it's interesting someone has said this publicly. Should we reply and see if we can get some more information?"

Addie pours her coffee down the sink. "Maybe. Do you mind if I think on it first? I don't want to be too hasty." *After last night,* she wants to add, but doesn't.

"Of course." Toby narrows his eyes at her. "What's going on? Why does it look like you're in a hurry to go somewhere?"

"That's because I am. I want to head up to the church and see Walter before we open. Will you be okay if I'm not back in time?"

Toby glances at the clock on the wall. "A little early for house visits, isn't it? And why the rush to visit him? I think you should be resting today—you must be exhausted after last night."

"I'd like the distraction, honestly. And there's no rush. I just noticed that the sponsorship money came back into our account, saying the details were wrong. I wanted to sort it out. Walter responded to my text this morning, so I know he's up and awake."

"You don't fool me, babe." Toby sighs. "Just say you're going up there to pick his brains about this town and all its deaths."

"You got me. I'm not exactly subtle about it, am I?"

"Not in the slightest. Maybe get that game face of yours on. Nobody stands a chance when you are in the zone." Toby chuckles.

Except for Beatrix, she thinks.

"I'll do my best, even if I'm a little rusty." Her heart isn't in it like it should be; last night has rattled her. She picks up her phone and water bottle. It's only just after six in the morning, but as soon as the sun comes up, the heat will be unbearable.

"You aren't taking the car?" Toby reading her mind again.

"I thought I'd walk. It seems silly to drive when it's just down the road."

"Take the car. You'll be gone for ages, and if I'm left in charge of that coffee machine, no one will ever come back." He's joking. They both know he's as good as she is with the machine.

"Fine. I'll take the car."

He nods, already deep in thought about something he's reading on his own phone. Probably the financial news.

Addie gathers her things and jumps in the car. It's only a quick drive, so she's in front of the church in a matter of minutes. A murder of crows lands in a large tree as she steps out. They caw at her as she walks up the dirt path leading to the back of the church.

"Shhh," she calls up at them. "You'll wake the whole bloody town."

The church is quaint and typically country. A tall, thin bluestone building with a beautiful single arched wooden door leading inside. A circular stained glass window adorns the middle of the front facade, with a large cross centered in the high peak above it.

Addie picks her way around the untidy path, which clearly hasn't been maintained for years. The sun peeks over the land around the church. Its bite already taking effect by sending lazy drips of sweat down her back.

She rounds the length of the church to see a small cottage extended off the rear. It looks like it's been added on because it's built out of brown brick and not the bluestone of the church. There's a small window next to the emerald-painted door. Walter's face appears, and he waves. Addie waves back. The door opens soon after.

"Welcome, welcome," he says, beckoning her in. He's got on his jeans and a faded oversize *Jaws* T-shirt.

"Good morning. I hope it's not too early—you said you were awake," Addie says as she steps through the door into an open-plan house, where the kitchen, living room, and dining room are all in one space. There's a door on the other side of the room that must lead to the sleeping quarters, she figures. There's a musty smell that lingers in the quaint cottage.

Walter sees her scanning the room. "It's not much, but it's home."

"I like it," Addie says, meaning it. "It's much cooler in here too."

He taps his boot on the floor covered in a large rug. "Cement under here. Great for when it gets hot. Great for when it gets cold. Now what can I get you? Tea? Coffee? I have some freshly laid eggs, if you want me to whip you some up."

He moves over to the small but functional kitchen as he talks, already pulling down mugs and filling up the kettle.

"Really, I am okay. I can't stay long. I've got to get back and open the store with Toby."

His face falls slightly, but he puts the kettle on anyway. "I understand. I miss those days of having a lot to do to take my mind off things."

Addie gives him a weak smile and instantly feels bad. Wishing she had the whole day to gossip about this town and all its secrets. Anything to not think about last night and how scared she was seeing that door open.

She pulls up the screenshot she took on her phone of the payment that didn't go through. "Like I said in my text, the banking details you gave me were wrong and the sponsorship money you need came back to us."

She hands him the screen, but he doesn't look at it. "I must've sent you the wrong details. I do apologize."

"It's okay. If you have the correct ones, I can do that transfer now. I know you needed the money for the marketing."

"I did. I do." He frowns, causing deep crease lines between his eyes. "I actually wanted to show you something first. I heard you were a journalist and are doing those little blog things."

Little blog things. *That's fair,* she thinks. Still it's surprising everyone seems to know about it so quickly.

He goes over to a pile of papers on the kitchen counter and picks up the top one. It's a letter-size piece of copy paper.

He passes it to her with a tremble in his hand, and she reads the handwritten note:

> HAVE THE FAIR AND SOMEONE ELSE WILL DIE.

Chapter Twenty-Three

"Who do you think sent this? Do you recognize the handwriting?" Addie can't stop staring at the words.

> HAVE THE FAIR AND SOMEONE ELSE WILL DIE.

The kettle boils, and its whistle gives her goose bumps. Walter turns off the stove and holds up an empty mug as a question.

"Um, yeah sure. Let me text Toby and tell him I'll be a little late." Addie pulls out her phone as Walter prepares two cups of tea. While his back is turned, she takes a quick photo of the threatening message and saves it. Then she texts Toby that she might be a while and to call Clancy in early.

Walter brings their mugs over to his small table and puts them near the note Addie has placed there as well. "In answer to your questions, yes, I do know whose handwriting this is and who sent it. I actually—"

Addie's phone beeps with a text from Toby. A thumbs-up, which is always the most annoying response in her mind. She turns her phone over and sits down with Walter.

"Go on, you were saying . . ." Addie leans forward. *Forget about appearing too keen,* she thinks. *This is wild.*

Walter picks up his tea, blows on it, and then puts it back down. "I returned from doing my groceries in Kerrindale yesterday and found Gale trying to slide this under my door."

Addie has heard that name before. The post office lady who never showed up. Clancy called her *the real wicked witch*. "So you caught her red handed. Wow, good timing."

Walter looks exhausted all of a sudden. "I doubt that. I think Gale had been waiting for me, heard my car pull up, and then made sure I knew it was her delivering this ridiculous message."

Addie has so many questions, but only asks one: "Why would she want for you to know it was her?"

"Because that's how Gale is. Have you met her yet?" Walter spins the ominous note around in his direction and stares at it.

"I haven't, no. She was supposed to help us on the first day with the post office training, but she never showed. This is a threat, Walter. Have you shown the police?"

A tired, breathy laugh comes out of his mouth. "I haven't and I won't. That's exactly what she wants me to do. She's been trying to shut the fair down, and this is just another ploy to do so. That's the reason the money didn't come through. It seems she's closed the bank account that dealt with any fair incomings and outgoings."

Addie's missing a few dots here. "Okay, you may need to go back a bit. How would Gale be able to shut the bank account down? And I am still unclear why she would want you seeing her leaving this note. It has no impact if you know who sent it."

"Forgive me. I have jumped too far ahead. I forget you don't know all the players in the mystery that is this town. Let me catch you up."

Walter's speaking her language if he wants to give up that information readily.

"Gale used to help me run the fair. She was probably what you would call the treasurer. A good one too. But after she lost her sister a few months ago, she quit suddenly and has been wanting me to shut it down ever since."

"Her sister? Was she one of the . . ." Addie isn't sure how to word it. "The seven deaths recently?"

Walter picks up his tea but still doesn't drink it. Addie's also remains untouched. "Yes, that's right. Janet was her sister's name. A nice lady. Quiet. Kept to herself most of the time, not like her sister, Gale, who likes causing trouble. Janet used to run the coffee shop near you."

Addie had been meaning to ask someone about the café, but things had been a tad hectic. "Toby and I stopped in on our first day, but there was a sign on the door saying it was closed because of Mary's funeral."

"That sign has been up there for a lot longer than Mary's passing." Walter does four points of the cross. "Janet was the first local to die out of the recent tragedies."

Addie hasn't gotten around to doing a deep dive on the timeline of all the deaths yet. Again, hectic. "What happened to Janet? I presume it was another accident?" It takes all her control not to do air quotes around "accident."

"No accident. This was a suicide. Gunshot to the head. Gale was the one who found her." Walter shakes his head. "Terrible business."

"I'm so sorry to hear that." She has a little more sympathy for the woman who didn't show that first day to help them with the store. "I'm still not making the connection with the fair, though, and why Gale would send you a threatening note or shut the bank account down without telling you."

Addie suddenly wishes she brought a pen and paper to take notes, even if taking any would be incredibly rude and give away her cover of trying to blend in with the locals.

"Janet had helped me run the fair for years. Along with the café, it was her passion project. She loved this town and was very big on keeping up community where possible. Once we lost Janet, Gale asked me if she could fill in instead—which I happily obliged. Keeping the fair running this year in honor of Janet was a priority, and I thought it would be good for Gale to keep busy."

Addie's phone buzzes with a text. Toby again, telling her Clancy will be there for the mail delivery and to not rush back. *Thank goodness.* She sips her tea, grateful to take her time because these dots are yet to connect.

"Walter, I'm still not understanding. Why would Gale deliberately sabotage the fair if this year's event was honoring her sister?"

Walter stares at the threatening note again. "It's a good question and one I still haven't gotten to the bottom of. I thought maybe when she dropped off the note she would tell me finally, but instead she just handed it to me and said, *Don't say I didn't warn you.*"

Addie stares at the note, too, her brain firing. "Warn you about someone else dying at the fair? But how would she know that, unless . . ." Her voice trails off.

They look up at each other, and Walter says, "Unless she knows something and is too scared to say."

Chapter Twenty-Four

Addie could stay and talk with Walter all day, but he complains of lightheadedness and an oncoming headache and says he needs to lie down. He puts it down to too much excitement, but she wonders if the tremor in his hand is something more.

There are so many questions she still has about the deaths, both past and present. But they will have to wait. Addie has a strong lead now. Gale knows what's been happening around town, and talking with her is Addie's first priority.

Addie is already feeling better now that she has something occupying her mind, and in the brightness of the day, last night's events seem like they might have been an overreaction on her part.

She pulls the car out from the church and passes Clancy's place as she heads back to the general store. No sign of Beatrix out front, thank goodness. Whatever that wedding ring nonsense was, she's happy to not revisit it.

She puts on the blinker to turn in to the general store but sits in the deserted main road. There are no cars in the dirt parking lot and no obvious customers inside.

Toby did say there was no rush, she thinks.

She flicks off the turn signal and heads toward the coffee shop where she and Toby stopped on arriving in Boney Creek. The picnic tables are still set up, but no cars are in front of the cottage.

Addie parks and exits the vehicle, inhaling the baked-manure stench and being reminded of the day they arrived. The smell doesn't seem to bother her as much as it did that first day.

She steps up onto the wooden veranda and peers into the glass door with the faded sign still stuck up inside: **CLOSED FOR FUNERAL.**

So not Mary's funeral but Janet's, she muses.

She knocks on the door and calls out, "Hello? Is anyone in there? Gale?" After no answer, she knocks a few more times.

No one's here. She's not even sure if this is where Gale lives.

Addie steps back down onto the open space covered in red dirt for customer parking and has to shade her eyes with her hand from the glare. She opens her car and leans in to get her sunglasses.

"Who are you?"

Addie spins around to the voice with her sunglasses in her hand. "Hello, hi. I didn't see you there."

It's a kid. A girl maybe five or so with dirt-marked, pale skin that matches the filthy, well-worn doll hanging from her hand. She stares at Addie. Not saying anything.

Addie bends down, mindful not to get too close or she'll scare her off. "I'm Addie. I run the general store now. What's your name?"

The girl bites her bottom lip and frowns. "You're a stranger danger."

Addie can't help but laugh. "Yes, I suppose I am. Where's your mommy or your daddy?" She puts on her sunglasses and scans around them.

There's no obvious house anywhere nearby, except for the cottage that's been turned into a café that they are in front of. Addie stands and offers her hand to the girl.

The girl just gapes at it.

Addie tries again. "Do you have a name?" There's nothing in response but the blinking of wide eyes. "Do you live here?"

Blink. Blink.

Addie sighs. "Does Gale live here?"

The girl's face lights up. "Granny Gale!"

Finally. "Yes, that's right. Granny Gale. Is she inside?"

The girl pouts her lips and cocks her head in a specific direction. "Granny's where the dead people are."

Before Addie can say anything else, the girl bolts off toward the back of the cottage, her doll dragging on the dirt beside her. She studies the direction of where the girl was looking. Down the road, back toward where the town exit is.

And before the exit, Cemetery Lane.

Addie jumps back in the car and drives until she finds the small dirt road that leads to the cemetery. She can see one other car parked in front of the large plot of land that houses headstones of various shapes and sizes.

It's not her finest moment—she's well aware of that—but she's also not going to lose the opportunity to speak to Gale and find out what she knows.

Addie keeps her sunglasses on and tucks her phone into her back pocket, so she isn't carrying anything, which makes her even more self-conscious walking into a graveyard empty handed.

Gale is on the other side of the cemetery, standing in front of a headstone, but her back is to Addie—so she takes the opportunity to pick a bunch of purple wildflowers near the front fence surrounding the cemetery.

She walks under the rusted metal arch acting as an entrance and strides directly toward Gale, following a worn-down path made by people's footsteps versus any permanent path. The grass is dried and long in most areas, neglected as the many headstones in among it.

Gale turns as she hears Addie crunching through some of the longer grass to get to her. Addie waves with the hand containing the wildflowers. She hopes she looks legit.

"Hi! I'm sorry to bother you. I'm Addie. The new owner of the general store. I was hoping you could help me." She pulls back her sunglasses to the top of her head so as to not appear rude.

Gale's face is lined and hard, tanned brown from the sun. Her hair a mix of grey and mousy brown that sits bluntly on her shoulders. She's dressed in smart casual as if she's come from working in an office. Her lips thin as she sizes up Addie.

"Hell of a place to corner a person." Gale's voice is strong, no nonsense.

"Oh, no." Addie waves the wildflowers in her hand, coming within striking distance of Gale now. "I thought I'd pay my respects to Mary, who owned the store we bought. It felt like the right thing to do."

Addie is grateful her brain is still firing even if the heat is slowly cooking it.

Gale gives her flowers a quick scan and then gives Addie an even longer one. "You think I'm stupid?"

"What? No. Why would you say that?" She kicks herself. Never ask a question you don't know the answer to. Even before Gale speaks, Addie knows she's fallen right into something.

"You think you are fooling anyone coming in here with that ugly weed in your hand? Put those on Mary's grave and she'll curse you every day except Sunday."

Addie looks down at the wildflower, which isn't a wildflower but a weed. *Not great.* Kicks herself again for not coming prepared.

"Find someone else to bother. I've seen that blog you're writing. Thinking you're some hotshot from the city who has a right to tell this town's story like it's your own." She gives a quick glance to the headstone she's in front of and moves away. "Now leave me alone."

Gale follows the trail back to the metal arch without hesitation and is in her car before Addie can collect herself and come up with a genius reply. Not that there is one. Gale will be a hard nut to crack.

Addie looks down at the bunch of fresh flowers—real ones, not weeds—that Gale has left in front of a temporary headstone. She reads the inscription, expecting to see the name of Gale's sister, Janet.

Only it's not for Janet—it's for Kip.

Clancy's best friend.

A TOWN CURSED?

The Death of Kip Shaw
Third blog.

Posted by Addie Clarkson.

At around three o'clock on a Sunday afternoon, Kenneth "Kip" Shaw (18) was grooming his horse, Smoke.

Kip had raised Smoke since she was a foal, and the bond these two shared was better than most humans. Smoke was a passive, gentle horse of ten years who was renowned for her patient temperament and was often used at the yearly Boney Creek fair to take kids on horseback rides.

Yet on this afternoon, something spooked Smoke enough for her to lash out and kick her owner in the head. The kick landed with enough force to kill him.

Kip was the sixth person to die in Boney Creek in a matter of months by way of "accident."

The official coroner's finding is still pending, but all initial reports state that Kip had suffered a major blow to the right side of his head just above his temple and had the distinct markings of a horse's shod hoof. The blow caused an artery to rupture in Kip's brain, and the findings suggested the teen did not suffer, or likely even have enough time to know what happened.

Kip wasn't found until later in the night when he hadn't returned for dinner. His body was discovered by his father, Kenneth "Ken" Shaw.

Clancy Myers (16), who was Kip's best friend since they were children, told me that Smoke has not been the same since the accident and no one has been able to ride or groom the horse since.

Clancy also confirmed Smoke was a well-behaved and friendly horse, having no past signs of flightiness or kicking due to a sudden noise or event.

Although no one can ever predict how an animal will react and given no one knows what caused the horse to spook, it is likely that this is just another unfortunate accident.

Kip was a bright student who had plans of studying graphic design so he could work from home and still help his father maintain the property that has been in their family for many generations.

Kip was active on different social media sites and had a decent following across his platforms, his videos sometimes going viral. Most of his content was life around the farm, set to popular, trending music, and always with splashes of humor. Kip's horse, Smoke, appears in many of his videos.

One of his most popular clips was of Kip standing on Smoke's bare back doing the old trending "floss" dance. The horse is notably docile and completely stationary the whole time Kip is dancing on its back.

What is strange is that Kip released a series of videos just before his death explaining he had discovered something he was afraid to share for fear of being hurt—by whom, it is unclear. His last video was posted a day before his death, where he spoke late at night in his bedroom, saying he felt like he was always being watched.

The next day Kip was dead.

Kip's father, Ken, has since removed all traces of his son's social media presence off the internet.

Having sourced a couple of the videos myself, it is clear that Kip was afraid of something. Or someone. He is often talking in a whisper and looking over his shoulder, even in the comfort of his own room.

Any reports I could source on this alleged accident commented on how police investigated Kip's strange videos and could find no evidence of anyone stalking him or any foul play in his death.

I reached out to the local police investigating the mysterious tragedies befalling Boney Creek but was told no further comment would be made at this time.

Why Smoke kicked out that day, killing her owner, is a mystery. Who, or what, Kip was alluding to in his online videos is also a mystery. Mysteries that are now buried with Kip in the local cemetery of Boney Creek.

Addie Clarkson has a degree in journalism and now runs the general store in Boney Creek with her husband and an absent cat called Gravy.

If you are passing through, mention this blog to get a two-for-one coffee deal.

COMMENTS:

UserBC217: You call yourself a journalist? All I see is brown nosing and friendly chats with the locals. When are you going to see what's right in front of you. The Highway Reaper is back and he's hiding behind a stupid curse. Open your eyes.

UserLocalGal: See through the smoke and get to the fire.

Chapter Twenty-Five

DAY FIVE

The store is busier than normal.

It's Friday, so people collect mail and supplies before the weekend. But the main attraction is that Toby has finally gotten the fuel pumps back up and running.

Clancy's father, George, has apparently found the source of the problem, and it's either something obstructing the pipes or lack of maintenance. Addie wasn't really listening as Toby explained it to her.

She doesn't care what is wrong, just that the pumps are fixed and operational. Anything to get more money flowing in versus out. Especially as she has another bill to pay for George's services, his handwritten invoices barely readable—but the total amount unmistakable.

The news has spread, and every car and gas can in town has been filled now that locals don't have to drive for nearly an hour to get fuel. It's like the general store has discovered gold, the way everyone is acting.

Toby waves a customer goodbye from the post office window and smiles at Addie, knowing she's staring at him.

"Checking me out, hey." He twirls as he comes back behind the counter with her, the store finally quiet. "Like what you see?"

"I like watching you work. I know you loved heading up the accounting practice, but this place suits you." She smiles, and it's nice to have a genuine good feeling about how things are going around here for a change, especially after an uneventful night.

Toby balks. "I'm not sure *love* is a word I would use to describe my previous job. Tolerated, more like."

"Well, you seem in your element after saving the town by getting the fuel pumps working again. My knight in shining armor."

He takes her hand and gives her a twirl. "I know, right? Such a simple fix too. Who knows why Mary didn't get them looked at before now."

She spins into him and gives him a quick peck on the lips, conscious of being caught kissing in front of the locals. They aren't that comfortable yet.

Addie figures he'll be worried about the cost. "I know it took a bit out of the budget, but the sales we've made today will make up for it in no time."

Toby nods, his hand still in hers. "Agreed. It was a good investment."

"So why did Mary not fix them, do you think?" Addie can't stop staring at her handsome husband, the spot of oil on his cheek incredibly sexy.

"Not entirely sure." He shrugs and drops her hand. "George found a tattered shirt blocking one of the pipes. How it got down there is anyone's guess."

"Strange. But pipes are always blocked with all kinds of crap. Pun intended."

They both laugh, and Toby says, "Not fuel pumps apparently. It's not like anyone can access them without knowing what they're doing."

"Well, crisis averted. When is Clancy back? Should we think about lunch soon?" She peeks into the sweltering kitchenette, which currently has the back door open for any kind of breeze. Air-conditioning will be their next big investment, and then they can keep the door permanently secured—especially after having the locks changed.

"Clancy was helping her mom with something. I'm not sure when she's due back. I'll make us some sandwiches if you can watch the store?" Toby picks up George's invoice and winces at the price.

"How about I make the sandwiches and you can man the front? You always get to leave the counter," Addie pleads.

"That's fair. I still have to get some of the mail sorted anyway." Toby gives her a quick peck on the lips and moves into the post office section of the store.

Addie hums as she goes into the kitchen and pulls out things she needs for sandwiches. They have a bread-and-milk delivery every day except Sunday, so fresh bread is always a good option for a quick meal.

She slices into a tomato as Clancy comes in through the back door, panting. "I'm sorry. Mom had to load up the car with some of her candles and teas, and then she decided we had to clean out the craft room so she can get ready for the fair and, well, sorry I'm late."

Addie grins. Clancy's energy never wavers. "It's alright, we did okay by ourselves actually. Want a sandwich?"

"Sure, I'll take one." Clancy puts her hands on her hips. "And I hope that doesn't mean you don't need me anymore."

Addie pauses pulling out two more slices of bread. "We will always need you from now until eternity. I'm already dreading you going back to school in Kerrindale next month."

Clancy flops into one of the chairs at the table. "I am dreading school too. Nothing feels the same without Kip. I'll never have a friend like him."

Addie keeps making the sandwiches, letting Clancy cry or talk or grieve how she needs to.

"I saw the blog post you did on him. I thought you were going to talk about Kip more as a person. That's what you told me, that you were going to write about the people *behind* the deaths."

She doesn't recollect saying that, but also doesn't want to get Clancy offside. "I can add anything you like to the post if there's something specific you want to include. That's the beauty of blogs—they can be updated at any time." Addie slices Clancy's sandwich and hands it to her on a plate.

"Thanks." Clancy stares at it, her mood now changed.

Addie feels for her. Losing someone close is something she has knowledge of. "Anytime you want to talk about Kip, I am always happy to listen."

"Yeah, okay." Clancy is clearly not herself today. "Um, Addie . . ."

"Yes, Clancy." Addie cuts Toby's sandwich and places it on a plate.

"I kind of have something awkward to talk to you about."

Nothing good ever starts with that sentence. "Okay. What is it?"

"Um . . ." Clancy shuffles in her chair. "It's about Mom."

Addie takes a breath, having no idea what's about to come out of Clancy's mouth.

"She said she doesn't want me talking to you about the blog anymore"—Clancy holds up her hand—"but don't worry because I'm still totally going to. It's just that she doesn't want you putting my name in the blog or you mentioning me at all."

Addie puts down the knife she's holding. "Clancy, you told me your mom was okay with me using your comments for the blog. You *told* me she said it was fine. Did you even ask her?"

"I didn't," Clancy mumbles. "I was mad at her and knew she'd say no anyway."

Addie kicks herself for dropping the ball and being too eager to get the post up. "It's my own fault for not asking directly myself. I shouldn't have put you in that position. I'll take your name off of the blog now."

"I'm sorry. I didn't mean to make trouble. I just really wanted to be part of it all." Clancy bows her head. "It felt important."

"I understand. I'm not mad, don't worry." Addie hands Toby's plate to Clancy, annoyed at herself for making mistakes already. "Take this out to Toby. You can both grab a seat at the table I set up at the front of the shop. If anyone comes in, just holler and I'll serve them. I must get a bell for that door, too, while I think of it."

"I really am sorry." Clancy stands with the two plates. "Mom was going to call you, but I told her I'd sort it out."

"I'll go and see your mother and apologize. This is my fault." Addie puts the breadboard and knife near the sink and pulls her laptop out of her bag to update the blog. "Is your mom at home today?"

"She should be."

"And Dad? He was here earlier fixing the fuel lines."

Clancy shrugs. "I think he's down at the park doing some work for the fair."

Addie makes a note to drop off some drinks for him on the way through to seeing Beatrix.

"Maybe Mom can read your jewelry again if you go over." Clancy's words come out flat, almost bitter.

"She told you about that?" Addie's annoyance is more obvious than she planned.

"No." Clancy stares at the plates she's holding. "I listened under the kitchen window. If you sit in just the right spot, you can hear anything going on. It's how I know when my parents are fighting. It's how I knew Kip was dead before they told me."

"That's a horrible way to hear about your best friend. I'm sorry." Addie sits at the table and opens her laptop to change the blog, her own sandwich just near it. She keeps her tone neutral, "But it's not a good idea to listen into people's private conversations, Clancy."

"I wouldn't if people actually included me in things. I'm always the last to know, even the big stuff." Clancy's eyes well up. "Sometimes I wish I'd never been born and then none of this would have happened."

"Clancy—"

The teen ignores her and trudges toward the front with the sandwiches.

Addie closes her eyes, a headache brewing. They've been constant since the blow to her head. She decides to go and visit Clancy's mother next.

They have some things to discuss.

Chapter Twenty-Six

Addie swings by the grassy reserve in the middle of town with a coffee and two bottles of water for George. She parks in a small cleared area in front of a toilet block, and a basic kids' playground with two swings and a slide.

Clancy's father stands in the hot sun in a tank top and shorts but no hat.

Has he lost his mind?

He waves at her to join him, which Addie does. Going down a small incline to get to the large browned grass area that the local council maintains.

Addie goes to say hello to George as she nears him. Then splutters and spits out whatever saliva she has in her mouth.

George laughs. "Fly got ya."

Addie opens her own water bottle, takes a sip, swills it around in her mouth, and spits. "That's disgusting."

"That's country life for you. Although, I don't think you ever get used to these flies." George accepts the drinks she hands him and puts the water bottles on the ground.

"I've only ever lived in the city, so I'll take your word for it."

He's still chuckling to himself as Addie takes a long drink of water to rid her mouth of the taste of fly.

"And your family? Where are they?" George sips on his coffee and gives a satisfied *ahhh*.

Addie has a speech she recites for any family questions, which usually doesn't invite further conversation. "I was raised by my gran, but she died a few years back. Mom wasn't really interested in having a kid, so she lived her life without me, and I never knew my dad."

George nods, not sure what to say.

Works every time.

She doesn't add that when her gran died, her mother was quick to return, thinking she would get her mother's inheritance, only to find what little was left had gone to Addie. She wants to believe her mother is repentant, but deep down she knows her mom is still sniffing out what her daughter might give her.

Addie changes the subject. "How do you stand it being out here in the heat? And with no hat."

"Got used to it, I guess. Bea says if I get skin cancer, it's my own bloody fault and she'll have no sympathy. Fair enough, I say." George's tanned brown skin creases deeply as he smiles.

"That's where I'm off to actually. To see your wife."

He blinks quickly at her, and she wonders if something has gotten in his eye. She comments on the fluorescent-pink sprayed lines all over the grass. "What are you up to? I didn't catch you in the middle of some kind of graffiti situation, did I?"

"Back in the day, yes. Got up to a bunch of mischief then." George winks like they share a secret. "Nowadays, nothing so interesting. Just marking up the spots for where everything will be for the fair."

"Ah, okay." Addie sees it now that she knows what she's looking for. All around the grass are blocks of spray-painted squares and circles in various sizes. "How do you know what goes where?"

George taps the side of his head. "All up here. Been doing this for so long now, I reckon I could come out here in my sleep and not have any trouble."

Addie walks around taking in how the fair will roughly look, careful to not step on George's handiwork. There are numbers in every box but nothing inside a set of eight smaller circles in a straight row.

"Numbers are the stalls, I take it?" Addie nods at the circles. "But these? What are they for?"

"Now *that* is a great question." George jumps into one of the circles, suddenly excited. "It's for the wood-chopping event. There are eight competitors, and each one will chop, chop, chop their little hearts out to win this highly contested event."

"I've never seen one before—it sounds interesting." Addie walks around one of the circles. "If a little dangerous."

Gale's note she left for Walter flashes in front of Addie. *Have the fair and someone else will die.*

"Nah. These guys know what they're doing. Completely safe. Blink and you'll miss it, honestly. They are that fast." George hops back out of one of the circles and picks up the spray paint from the grass.

"It's a good spot for the fair. A decent piece of land right in the middle of town," Addie muses.

"It wasn't always like this." George looks around. "The town's pub and hotel used to sit right here before it burned to the ground. Where I'm standing used to be the heartbeat of Boney Creek, and now it's just a whisper of a better time. Sad when you think about it."

"When did the pub burn down?"

"Not sure of the exact year. Late eighties, early nineties? I was only a teen back then. Ask Ken about it—his family lost the pub and his dad all in one night."

"Ken, as in Kip's father?"

"That's the one. I'm sure he'd love to tell you all about his old man—maybe you can write about it." George shakes the spray can in his hand. "I should get back to it."

Addie makes a note to put Ken on her list of people to speak to. "Of course, don't let me keep you."

"If you do one of those blog thingies on the fair, make sure you mention how the wood-chopping event is gonna be extinct soon enough. Might even be the last year, you never know." George shakes the paint can.

"Oh, yeah. Why's that?"

"Supply shortage of the wood we need. Had to source local this year to get those environmentalists to shut up. Gonna make it interesting, though." George must know he's leading her.

"Go on then—tell me why." Addie smiles again at how similar George and Clancy are.

"The wood we are using is tough as nails, apparently. Gonna make things a bit harder for our competitors, that's for sure."

"Sounds it. Are you competing?" Addie asks.

"Nah." George holds up his left arm and turns it to the whiter, fleshier part. There's a nasty long scar running almost to his elbow. "Had an accident when I was a kid, and that ruined me. Lucky for those blokes, though. I'd smash them out of the water if I was competing."

"I'm sure you would." Addie smiles. "Anyway, I'll leave you to it."

George nods and shakes the spray can again, already leaning over an area of grass yet to be marked off. "Anytime you or Toby want to join me for a beer, you're more than welcome. Got a nice little setup going, with a barbecue and everything." George looks proud of himself.

"The yellow table and chairs in front of your place, do you mean? I didn't see a barbecue, but it looked like a perfect spot to me. We would be happy to join you." Addie knows Toby isn't big on socializing, but they need to get out of the store every now and again, as its walls are already closing in on them.

"Yellow chairs?" George looks confused for a moment, frowns. Then hastily adds, "Right, the yellow table and chairs in front of Bea's place. Clancy and Kip painted those."

Addie nods, knowing she's caught George lying but not knowing about what. She says goodbye and heads off, ready to get inside and out of the heat.

As she walks away, she wonders why he called it Bea's place when Addie figured he lived there too.

Chapter Twenty-Seven

Beatrix has her long hair scraped off her face into a bun and wears minimal makeup. She's already said she has a shift at the hospital in a few hours and has accepted Addie's apology for putting Clancy's name in the blog.

Addie's been putting it off until now, but with a lull in the conversation, she's aware she needs to bring it up, work out what Beatrix knows and if she plans on sharing any of it.

"So the other day, with the ring . . ." She hopes Beatrix will fill in the rest.

"I wondered when you were going to bring that up." Beatrix sips the tea she has prepared for them, the same calming blend they'd shared previously. "I do apologize if I made you uncomfortable. It wasn't my intention."

"I did some research on how it works. Psychometry. The reading of jewelry or personal items. It was really interesting." Addie keeps her tone light. Just shooting the breeze with a friend.

Beatrix, of course, sees through her. "What is your question, Addie? I can sense something is troubling you."

Addie sighs. "I need to know what you saw or felt, or however it works. I need to know what you know."

"Why don't you tell me what's bothering you? This is a safe space." Beatrix sits forward, nods as if she's inviting Addie to spill her guts.

She waits for more, but Beatrix is done. Addie isn't used to someone else using her style of getting information. It's frustrating. "Fine, I have a question for you." Addie is tired of being polite. "Why don't you use your magic tricks to find out what's been going on around here?"

Beatrix takes her time answering. "They are not tricks, but connections, and it's not like having a conversation. I might see colors or shapes. A word, or initial. Maybe a particular smell. I don't always understand the message being presented to me."

Thank goodness, Addie wants to say, but says instead, "So you can't just get the Ouija board out and talk to Kip or Mary, ask them what happened to them." Part of her wishes she could talk to her gran one last time while they are at it, even if she's not really sure she believes in all this.

Beatrix leans back, visibly uncomfortable with the question. "It is not always wise to invite the dead back."

"Why not? If it can answer a lot of questions, then what's the harm? Surely giving Clancy some peace about Kip's death would only be helpful."

Beatrix looks out the kitchen window. "Clancy has been obsessed with my mother's spirit board since long before Kip died. She and Kip would sit in her room for hours communicating with who knows what. I thought it was harmless fun, but Kip started getting paranoid, saying he thought someone was after him."

"Wait." Addie jumps in. "Are you saying he was not scared of someone who was living but of someone who had passed?"

"That is my belief, yes."

"Was he taking drugs?"

"Not to my knowledge," Beatrix says lightly. "Something came over that boy long before he died, and his obsession with communicating with the dead got out of hand. It's why I asked Clancy to lock the board in the shed. It's why I don't want her using it as some sort of toy."

"Who do you think he was scared of?" Addie isn't really keen on adding ghosts to her lists of suspects but has to ask.

"I couldn't answer that. Kip had changed in the last year before he died. I know he'd just turned eighteen and was expected to work for his father on the farm, but something really shifted in him."

"What does Clancy say?"

"If she knows what's going on, she hasn't told me." Beatrix finishes her tea and stands, her tone clipped. "I should get ready for work. Thanks for dropping by."

Addie's heart sinks. She still has so many questions, and all they talked about was ghosts—and she has enough of her own without adding more. "Of course, I appreciate you seeing me and your understanding about the blog." Addie hands her empty teacup to Beatrix, who takes it to the sink.

There's a stillness in the kitchen. Beatrix's shoulders sag as she leans against the counter.

"Are you okay?" Addie slides back her chair.

Beatrix waves a hand at her. "Don't get up. I do want to mention something before you leave."

Addie stays where she is, almost afraid of whatever Beatrix has to say.

Beatrix turns around, her eyes wet. "What happened in the city, with your loss. I really am sorry, Addie. I know what it feels like to lose a child, and I want you to know you can always come to me if you need to."

Addie slowly lets out a breath. She can do this. "Thank you, I really appreciate that. Toby and I don't talk about it nearly as much as we should."

"You should let him in," Beatrix says with sadness. "Secrets burn a hole in you, force your hand in the darkest of ways."

She definitely knows. But there's something else . . .

"You sound like you're speaking from experience," Addie says with a lowered voice.

Beatrix looks out the kitchen window again. She takes a moment to answer. "I lost multiple pregnancies. I got lucky with Clancy."

She's lying. Addie is sure of it the way her voice lifts at mentioning her daughter's name. But why? "I'm sorry to hear that, Beatrix. It must have been hard on you and George."

If Addie wasn't looking for clues on Beatrix's face, she may have missed the subtle twitch in the corner of her eye. "It was hard. Very hard. We even broke up for a while after trying for so long."

Addie looks at Beatrix's hands. No wedding ring.

Beatrix follows Addie's gaze. "George and I never got married. It wasn't ever something we felt like we had to do. When I got pregnant with Clancy, we had everything we needed."

"And now?" Addie prompts, thinking about her conversation with George as he was preparing for the fair, having a suspicion he doesn't live here anymore.

Beatrix comes and sits down again. "I wondered if you knew. Did Clancy tell you?"

"No, she never said a thing."

Beatrix nods, wringing her hands together. "George moved out six months ago, but we were having problems well before that."

Addie knows whatever questions she asks will be the wrong ones and waits for Beatrix to explain further.

"George and I both had complicated pasts, and they caught up with us. We tried to work it out for Clancy's sake, but there are some things that can never be forgiven."

Addie understands more than Beatrix will ever know. "It's like you said: secrets will burn a hole in you."

"Exactly. I knew you would understand." Beatrix rubs the base of her neck, lost in thought.

Addie wishes she had the perfect words to say.

"I really should get ready for work."

"Of course. I'll leave you to it." Addie gathers her things and stands. She should get back to the store anyway. "If there's anything you need, just let me know."

"There *is* something you can do." Beatrix grabs her arm lightly. "I'd love for Clancy to not be on her own so much when I'm working. Mary used to help me look after her, but . . ." Beatrix's eyes fill with tears.

Addie puts her hand over Beatrix's. "Of course, Toby and I would be honored. Anytime. She's a good kid."

"She really is." Beatrix sniffs. "Best thing to ever happen to me. She doesn't like going to George's trailer out in the middle of nowhere. She says it reminds her of Kip and how he'd always go and stay with Frank. I don't want to push her."

"Frank?" Addie frowns. "As in Mary's husband, Frank?"

"Yes, that's right. Although they haven't been husband and wife for some time." Beatrix gets up and pulls a tissue from its box. "I don't suppose you've met him; he's been a recluse for a long time now. Apart from Walter, Kip was the only one who visited Frank. Those two used to spend hours together, shooting at targets. Clancy said she couldn't stand the noise the gun made and hated going out there."

"I just presumed Frank was dead or had left town. His son, Gary, didn't mention anything about him still living here." Addie thinks back to when Gary showed them the store for the first time. She's sure he didn't say anything about his father, other than him being a hero.

"Typical Gary. Always was an arrogant child, one who hasn't spoken to his dad in years." Beatrix shakes her head. "I don't suppose he would tell you given Frank is now living on your land."

"What do you mean?" Addie asks.

"You own a lot of property, Addie. Most of it hard to access in a car or on foot. Frank lives far back among the dead and dying trees, in a trailer that he barely ever leaves."

"How am I only just learning this?" She now understands why Toby was asking about Gary's father the day they arrived; he must've been curious where Frank had ended up.

"I imagine people either thought you knew or didn't want you going over there unannounced. Frank has been known to use that gun of his on anyone trespassing."

"But if we own the land, we aren't trespassing."

"Try telling him that." Beatrix laughs. "Frank is a crack shot. You'd be lucky to get anywhere near him."

Chapter Twenty-Eight

DAY EIGHT

Night hovers around her as Addie sits in the shed in a T-shirt and cutoff sweatpants. The overhead light buzzes with a cacophony of flying insects.

She's been in here for almost an hour now, another restless night forcing her out of bed at 2:00 a.m. A fresh nightmare hangs heavy on her shoulders, the scraps of what she remembers now fading. What she does know is that two of the worst experiences of her life are now merging. The break-in and finding her gran's body. It's enough to never want to sleep again.

She shivers, even if the night air is sticky with heat. The dirt permeating her skin and lungs as she sits on an overturned rusted bucket. Around her are Mary's archive boxes with old clippings of the Highway Reaper disappearances and murders, Gary's old schoolwork, piles of vintage women's magazines, and old photos of Mary when she was younger.

Addie's restless, and not only because of the nightmare.

Her anxiety is in full force after a week of dead ends and feeling like a hack. Which she is. Writing a silly blog for her own personal gain is the definition of an amateur.

If she listens hard enough, the constant chirping of the insects merges with the voice of her previous editor chastising her for thinking she has what it takes to be a "proper" journalist.

Impostor syndrome is settling in like an unwelcome friend. She has no business trying to uncover what has been happening in this town—both past and present. She's not an investigative journalist, not even close.

Her editor was right: she doesn't have the instincts to go all in on a story. Not to the detriment of anything else.

She tried to go all in before, and look how *that* turned out.

Addie kicks the dirt, trying not to suffocate on her failings.

She's been here before. With these bad thoughts, pushing her to do something she doesn't want to do. All for the *story*. This time will be different. No one is stopping her from doing this blog or telling the truth in her own words—even if it's not in a typical journalistic style.

She promised Toby that she would try to find out who killed his uncle. She promised Clancy that she would help find out what happened to Kip.

This isn't about her. This is about them.

Liar.

Here she is, back here again. Trying to prove herself and going about it in all the wrong ways. This was a vocation she was drawn to because it falsely promised if she got to the heart of other people's truths, she could escape her own. If she focused her time on uncovering the mystery of the why through her stories, then she could forget about why her own mother left her.

A therapist would have a field day with my mommy issues.

Addie picks up one of the old newspaper articles about the Highway Reaper, determined to stay focused and not second-guess herself or her bad decisions. The article tells the story of two female backpackers in the late eighties. One found fatally shot just near the Boney Creek bridge, and the other is still missing, presumed dead.

She shuffles the papers, looking for more information on Toby's uncle, Steve, but finds only what she already knows. He was last seen at the Boney Creek pub, where he was staying overnight. He had also withdrawn money from the town that day, the last known activity on his bank account.

Police were slow to act when Toby's father reported him missing, saying he was an adult and would show up eventually. They were also dismissive of the family's concern, saying it was Steve's fault by engaging in risky behavior such as hitchhiking and traveling alone.

When weeks passed, the police were still slow to act, saying without a crime scene or any evidence, they had nothing to go on. Basically they were hoping a "body would turn up," but until then, their responses were lukewarm at best.

There is also mention of how the town was not forthcoming with any last known sightings of Steve, and the police were open in their remarks of how the locals of Boney Creek were probably protecting a predator.

A reward of $20,000 was offered by the family, but even this was not enough of an incentive for someone to step forward. A coroner eventually concluded he was "satisfied that missing person, Steven Clarkson, was dead due to reasons unknown."

In total there were three confirmed dead and four missing (presumed dead) over the two decades the Highway Reaper was said to be active.

Addie scans the articles, looking for any clues or signs that this predator is a local from Boney Creek or could be still active in some way with what has been happening recently.

Only there's no connection there. The Highway Reaper engaged in crimes of opportunity and attacked people not associated with the town in any way. Yet the current deaths have *all* been locals.

She looks up. *What is that?* A ringing noise.

Her breath comes out shaky as her heart speeds up. She glances at her phone. 2:50 a.m.

It's the phone inside. Someone pranking them again. Addie has no desire to go and pick it up, not after last time. The phone rings during the day when the store is open, but there's always someone on the other end.

These late-night calls are something different. Something personal. The first one having come just as she posted the blog on Mary Peterson.

Someone scaring her, obviously.

It's working too.

She gets up and wipes her bottom. She'll clean all these papers up in the morning.

Like on cue, Betsy barks from inside Mildred's house. The dog did the same when Addie came out to the shed, and now that there's activity again, Betsy is like a sensor light reacting to any movement.

The phone still rings inside, and Addie glances up at their bedroom window. It's dark. Toby obviously sound asleep like always. Having nightmares is clearly only her burden to bear. It's a wonder he even woke up the night of the break-in when he can sleep so soundly now.

She curbs her resentment as her unlaced boots crunch on the dirt and something scampers off into the surrounds. The stars speckle the night sky for as far as she can see. It's breathtaking.

She comes to the back door and steps inside. The old rotary phone is silent now as she closes the door behind her, locking it. The partial moonlight giving her enough light to see by.

Betsy is still barking, but now that she's inside, the dog should quieten. Addie treads across the kitchen floor toward the stairs. She's already looking forward to closing her eyes and snuggling back up to her husband.

A piece of paper on the table catches her eye. She cleaned before she went to bed, and nothing should be on there.

Had Toby come down after all?

She picks it up and flips it over.

In cutout letters of various sizes and colors, someone has spelled out the message:

KEEP DIGGING AND YOU'LL BE NEXT.

Chapter Twenty-Nine

Addie calls the police as soon as the station opens and tells a young officer about the threatening note. He recognizes her from the previous times she's been trying to get further intel for her blog—not surprising given there are only three active staff members at the police station in Kerrindale.

He says it's probably just a prank and even insinuates she's done it herself to get more clicks on the blog. He does say that if she wants to pop into the station, they'd be happy to make a formal report.

She knows she won't be doing that anytime soon.

Addie blames herself for not securing the back door to the kitchen. She closed it but didn't lock it when she went to the shed. What was the point of new locks if she wasn't going to use them?

Too many late nights and not enough sleep are the only excuses she has. Toby does his best to comfort her but isn't really sure what to do either.

She decides to go and see Walter and get his take on it. Something tells her this is very different from the note Gale left. And if she asks Gale about it without a reason, she may never get anything out of her.

As Addie pulls up at the church, Walter has on a wide-brim straw hat, gardening gloves, and a pair of pruning shears in his hand. He is sweating and flushed from the morning sun.

As Addie walks toward him, Walter taps the brim of his hat, which has bright sunflowers dotted around the rim, and chuckles a little. "Someone left this behind many moons ago and never claimed it, so now it's my best gardening hat. The flowers bring out my eyes, don't you think?"

"It's very becoming." Addie pulls her sunglasses up as she approaches him. "I hope I'm not intruding. Like I said, I had something I wanted to show you."

A black SUV drives past and beeps its horn at them. Walter waves, and Addie squints, not making out who is driving.

"That's Larry," Walter says, watching the vehicle travel back toward the town's exit and the bridge sitting above the town's nonexistent namesake. "You met him yet?"

"No, not officially. I heard he also tried to buy the store, though."

"Sounds about right." Walter kicks at some stones around the dead-looking bush he's pruning. "Not really sure what I am trying to do out here, to be honest. Most of the garden is dead, and I should have cut these back months ago. How about we head inside, and you can show me what you have?"

Addie nods and follows him behind the church to his dwelling. They step inside, and it's instantly cool. Addie takes off her sunglasses and puts them on the table as Walter does the same with his hat.

He pours them both a glass of chilled water and empties half his glass in one gulp. "Oh, and before I forget, thanks for that money. Received and already spent."

"That's good to hear. Seems like everything is ticking away for the fair on Saturday."

"It is. No more threatening letters." Walter pulls out a chair and sits. "For now anyway."

"That's actually why I'm here." Addie sits across from him and pulls out the note from her bag, which Toby has put in a plastic cover. "Someone left this on my kitchen table late last night."

Walter frowns. "Did you see who it was?"

"No, but someone came into our home uninvited and left it for me to find. Do you think it could be Gale again?"

Walter continues to frown. "This doesn't sound like her, and hers was in her own handwriting. Whoever left this is trying to scare you."

"Agreed. We've been getting prank calls late at night too."

Walter finishes off his water. "I'm sorry this is happening to you, Addie. I imagine that blog of yours has set a few people off."

She's come to the same conclusion. That or someone from their attack is trying to scare her ahead of the court case they are still waiting on a date for.

"Should I be worried?" Addie asks.

"Like I said, I think you've ruffled some feathers and people are just trying to remind you of your place."

"Which is?"

"That you are new here and have no right to air out this town's problems." Walter hands the threatening message back to her, the tremor in his hand slight but obvious.

Addie isn't in the mood to argue about what is right and wrong; she has enough of her own demons. "And you? Have you been here long enough to be considered a local?"

"I doubt it." Walter's hand shakes slightly on the table, and he moves it into his lap. "I came here in my midthirties and have been here ever since. I got a couple of other offers for postings, but I liked the town and its community and starting over again didn't feel right. So I was lucky enough to stay all these years."

Addie has to do the math in her head. "So you got here, what, mideighties or so?"

He thinks about it. "Something like that. Seems like a lifetime ago now."

Addie knows the timing is off for Walter to be the Highway Reaper. Not that she really has any reason to suspect him, but it's good to cross him off the list for now.

"You're not thinking of writing one of those articles on me, are you? I can't say I'd like that." Walter nibbles the bottom of his lip.

Addie dives on his statement with a lightness to her voice. "Why wouldn't you like that? Something to hide?"

He chuckles. "I'm sure if you went looking for the skeletons in my closet, you'd find some. No one is without secrets."

"Sounds intriguing." Addie keeps the lightness. "For now, I am just focusing on the locals who have passed in the last three months, but I'd love to hear more about your life—totally off the record if you'd prefer."

"I am always up for a chat as long as it doesn't end up in some gossip rag." He looks at her pointedly.

"You think that's what I am doing? Fueling gossip?" This is not something that sits well with her.

"I'm not quite sure what you are doing, but I urge you to be careful." Walter pushes back his chair and stands. "Small towns like their gossip to stay local. Simple as that."

"I think people have a right to know what's been happening around here, especially if there's any doubt the tragic events weren't accidents." Addie stays seated—she's not done yet. "Look at the Donolly family. How did that whole family perish from a faulty portable heater? Doesn't that seem suspicious to you?"

Walter scratches above his eyebrow. "There was a thorough investigation on what happened with the Donollys, especially as young kids were involved, and from all accounts, that heater had been accidentally left on. Everyone knows how dangerous they are. It was the gas fumes that killed them, but it was the heater's proximity to the flammable curtains that caused the fire."

"So you have no doubt that all of the incidents over the last three months have been accidents?" Addie still isn't budging until she gets some answers, even if Walter hovers above her.

"I'm just saying that some things are better left buried. You stir up the dead and the living come a knockin'—and not the living you want knocking, if you know what I mean." Walter takes their water glasses and places them in the sink, his back to her as he leans against the counter.

"Are you saying I'm in danger?" Addie takes a breath, getting out her next question quickly. "Is it because of what happened back when the Highway Reaper was hunting people who came through this town?"

Walter spins around, his face flushed. "What did you say?"

"You heard me." Addie stands and grabs the back of the chair for support. She hadn't meant to bring up the past so quickly, but she's in it now.

"The deaths recently have nothing to do with the deaths back then. The Highway Reaper, as he was known—stupid name, honestly—preyed on people passing through. If it was someone living here, we would have known." Walter fires his words out equally as quickly. "That's all in the past. Some sicko taking advantage of a small town and the drifters it attracted—nothing more. What's happening now is a series of unfortunate tragedies that have all occurred in a short period. God works in mysterious ways, and we don't always have to understand it."

Addie listens to his monologue with interest. It's like he's defensive of not just the town but its deaths, past and present. "So you don't think there's any connection to the two events? None at all?"

"I don't, and you'd be wise to not publish any of your thoughts on what you're clearly making up out of thin air."

"Thin air? Hardly seems fair when a small town has had more than its share of bad luck. Or bad people." Addie can feel herself getting defensive at how dismissive he is being.

He steadies one of his hands. "I'm just saying it's best to let sleeping dogs lie."

"Why? You think that the Reaper is still alive?" Addie watches his face for any tells.

Walter walks to the door instead, his voice now upbeat and casual. "Have a nice day, Addie. I'll see you at the fair, no doubt."

The door closes behind her, and Walter's words linger. *I'll see you at the fair.*

It could be fatigue, but she's almost positive it sounded like a threat.

Chapter Thirty

DAY TWELVE

It's the day before the fair, and things are surprisingly calm.

Toby has all the extra stock and deliveries organized. He's sorted the mail early. The fuel lines are full. And if she squinted, Addie could almost convince herself the store sparkles from cleanliness.

Having everything right with their new business dilutes the chaos of everything else in Addie's head, including the dull headache that sits at the back of her skull.

It's early evening, and they've closed an hour before they normally do. Tomorrow will be busy and long, and they will need all the rest they can get. It's just her and Toby at the kitchen table now. He's in front of his favorite thing: a spreadsheet, and she's holding a glass of wine. Perfection.

She sighs deeply. Enjoying a rare quiet moment with her husband. The only time they seem to connect properly these days is when they go to bed, and that's if Toby can keep his eyes open now that the new mattress has arrived.

Toby groans, his fingers rubbing his scalp through his hair.

"Penny for your thoughts?" Addie says, hoping he'll pack it in soon and share the wine with her.

"I need more than pennies. I need a miracle." She hands him her wine, and he takes it, gulping down a large sip.

"That bad, huh?" Addie gets up and pours him his own glass. From the looks of things, he'll need it.

"Thanks." He takes it. "No matter how many times I've gone over these books, they just don't add up."

Addie clinks her glass with his. "You are on your own there, my darling husband. Numbers and I are not friends."

He stares at the laptop screen in front of him. "Usually numbers are the only thing I seem to understand, but not this time."

"Should we be worried? Maybe I can get some freelance writing work on the side if we need extra income."

Why doesn't he ask me for my grandmother's inheritance money? He knows it's there, sitting in a high-yield savings account he can access—but would never touch because it's "her" money.

Toby bites his lip, then says, "At this stage, I'm not sure what we need. From inspecting these books, Mary should have been coming out even. She's had steady sales and just enough profit to keep her afloat."

"But?"

"But cash amounts seemed to be going out at a steady rate, and it's not accounted for."

Addie sips her wine, half listening. "Maybe she had a secret love child she's been supporting all these years?"

Toby ignores her joke.

"Why don't you ask who did their books? Surely Mary had a bookkeeper."

Toby rubs at his eyes. "That's the thing, Eddie Donolly was her accountant."

"Donolly?" Addie recognizes the surname. "As in, one of the family members who died in the house fire recently?"

Addie needs to do more research concerning what happened to the Donollys, but this connection to their store is a lead worth following up on.

"That's the one. I need to speak to Gary. I'm hoping he might know more."

"Good luck with that. I doubt he knows anything, and even if he did, he wouldn't say." Addie remembers the bumblebee necklace sitting upstairs. "Did you end up asking him about the necklace I found?"

Toby is distracted. "Not yet."

"And Frank? Have you spoken to Gary about his father living on our property without our knowledge?" She already knows Toby hasn't, but she hopes another nudge will get him to do something about it. The idea of this elderly stranger being on their land somewhere is not exactly comforting.

"Not yet," he repeats.

"What's the plan for how we deal with Frank? Do we warn him ahead of time or just show up at his trailer? Beatrix mentioned he has a gun."

Toby types something on the laptop. She knows she's talking to a brick spreadsheet.

"Are you listening to me?"

He looks up. "I'll call Gary, don't worry."

"Why don't you put all that away for now. Hopefully after the fair tomorrow, we won't need to worry so much about the budget. Or maybe we can charge Frank rent and get some extra income?"

He mm-hmms as a response, his eyes back on the computer screen.

Toby isn't listening to her; she knows his intense work look, and nothing is cutting through that. Addie gets back up, suddenly starving, and grabs a bag of corn chips from the cupboard. "Should I make us some nachos for dinner, keep it simple tonight?"

She pulls out the ingredients and preps around him without waiting for an answer that may never come. It should frustrate her, but she finds it sexy when he's so focused like he is now. The crinkle in his brow. His fierce gaze at the budget in front of him. She wonders if she looks similar when she's typing up a story.

Doubtful. Addie figures she would look more like she is in pain when she's drafting something. Sometimes the words come easily to her, but most days it's a struggle to get them on the page.

Toby clicks the laptop shut and leans back in his chair. He ducks his head under the table. "Where's Gravy? I haven't seen much of that cat since we arrived."

"He does as he pleases." Addie squirts some lemon juice into the bowl of mashed avocado. "I think he must have a better offer."

Toby pulls over a block of cheese and starts grating some onto a plate. He keeps looking up at her.

"Out with it," she prompts. Toby is never subtle when he has something to tell her.

"Do you want the good news or the bad news?"

"Bad. You know I always start with the bad."

"I know, but I'll never stop asking." Toby smirks or frowns, she isn't sure which. "We got a letter today, from the court."

Addie wants to be sick. She knew it was coming, but she also hoped it would never arrive. "And? When do we have to be there?"

"Two weeks."

"Two weeks?" Now she really wants to be sick.

Toby closes his eyes and rubs them again. "Our mail redirection took a while to get here. I'm sorry, babe. It's not ideal, but the quicker we do this, the quicker it will hopefully be over. Let me find out exactly what happens and what we need to do, okay?"

Addie takes a long sip of her drink, not wanting to even think about sitting in the same room as their attacker.

"You okay?" Toby reaches out for her hand. "Not just about this, but about everything. I haven't really checked in with you."

"I'm okay. Some days are better than others. You know?" She clutches at his hand.

"I do." He entwines his fingers in hers, takes his time in saying "Maybe we can start trying again?"

Oh. Addie knew that was coming too. She squeezes his hand back. The word is stuck inside her because she's not sure she'll ever be ready. *Yes.*

Toby brightens, even if his eyes are watery. She loves this man more than anything else in the world and knows she should tell him about that night before trying again.

He lets go of her hand and lifts up his glass of wine. "So now do you want the good news?"

"Always." *I'll tell him another time,* she thinks, knowing damn well she's lying to herself.

"You'll never guess who came in today asking after you."

"Who?" Addie sprinkles some salt and pepper onto the avocado.

"Gale."

"Gale?" Addie hovers her hand over the bowl. "As in the woman who was supposed to come in and help us with the mail and never did."

"The one and only." Toby smirks. "You mentioned she would be a tough nut to crack, and it looks like she's come to you."

"What did she want?" Addie hasn't seen Gale since accosting her in the cemetery, and Toby's right, she's been wanting to talk to her ever since.

"She said she has something to tell you."

"That's it? No handwritten letters warning us someone is going to die tomorrow at the fair?" Addie wants to laugh, but it's not exactly funny.

"You know I'm not good at getting information from people like you are. I told her I'd pass over the message, but I knew you'd be excited."

Addie is excited. It's always much easier to extract information from a willing party. "How did she seem? Nervous? Hostile?"

Toby looks at her with a *you've got to be kidding* look. "Reading people is your thing, not mine."

Addie stirs the guacamole slowly, her mind racing at all the questions she has for the woman who lost her sister.

Toby smiles. "It's early. Why don't you go and visit her after dinner?"

Addie could kiss him, and she does. "I knew I married you for a reason."

Chapter Thirty-One

The sun is setting, casting a pink-and-orange glow across the town. A chill starts to creep in. Nights are weird up here: sometimes they are as hot as the day; sometimes they are as cold as winter.

I should have brought a jacket, Addie thinks as she walks up to the café's veranda with the CLOSED FOR FUNERAL sign still taped inside the door. She knocks, but the interior is dark and silent.

It'll be night soon, which doesn't sit well with her, so she walks briskly to the rear of the café. Addie figures the living quarters must be in back, like at their own store, and it was the direction the child ran toward the day Addie was looking for Gale.

Addie follows the length of the café until she comes to a security screen that has the door behind it open. Inside, she can see a light coming from one of the rooms off the hall.

Addie looks for a doorbell, finds none, so knocks on the security door frame. The metal rattles heavily in the quiet evening air.

Gale storms out into the hall in grey sweats, a dish towel in her hand and a scowl on her face. "Oh, it's you."

"Is this a bad time? My husband said you wanted to—"

"Keep your voice down. I just put the little one to bed."

Addie covers her mouth and whispers, "I'm sorry. I didn't mean to intrude."

It sounds sincere even if she absolutely meant to intrude.

"Come in then." Gale opens the screen door and looks around behind Addie. "Watch the toys on the way through. I haven't had time to clean."

Addie walks into the hall and takes it all in as she comes into the small living space. There are indeed toys scattered across the floor, but otherwise the place is tidy. It's filled with oversize outdated furniture, lots of knickknacks, and framed photos.

"No need to sit down—we'll keep this brief," Gale says as she comes up behind her, the tea towel now over her shoulder.

"Um, okay." Addie swallows as the saliva builds up in her throat. Gale's hostile manner is jarring.

"I want to make a few things *very* clear to you, and I will only say this once."

Addie desperately needs to sit down for whatever this is but stands beside one of the armchairs instead. Realizing Gale is waiting for some kind of response, she nods.

"I've seen those blogs you've been posting. One after another on the deaths that have been happening around here lately, and I know damn well you think you're writing one on my sister, but if—" She holds up her hand as Addie goes to say something. "Let me finish."

"Of course, sorry." Addie holds on to the armchair for support. This is not what she had in mind when she came over here; she was hoping for some answers, and instead she's getting a scolding.

"Janet, my sister, is off limits to you. You will *not* write about her; you will *not* ask about her; you will not even utter her name. Do I make myself clear?" Gale's words sink in like venom.

There are two ways Addie can play this. One: agree and leave. Or two: talk Gale around and get what she came for. She has had two glasses of wine already, so option two is where she's at on the rationale scale.

"With all due respect, Gale, there is something going on in this town, and I believe it is in the public's best interest if they are kept abreast of the truth." Addie plops into the chair in defiance. She's not going anywhere until she sorts this out.

Gale's eyes narrow. "I'll sue you."

"For what? I haven't done anything."

Addie notices something on Gale's face other than hostility. If she were to place a bet, she would say it was uncertainty.

"If you write a word on my sister, I *will* sue you."

"I'm only after the truth."

"What would you know of the truth?" Gale spits out.

Addie gets up and steps toward Gale. "That's what I'm trying to find out, and I'd like your help."

If her instincts are right, there is a vulnerability to this woman who has been through so much and the hostility is merely a protection from her grief.

Gale pulls the tea towel from her shoulder and walks out of the room.

Great. I've lost her. Addie sighs and heads for the door. She should have known this was a long shot. Gale was never going to give her answers.

"Where do you think you're going?" Gale has ditched the tea towel. "I had to check on Myah and make sure she was asleep."

Addie is getting whiplash at this point. It's like Gale wants to talk but won't let her guard down either. This is new territory, and she's unclear how to navigate it.

"Sit down. I'll get us a drink." Gale leaves the small room, and there is clinking of glasses next door.

Addie takes a seat again in the chair she was using for moral support. She really can't work Gale out but will take what she can get, even if it's anger.

"Not that one," Gale says as she comes in with a bottle of scotch and two glasses. "That's my chair. Use this one."

Addie does as she says and moves to the two-seater couch. Gale pours a splash of scotch into each of the glasses and hands one to Addie. "I don't really care how you take it."

"Straight up works for me." Addie can't stand scotch, but there's no way she'll let Gale know that. "So is Myah your grandchild?"

Myah must be the child she met the other day with the dusty face and well-loved doll.

"She's my niece." Gale takes a swig of her drink. "Someone tell you she calls me Granny Gale?"

"I might have heard it around." Addie swirls her drink, not thinking it wise to mention she's already met her niece. "Why does she call you Granny Gale, if you don't mind me asking?"

"Auntie Gale didn't sound as fun, I guess. You know how kids are."

Addie feels a tug in her stomach but ignores it. "Was Myah your sister's child?"

Gale leans forward in her chair. "What are you trying to prove writing that blog? All you are doing is stirring up trouble, and if no one else in this town is going to call you out, then I will."

At the mention of being called out, Addie has to ask, "Is that you writing those comments, BC217?"

Gale huffs into her glass. "Why write something when I can say it to your face? Only cowards hide behind a keyboard."

The rebuke to hiding behind a keyboard is not lost on Addie. "What about the letter you wrote to Walter, about the fair? You didn't say *that* to his face."

Gale shifts slightly in her chair. "I'm not ashamed of that note, and I don't care who knows about it. And for your information, I *handed* it to Walter, which is as good as saying it to his face."

"Why did you say someone is going to die at the fair? What do you know?"

Gale laughs, then quietens down as she glances behind her to where Myah must be sleeping. "I don't want that fair going ahead, is all. It doesn't seem right with Janet not being here, the whole town getting on with their lives like nothing has happened."

Addie doesn't know whether to believe her or not. "I'm sure if you had explained that to Walter, he would have understood."

"You know nothing of this town." Gale sips her drink. "Or Walter."

Addie wants to ask about the other threatening note found in their kitchen, but something tells her it wasn't the lady sitting in front of her. Gale seems the type to not hide behind a threat; plus Addie is finally getting her to open up.

"So why don't you tell me? I want to find the truth." Addie meets Gale's gaze. "Don't you?"

"You don't know what you're playing at." Gale finishes her drink and pours a larger shot in its place.

"So I keep being told, yet no one will say why." Addie takes a small sip, and her mouth burns in protest. "What happened to your sister?"

Gale gulps down the scotch in one go and licks her lips. "You *know* what happened to my sister—she took her life."

"But how can you be sure? I heard it was a gunshot to the head. That's not exactly a common method among women." Addie keeps her words light. "Did she leave a note or . . ."

"Is all the trauma we've suffered just a mystery for you to solve? Is that it? Some kind of game where the winner gets a gold star? You don't know anything about my sister or what she did."

"That's why I want to find out." Addie sees water collect at the corners of Gale's eyes. "Don't you want to know for certain? Don't you want to make sure no one did this to her?"

"Not everything can be wrapped up in a nice pretty bow, little miss nosy," Gale slurs the word *nosy*. "Some people just make a choice and stick with it."

"Are you saying that you have no doubt your sister did this? That you've never suspected anything more, even after other locals died in the months afterward?"

A tear falls down Gale's flushed cheek. "That's what I'm saying."

"But how can you be sure?"

"Because I saw her do it with my own eyes."

Chapter Thirty-Two

DAY THIRTEEN

The day of the fair is hot and windy. Perfect fire-season weather.

No one seems to care. The stalls already set up, the ice cream already melting down children's arms, and the sweat already pooling at the base of everyone's backs.

Addie has left Toby at the store with Clancy, who is a wiz on the coffee machine now and will pump out hot drinks as he mans the register. Thankfully, being a Saturday, the post office is closed.

She still has a dull headache from the night before, Gale's confession throwing her. Addie has been thinking about it ever since. She knows not to look for Gale today, as both she and Myah will not be attending the fair. In some ways Addie's glad—it won't matter what she says, not after everything Gale has been through. All she can do is respect Gale's wishes and not write about her sister. Which she plans to honor.

Addie has brought down the mobile ice cream freezer they rented for the event to the fair site and stands under the large bright-yellow umbrella with red branding, so everyone knows what she's selling. At the rate she is going through the packaged ice cream in the freezer, they'll be out before lunchtime.

Walter wasn't wrong. The fair brings a lot of traffic through town, and cars line both sides of the main street. People are everywhere.

Addie feels like a local for the first time, with everyone waving and saying their hellos. Asking after Toby and the store. Thanking her for getting the fuel lines working again so they don't have to drive forever to fill up their gas cans.

If she was going to admit it to herself, she's warming to the sense of community and can see why people stay in a small town. Despite the lingering threat of a killer in their midst, she just might be happy here.

She sends Toby a quick text asking how they're doing and that she might have to bring all the ice cream down from the store at this rate. He doesn't answer and that's good. It means he is busy.

A good day of profits is exactly what they need. Take some of the pressure off their ever-mounting bills and the mess Mary left them in. This fair could just turn things around.

She scratches the base of her throat, the bumblebee necklace she found in the store itching her neck where the tiny wings tickle her skin. No harm in wearing it while they are waiting to talk to Gary.

A gust of wind whips the sun hat off her head before Addie can grab it. She chases after it, just missing each time she reaches out. A boot comes down, stomping on the hat. A man bends over to pick it up. It's Larry, the man who is playing Monopoly with the town and its land. He has a scowl on his face as he holds her hat to his chest.

"Thank you." Addie pants. "I can't afford to lose that today."

Larry doesn't move. His eyes roaming over her face like he's looking for something.

Addie glances over to the ice cream refrigerator, where two kids stand waiting to be served. "Thanks again. I better get back." *Give it to me,* her fingers say as she wiggles them at him, her hand still hanging there.

Larry's eyes don't move from hers. It's unnerving.

Deciding to be more like her diplomatic husband, she reaches out for a handshake. "We haven't officially met, I'm Addie."

He glances at her gesture but stays silent.

Addie doesn't have time for this and grabs at her hat. He lets her take it, a slow snarl creeping up his mouth.

"Have a great day, Larry." Addie stalks off, leaving her obvious sarcasm as a poor man's mic drop.

What's his problem?

She glances behind herself, and he's still standing there, watching her. She shivers even in the heat.

"Sorry, kids. What can I get you?" Addie pulls out the ice cream treats they point to and takes their money. When she looks again, Larry has gone.

Addie scans the stalls closest to her. Mildred is doing a roaring trade with her pies and baked goods. Beatrix has a few customers sampling her teas or smelling her candles. George is setting up the wood-chopping event with some helpers she doesn't recognize.

Addie checks her phone. Still nothing from Toby.

More cars. More children. The ice cream is now gone. Toby will be thrilled. Addie thinks about going to get the stock up at the store but decides to look at the stalls first. An hour won't hurt.

She waves at Mildred, who is busy taking money from her chair that she doesn't have to move from. People pick up their purchase, hand her their cash, and Mildred takes it with what looks like a smile and pops it into her lockable money box.

Sitting under the pop-up marquee, the old lady even has some color in her cheeks. If Addie was to guess, she'd say Mildred was enjoying herself.

Addie stops at a stall that is three tables' worth of knickknacks, old books, and various lamps and small furniture items. She looks through the books, quickly pulling out a ratty paperback thriller she knows she doesn't have in her own collection.

"You have a good selection here," Addie says, handing over her two dollars for the book to a woman she recognizes. It's Sharmi, who normally comes into the store alone and in her horse-riding attire. Today she is in jeans and a tucked-in black T-shirt.

Sharmi surveys the goods on the table in front of her, her face a little grim. "Most of it is from the Donolly house. We salvaged what we could and thought we'd sell off a few things to donate to an animal shelter they supported."

Addie nods. Not really sure what she can say about the family who died in the house fire.

"You should come out sometime and see if there's anything you can use at the store." Sharmi looks hopeful.

"Of course. Thanks for the offer." Addie has been wanting to visit the house since she heard about the gas and subsequent fire that killed the whole family as they slept. A snoop around disguised as something else is always less evasive. "Maybe I can call you this week and we can go out together?"

"I'd like that. I never enjoy going out there alone. Too many memories. Too much pain."

Addie gives a sympathetic nod. "Who owns the property now?"

"Larry and his kids. They swooped in and bought the land before it even went on sale."

Larry again. The way he looked at her before sends another chill up her spine. "I'm surprised he's letting you anywhere near the place if he owns it."

"It's not his yet. They settle the sale in two weeks. Anything not fixed down he has no claim over, so there isn't much he can do about it."

Addie's radar goes off. "He sure is buying up a lot of land around here."

"He is, yes." Sharmi's tone is a little clipped.

Addie can't tell if her tone is directed at Larry or at her for making the observation. She doesn't want to upset Sharmi. "Forgive me, it's none of my business."

"It's okay—it's not a secret." Sharmi gives a weary smile. "We can chat more when you come out. It'll be nice to catch up properly."

Sharmi moves behind the other table as a potential customer asks about a vintage perfume bottle, the conversation over. Addie holds the book to her chest and pulls her hat down as she walks over to Beatrix's stall. There are a few customers already there, so she feels comfortable going over.

Addie sips a small cup of the sample tea on offer. It's different from the one she tried at the house. This tea is equally delicious. A berry flavor of some kind.

Beatrix smiles at her. Her face open and not judging. Not yet anyway. Addie tucks her wedding ring behind the book in case it gives away all her secrets again.

"That one's Berry Blast. It's good for getting your brain working midafternoon. Suppresses those cravings for sugar too."

Addie picks up a box and adds the mint-and-lavender one she's already tried. "I'll take both of these. How much?"

"I'm not taking your money, Addie. I already told you—you can have as much as you like, no charge."

"I couldn't. Please. I'd like to pay," Addie pushes.

Beatrix pulls out a canvas bag from behind her and places the tea inside. "Take this. Put your book in there too. Keep it or return it another time if you like."

"Thank you. That's very generous." Addie puts the bag over her shoulder. "I'd still love for you to consider us stocking them at the store."

Beatrix doesn't say anything, now looking at the bumblebee chain around her neck.

"I'm sorry, I shouldn't have worn it out." Addie fiddles with the pendant. "I found it at the store. I'll return it to Gary, don't worry."

Beatrix frowns. "Why would you return it to Gary? It's not Mary's, it's mine."

"Beatrix, I am so sorry." Addie flushes with shame and immediately removes it. "I didn't know."

"Why would you? It's okay, I appreciate you keeping it safe for me. I have been looking for it everywhere."

Addie hands the chain over, and Beatrix takes it, a wave of sadness falling over her face.

"It looks like it meant something to you."

"It did. It does." Beatrix gives her a forced smile. "Someone from a long time ago gave it to me."

Addie is intrigued. "Is the bee a reference to your name? Bea?"

Beatrix looks at her with a smile hiding obvious heartache but doesn't reply as she moves over to a waiting customer.

Addie jumps a little as a voice blasts out over a megaphone.

"Ten minutes, everyone. Ten minutes until the wood-chopping competition begins." It sounds like George.

Addie glances at Beatrix, seeing if she has a reaction to his voice. That must be who the sadness is about as she's heard George call her Bea before.

Beatrix returns her look. "You should check it out. It's quick but hard work—especially with that wood George has organized this year. I'm glad he doesn't compete. It's dangerous, if you ask me."

The word *dangerous* sets off a silent alarm inside Addie. Men with axes is certainly a dangerous combination.

Have the fair and someone else will die.

Gale's note flashes into her mind.

Addie hasn't thought about the curse all day.

Impossible to think of anything else now.

Chapter Thirty-Three

Addie heads back toward the wood-chopping event, where everyone is now crowding around. Walter spots her just as she sights him up at the pony rides, and he gives her a tentative wave.

She hasn't spoken to him since his borderline threatening behavior when she mentioned the Highway Reaper. He said he'd see her at the fair, and now he's in his usual uniform of jeans and a vintage T-shirt—this time with a movie poster from *The Shining* on it.

Addie waves back and takes a walk up to where three Shetland ponies carry small children, an adult leading each horse. There is a queue of three other children waiting. The ponies are all too small to be Kip's horse, Smoke. Clancy has said that Smoke was always used at the fair for the pony rides so the bigger kids could have a go.

Except Smoke is as traumatized as the rest of this town, apparently. It breaks Addie's heart that Kip's horse is another casualty of everything that has been happening around here.

"Addie, hello. I was hoping to run into you." Walter shades his eyes from the sun as he squints at her.

"Here I am."

"I must apologize for my behavior the other day. It was out of line and very rude of me."

Addie isn't sure what he's apologizing for exactly, so clarifies by saying "You mean for your casual threat or because you shut me down as if a serial killer didn't haunt this town decades ago?"

"For both. You caught me off guard and I wasn't feeling myself. I forgot my manners, and I hope you'll forgive me." He smiles and touches his imaginary hat like he did the first day they met. *His version of a wink,* she remembers.

"I'll happily forgive you if I can bend your ear. I have a lot of questions." She dips her real hat at him, playing him at his own game.

"I bet you do, and I'd be happy—"

"Excuse me, are you Addie Clarkson?"

Addie spins around to a young woman she doesn't recognize who looks to be in her early twenties.

"I'll leave you be." Walter bobs his whole head at her, already walking off. "Enjoy the fair."

Addie is annoyed at the intrusion and stares at the face of full makeup and long blinking lashes looking expectantly at her. The woman's curly black hair is parted in the middle, and she has on casual, baggy cotton clothing. There is not a drop of sweat in sight.

"I am Addie, yes. I don't think we've met." She doesn't feel like shaking hands, knowing hers very much *are* sweaty.

"Oh no, we haven't met. I'm Dalia. I don't live here. I'm from Kerrindale. I work at the local paper there. Do you know it? I've been following your new blog about there being a curse here, and it sounds super cool. My editor said I should come out and do a story." Dalia finally takes a breath.

Is this girl even old enough to be a reporter? Addie wonders. She glances around herself, making sure no one else is listening in. Talking to other reporters is not exactly going to go down well.

"Dalia, is it?"

Dalia nods.

"What story do you plan to write?"

"Write? On no, I don't write things. I do all of the online content. The paper pays me to create videos, do live reporting, that sort of thing. No one really reads that much anymore—who has time?"

Addie is pretty sure Dalia is being serious and doesn't know whether to laugh or cry.

George makes another announcement that the wood-chopping event is only moments away.

"Oh, I promised I'd cover this. I'm going to do a live in case any weird accidents happen while I'm filming." Dalia claps with excitement. "Imagine getting that coverage as it happens—I'd go viral for sure."

Addie thinks she might be in an episode of *The Twilight Zone*, which her gran loved, and wonders if Dalia even knows what *The Twilight Zone* is. Addie isn't that much older than Dalia, yet she suddenly feels ancient.

Addie doesn't hold back. "Did you really just clap at the idea of someone having an accident live on camera?"

Dalia thinks about it and frowns. "I mean, I don't *really* want someone to get hurt. I'm not a sicko. But I'd love to go viral. Isn't that what everyone wants?"

Addie is about to say something rude but stops herself. If she's honest, she has always wanted a front cover or feature article with her name in the byline, which is just an old person's version of going viral. How can she be angry at Dalia for basically being her?

Addie knows she's just mad someone else is on her turf, covering a story that should be hers. She kicks herself for posting the blog too early.

"Addie, I have to go live right now, or else I'll miss all the action," Dalia says. "Maybe we can catch up later and you can tell me about all these mysterious deaths around here. Or maybe we can even do a live together about it. Cool?" Dalia doesn't wait for an answer and pulls out a selfie stick from her bag, which she attaches her phone to.

Addie has never done a live on her own, let alone doing one with Dalia. She shut all her and Toby's social media accounts down after the break-in. Between the comments and the media taking their personal photos for stories, she felt violated.

Dalia steps away from Addie with her phone raised and starts recording.

@ReporterGirl20 has started a live video.

Hi, y'all! It's Reporter Girl 20 reporting live at the Boney Creek fair.

Behind me is the main event of the day, a wood-chopping thingo where a bunch of guys in tight shirts will chop some wood. I'm not really sure what it's about, but it looks like it could be fun!

A little bit of background on Boney Creek. Hang on, I'll check my notes here. Right, let me do my creepy voice:

Boney Creek. Population 217. A last stop on the road to nowhere. Life is quiet here. Simple. Nothing ever happens, and that's just how folks like it. Well, that is until all those strange deaths started happening. Seven bodies in a matter of months. All accidents. No connection. Coincidences, surely.

One suicide, a gas-leak-turned-house-fire killing a family of four, an incident involving a horse, and a food choking. A lot of deaths for a small town—

"Excuse me, but those are my words."

Y'all this is Addie Clarkson! She's the one who has been writing a blog on this town, and those are, in fact, her words. Super creepy, right?

"What do you think you are doing? You can't just plagiarize other people's works. Wait, are you filming me? Please don't do that."

It's a public space. I can film where I like, you should totally know that. Addie is a big shot journalist from the—

"No, I'm not. I'm not a big shot anything."

So, Addie, what do you reckon is happening in this tiny town? Do you really think it's a curse, or do you think a serial killer is murdering locals one by one?

If you were to take a bet, Addie, who would be the final girl in this scenario? "Girl" being gender neutral, obviously.

I can see all your comments and questions coming in, y'all, but it's hard to read them with this glare—

Oh, did you hear that? The wood-chopping competition is starting! Let me get closer.

Excuse me.

Reporter Girl 20, coming through!

Chapter Thirty-Four

Addie watches Dalia part the crowd with her phone on a stick above her head. Her rapid-fire way of talking, combined with high energy, is weirdly infectious, and Addie is exhausted just watching her.

She is also everything Addie is not. Young, eager, adaptable to the changing landscape of how media is now presented to the public. Her old editor would have loved Dalia and her unashamed approach to getting a story.

Part anger, part shame seeps in. Addie's going backward in her delivery of this story. A blog? What was she thinking? Maybe Clancy was right and she should have given podcasting a go.

Also, how dare she rip off my words as if they are her own. Addie will have to call the Kerrindale paper and find out what is going on over there. If this Dalia girl plans to steal her story from under her, she will have to get ahead of it.

The crowd claps all around her, and Addie focuses on the wood-chopping competition, which is about to start. Eight men are lined up in a row next to their very tall tree posts fixed to the ground. Each of them wear tank tops with sweat marks staining the various colors. They each have on long white pants and different shoes—some sturdy work boots, others plain sneakers.

A few of the men are already burned red on their shoulders and nose. Addie wonders if they've ever heard of sunscreen.

The whole fair seems to have stopped. The only sound is George announcing each of the contestants and going over the rules. If Dalia is still commentating to her viewers, Addie can't hear her over the loudspeaker.

Larry stands by as his two grown sons get called as competitors. If he's proud of them or has any kind of emotion other than scowling, he's keeping it buried like hidden treasure.

Sharmi comes up behind Addie and touches her lightly on the arm. "Have you ever seen an event like this?"

"No, never. It looks hazardous." Addie notices someone else is now manning the stall Sharmi was at.

"It can be, but these men know what they're doing. Larry puts in the prize money every year—that's why we get a few pros who turn up."

Addie nods as men hold up their axes when their names are called. "Seems unfair if there are some professionals. And isn't it a conflict of interest with Larry's sons participating?"

"Try telling Larry that." Sharmi swipes away a fly. "And they'll give some of them a small handicap. It's not fair otherwise, as you said. This event is the tree felling. The hardest by far. We usually have three events, including the underhand and the standing block, but with the tree shortage, they've gone with the most popular event this year."

"George mentioned something about that. So where is the wood from then? Those logs look pretty high."

"Not sure about the wood source, but it *is* high. This event is three boards, not two," Sharmi says like she's telling trade secrets.

Addie nods again, having no idea what mythical language she is speaking.

Sharmi laughs as she notices Addie's confused look. "You have no idea what I'm talking about, sorry. I was like that when I first watched it. It's better I don't explain—see for yourself. It'll blow your mind at how tough it is, and how quick."

"I'm looking forward to it." Addie gets her phone out ready to film; she wants to show Toby later.

"Keep an eye out for Larry's kids. They don't like being defeated on home soil."

Addie catches Larry's eye, and he gives her nothing but a scowl.

"What's Larry's deal anyway? I always get the impression he doesn't like me, or is he like that with everyone?" Addie knows she's fishing but doesn't care. She's still a little flustered from meeting Dalia.

"That's just Larry. He'll warm to you, don't worry. It took me a while too."

"Good to know. How long have you lived here again?"

"Coming up to ten years now. Not quite a local yet, though, according to most. I was one of the first to move into the cheap housing Larry has planned."

With the competition about to start, it's too noisy to ask what she means by *cheap housing*. All Addie knows is that Larry seems to have his finger on the throat of this town.

George finishes his announcing and now asks the competitors to get ready. He counts them in, each of the men starting at a specific number per their handicap.

Soon the axes are flying, and Addie isn't sure where to film. They start by making a couple of quick cuts into the log to insert a board, which they climb onto to then make another cut, inserting another board until all three boards are in place to get them to the top of the log, finally chopping to its center.

Then they scramble down and do it all over again on the other side.

Addie knows she's holding her breath as she watches. It's as fast as everyone keeps saying, but it's the men standing precariously on the boards as they chop so high above the ground that makes her nervous.

It seems like the wood is causing some of the competitors grief as they reach the top, and one of Larry's kids is cursing as he can't seem to make a cut impactful enough to move to the other side.

He calls down to his father, "This is bullshit. Someone gave me the dud position."

"Keep chopping and shut your mouth," Larry shouts back.

Wood chips are flying, and parents pull their kids behind them, knowing one of those to an eye would cause some serious damage. Addie wonders how Dalia is doing being so close to the action.

All but one of the men are onto placing their boards to get their final position of lopping off the top of the log, which apparently declares the winner. Only Larry's younger kid can't chop into his wood to save himself. His board bends and wobbles as he loses his cool and chops furiously to no avail.

Larry mumbles something under his breath and is shooting daggers at George with his eyes. George doesn't notice as he gives commentary on the event with his usual gusto and charm.

One of the men is now at the top, and people are cheering him on. Addie finds herself doing the same as she films the man, but keeping her eye on Larry's kid, who has given up and watches as he is defeated.

The man wins and the crowd cheers. George keeps calling until everyone has finished and gives a lighthearted chuckle to Larry's kid. "Looks like that new wood caused someone a bit of trouble. Better luck next year, Harrison."

Harrison jumps down onto his boards to get to the ground and shakes his fist at George. "You did it deliberately. I guess you're tired of me and my brother winning the money every year."

Harrison raises his axe, and for a moment, it looks like he's going to charge at George with it before Larry steps in and takes it from him, whispering something in his son's ear.

Larry then goes to his other son, who has placed second, and also takes his axe. No handshake, pat on the back, nothing. Larry wears his disappointment like he wears his hat, for all the world to see.

Ribbons are given, and Harrison cracks his knuckles, his face going redder and redder. Addie brings her camera up again, sensing something about to happen. Dalia does the same as her phone is seen hovering nearby.

The winner brushes past Harrison, deliberately provoking him. This man is huge and has nothing to fear from the smaller son, it seems.

Addie can almost see it play out before it happens as Harrison pushes the man from behind and the two quickly get into a fistfight. People are quick to break them up but not before Larry's older son slams the winner across the back with one of his boards.

The man staggers, and Addie gasps, her video still rolling.

Some of the other competitors step in, one with an axe raised to Larry's kids. Addie zooms her camera in to find Larry is watching on like he couldn't care less that his kids are publicly assaulting people.

Shouts come from the other side of the fair now and then a loud, piercing scream.

Then another.

It's enough for all the men to stop midfight, and Addie follows her camera to where they are looking. A group has gathered around Mildred's baked goods stall, and another lady screams for help.

Addie runs to the stall, her phone now by her side, her heart pounding in her ears. She has to push onlookers out of the way as she sees what everyone is staring at.

It's Mildred. She's lying on the ground with her dress hitched up and her knee-high stockings falling down. Her face is blue. A woman holds Mildred's hand and cries.

"Someone call an ambulance," Addie yells as she steps forward and moves the lady out of the way.

She gets on her knees and checks Mildred's breathing. No pulse.

Crap, crap, crap is all Addie can think as she tries to remember her first aid training.

Someone else is by her side now. It's Beatrix.

Good. Beatrix is a nurse. She knows what to do.

Addie makes way for Beatrix, who also feels for a pulse. Listens to Mildred's heart. Checks her airways.

"What happened?" Beatrix says as she begins chest compressions like she does it every day, which she does.

"I don't know. She was like this when I got here."

"I've called an ambulance," a young girl with a phone in her hand says. "They won't be here for at least another thirty minutes."

"She doesn't have thirty minutes," Beatrix says, her voice calm. "Go and get the first aid team over at the wood-chopping event. I told them to have an ambulance standing by, but no one ever listens."

Addie isn't sure if she's talking to her, but a young boy bolts off, so she figures he's on it. "Will Mildred be okay?"

"She's blue. Maybe some kind of asphyxiation. Did she choke on something?" Beatrix says to no one in particular. "Heart attack?"

Addie doesn't answer as she knows Beatrix isn't talking to her.

Two first aid members race over with their kits and sit across from Beatrix, who asks, "Do you have the portable defibrillator?"

One nods and pulls it out. Beatrix keeps pumping away at Mildred's chest.

Addie sees two kids run off with some of Mildred's baked goods and, like this is some kind of dream, can hear Dalia talking excitedly into her phone screen.

Another one dead. Is this really happening?

Chapter Thirty-Five

DAY FIFTEEN

Addie sits in the kitchen in the dark, a freshly made pot of Beatrix's tea beside her.

The only light is from her laptop, the blank page of her blog staring back at her. She doesn't even know where to start with what happened to Mildred.

What did *happen to Mildred?*

She's alive, for one. Beatrix finally reviving her. The report back from the hospital is that Mildred suffered sunstroke, but the patient herself has told Beatrix, who is nursing her, that that's a load of codswallop and someone did something to her. Put a spell on her is what she keeps saying.

So far no blood work has reported anything abnormal with Mildred, apart from elevated blood pressure and dehydration.

So maybe it *was* heatstroke, which can be fatal to the elderly.

Addie pours herself a cup of tea and sips on it. The lavender and mint aromas hitting her nose before they swarm her palate.

If it wasn't so late, she'd call Beatrix like she has for the last two days since the fair. Addie knows she has an ulterior motive for checking in on Mildred, and she suspects Beatrix knows that too.

The cursor blinks at her from the blog. She's been sitting here for an hour already—Toby went to bed hours ago—and the words are not coming. She's not sure what she even wants to say anymore—about this town, about a possible curse.

A possible killer.

And does she even want to put up a new blog post anyway with that young journalist Dalia, from Kerrindale, potentially stealing her ideas? No, it's best she hold off on posting anything new until she works out what she wants to do with her story.

If there even is one. She's yet to find concrete evidence linking any of the accidents together or even disproving they *were* accidents.

Addie clicks out of edit mode and checks on the latest blog comments. Mostly trolls. Except for the comments underneath Kip's blog post, which she hasn't seen yet.

UserBC217 again with a new comment:

> You call yourself a journalist? All I see is brown nosing and friendly chats with the locals. When are you going to see what's right in front of you. The Highway Reaper is back and he's hiding behind a stupid curse. Open your eyes.
>
> UserLocalGal: See through the smoke and get to the fire.

And there's that phrase again, similar to the one Clancy mentioned Kip had been saying before he died. *Wherever there's smoke, there's fire.*

Now this new blog comment. *See through the smoke and get to the fire.*

It's got to mean something. Who are these two users making comments? Why don't they say who they are? Give her the information firsthand?

Addie can't believe she wants this gifted to her on a silver platter. She's always been about getting to the truth herself, through her own volition. She's disgusted with herself for wanting the answers so easily.

Yet she knows why she's so anxious. Dalia is going to take this story from her if she's not careful. The live coverage from the fair has already racked up tens of thousands of views, and people are begging for a series on the cursed town of Boney Creek. She's even noticed an increase in traffic on her blog if she's being honest.

Addie should be happy, but how can she be when her one shot at being taken seriously as a journalist is being steamrolled by a rookie with a phone.

Ouch. Addie knows damn well she's just as much of a rookie at all this as Dalia is. Envy is never a welcome visitor. Her anger is with herself. She's lost her grit, her drive. This town, the break-in, her brush with the media, it's all made her soft.

No more. This is her story, and she's going to fight for it.

She knows she has something, even if what Gale told her is true and Janet's death wasn't foul play. That doesn't mean that something bad didn't happened to Kip, Mary, and the Donollys.

She scans over the comments on her blog again, her adrenaline pumping even with Beatrix's calming tea in her system.

What is she missing?

The comment says straight out that the Highway Reaper is back. So someone other than Toby thinks the same thing. Which means that an elderly killer is stalking the town, or a copycat of some kind, killing its residents, and hiding behind a series of well-staged accidents.

How is he staging them? Getting away with it? Does he have an accomplice? Multiple? Her mind flicks to Larry and his sons. Larry is the right age; his sons have access and the strength to pull off the killings. But why? What's their motive?

Has the Highway Reaper trained someone up? A protégé to take over from him? It's possible. But why now? And why the locals chosen?

The town has changed since the Highway Reaper had the means and access to drifters and passersby. A crime of opportunity is less of an option now with the highway gone and the jobs with it, and that may have forced the change in the pattern of behavior.

It all comes back to what is the connection between the recent deaths and finding a motive.

Addie makes notes as she thinks. Her stream of consciousness better on paper, where she can look at her words again and again, but only getting those fresh perspectives once.

Addie taps the pen on her notepad. Stares at the screen.

The last comment has her intrigued. What is this person's connection to Kip?

See through the smoke and get to the fire.

Is it a clue? Another warning?

A threat?

Addie shivers. Gets up to make a fresh cup of tea.

She looks out into the quiet of the night. The half moon casting a blue tinge over the barren pasture, trees creating long, creepy shadows.

Anyone could be out there, and she'd have no idea. She's grateful the light isn't on where she stands, certain she is mostly hidden in her own shadows.

In her own dark thoughts.

Open your eyes. See through the smoke and get to the fire.

She frowns.

It's got to be about the Donolly family. All of them perished in a fire.

She scrambles back to the laptop and greedily scans the UserLocalGal's comment.

That has to be it. The Donolly fire.

She needs to "open her eyes" and see the crime scene for herself. There has to be a clue out there, and if there is, she'll find it.

A TOWN CURSED?

The Tragic Deaths of the Donolly Family
DRAFT BLOG TEXT

NOT YET POSTED

Late one Saturday night, the Donolly family was sleeping soundly before a tragedy befell the household and led to their untimely deaths.

Eddie (43) and Shelley (42) Donolly were in their master bedroom, with their two children, Jacob (11) and Sally (7), tucked up in their own rooms.

At some point in the night a portable gas heater, which had been accidentally left on, would produce toxic fumes that suffocated the house's residents. Soon after the excessive heat and proximity to the living room curtains caused a fire that would burn down the house and its occupants.

Police reports say that all of the Donolly family had died from carbon monoxide poisoning before the blaze occurred and not from the fire. Little comfort for a much beloved family in the small town of Boney Creek.

Eddie Donolly had been part of the rural community for most of his life, his family farm going back many generations. He met his wife,

Shelley, when they were both at the same university in Bretford and married soon after graduation.

(ADDIE NOTE: Confirm Eddie and Shelley's occupations.)

Both of their children, Sally and Jacob, were born and raised in Boney Creek and attended the local school in Kerrindale.

The Donolly family tragedy was the second to occur in the small town in a matter of months.

The first being another permanent resident, (name withheld [38]), who took their own life for reasons unknown.

The Donollys' gas heater accident/house fire was one month later.

Kenneth "Kip" Shaw (18) was Boney Creek's third incident/victim after being killed when his horse spooked and fatally kicked him (see this blog post here).

And lastly, Mary Peterson (81)—who owned the general store that my husband and I took over—died choking on her breakfast cereal (see this blog post here).

That is four incidents resulting in seven deaths in the space of three months. All of them deemed accidental or by their own hand. None of them connected in any way that has been established and none have been considered suspicious.

(ADDIE NOTE: Find any connections and add here. Confirm someone who saw Kip riding Smoke through town the night of fire.)

(ASK SHARMI: about the heater and why it may have malfunctioned? Any enemies of the family? If there had been any other threats or suspicious behavior before the fire? If she knows what "if there is smoke, there is fire" might relate to?)

Addie Clarkson has a degree in journalism and now runs the general store in Boney Creek with her husband and a truant cat called Gravy.

If you are passing through, mention this blog to get a two-for-one coffee deal.

Chapter Thirty-Six

DAY SEVENTEEN

The gate of the Donolly farm is open as Addie drives along the lengthy dirt driveway leading up to the main dwelling.

She has to choose between looking out for potholes and staring at the black, charred skeleton of a house. Addie chooses the potholes, only because changing a tire in this heat is out of the question.

Sharmi waves as Addie pulls up and gets out of her car, noting a tall chestnut horse in full tack standing under a tree next to a trough of water. "Did you ride over?"

"Yes. He's an ex-racehorse I was supposed to rehome but decided to keep instead. His racing name is Strident Moon, but we just call him Blaze. Didn't win any races but won my heart instead." Sharmi looks over at him with pride. "I can't stay too long—do you mind if we get started?"

Addie takes in what used to be a home and shakes her head at how brutal it is now that she's close up. "This is horrific."

Sharmi sighs heavily. "It really is."

Most of the weatherboard house is burned all the way down to the floorboards. Blackened wood frames where a loving home once stood. The study, laundry, and bathroom—which are at the back of the house—are the only spaces that haven't been totally destroyed. Addie can see right through into these remaining rooms from where she stands, and it feels eerily invasive.

"Is it safe to go in?" Addie asks, grateful she wore her work boots.

"Given I've been going in for weeks now, I'm going to say . . . yes?" Sharmi shrugs.

"I'll follow your lead then." Addie waits for Sharmi to climb onto the wraparound veranda, which has black holes and splintered timber everywhere.

Sharmi takes each step carefully, until they cross the threshold into the house, and then walks normally. "Most of the flooring in here has been stood on, so anything that is going to give has already done so."

Addie looks down into a large hole, showing the dirt below. "I'll take your word for it."

Sharmi looks comfortable as she strides through what used to be the living room, pointing out a corner of the house that is completely decimated. "That's where the heater was. Gas filled up the house for who knows how long, and then the excessive heat caused the curtains to ignite."

Addie notes the hitch in her voice and asks her next question with as much compassion as she can. "Do you think the police were right and they were dead from the fumes before the fire started?"

"That's the theory, yes. We are still waiting on the official report from the coroner, which might be months off yet." Sharmi continues looking at where the accident happened like she can see something that Addie can't.

"I'm sorry, Sharmi. I totally understand if this is too difficult to talk about." Addie places her hand lightly on Sharmi's shoulder.

"I never talk about them. No one wants to. Like they never existed in this town or were part of our lives. I miss my friend."

Addie is reminded of Clancy saying something similar about Kip.

Sharmi's shoulder sags under her hand, so Addie removes it. "Shelley was your friend's name, right? How long did you know each other?"

The smell of the house is starting to bother Addie. Ash and soot still lingering.

"I called her Shell. My Shell. We actually went to university together. Both of us studying law because it sounded exciting, but the truth is it was far from it. Our priorities shifted after we got our degrees, and neither of us regretted that."

Addie is curious. "So you never worried you were going backward or not doing big enough things with your career coming to Boney Creek?"

"No." Sharmi's response is immediate. "That corporate lifestyle suits some people, but I didn't want to get caught up in the grind of it. Shelley felt the same way. I'd take horses over billable hours any day."

"Good to hear, thank you." Addie feels a sense of peace at hearing Sharmi's answer. "So you went to Bretford University? Isn't that where Shelley met her husband, Eddie? Did you know them both back then or just Shelley?"

Sharmi smiles. "I actually played cupid and introduced them. Eddie worked at the same restaurant I did, and I knew they'd hit it off. Eddie was hilarious and a very kind man. Shell deserved that."

Addie notes she has a lot of gaps to fill in her draft blog of the Donollys. "And how did they end up here?"

"Eddie always knew he was coming back to work on the farm. He was also a certified accountant and did a lot of work from home. Shelley wanted desperately to have a family, and the country lifestyle honestly suited her." Sharmi rubs a section of the charred wall absently.

"And you?"

"Me?" Sharmi looks confused. "Oh, you mean how did I end up in Boney Creek? Shelley suggested it. She told me how Larry had plans to set up cheap housing for people who can't afford to buy in the bigger cities. I've been helping with the legalities of setting up dozens of kit homes all around town, slowly building things up."

Now it all makes sense that Larry wants to buy so much land. "So what's the catch? With the cheap housing, I mean?"

"No catch." Sharmi laughs and wipes her hand on her riding pants, leaving a small black mark. "Larry wants this town to thrive like it once did. He said if he can bring more people into the town, it will create jobs and better infrastructure. I was his guinea pig, I guess. I'm not sure what I'll do now that Shell, Eddie, and the kids aren't here."

Addie hasn't heard about Larry's plans and knows Toby will be interested when she tells him. He's always mentioning the town's potential. "So how did Larry get possession of this place? Aren't there relatives who want to keep the property in the family?"

"That's a good question." Sharmi moves off, going down what looks like a hall. "Shell did freelance legal work from time to time, mainly with contracts, drafting wills, things like that. She loved all that stuff at school. I was more into corporate law."

Addie follows behind, taking in the devastation. Spaces that were clearly bedrooms come off from the hall. Toys, books, clothes are scattered everywhere. Some burned, some looking like they've been drowned by a fireman's hose.

Sharmi continues, "Shell redid their family will after both of the kids were born. She wanted to make sure if anything happened to her and Eddie that the kids would get everything."

Instead they all perished together.

Chapter Thirty-Seven

Sharmi explains, "She never expected the kids to die at the same time, and the only remaining member of Eddie's family was an uncle who lives in London. He sold the house quickly after the police investigation, and insurance inspectors gave the go-ahead to the first offer he received." Sharmi confirms what Addie already knows. "Larry."

"So what will happen to this place? Will Larry knock it down and build again?" Addie keeps her hand over her nose. The heat from the sun worsens the mildewy smell as they tread up the hall.

"I presume so." Sharmi sidesteps another hole in the floor. "That's why I'm collecting everything I can that's salvageable and either selling it off or keeping it so there is something to remember them by."

"You said there were some things that might be of interest to me? For the store?"

They are at the study now. Its doorframe still intact, which they stand near. "Most of that stuff is in the shed out back. Shell loved having parties, and I know there are some tables and chairs that might be useful."

The study is in pretty good shape. Smoke-and-water damaged, but for the most part intact. "Mind if I go in?" Addie asks.

"Be my guest. It's mainly paperwork and bills in here. Any photos or personal items, I've collected already."

Addie nods as she studies the room. A decent-size desk with notebooks and paper stacked up on either side of where presumably a computer or laptop sat in the middle. A bookshelf with white hardcover folders takes up most of the wall. Similar folders have fallen to the ground.

"So Eddie was an accountant?" Addie references the folders, even though she knows the answer. "How did this room not burn down like the rest of the house?"

"Eddie did taxes, accounting stuff, like I said. Most of it was remote, so he could work from the farm while they were renovating over the last couple of years." Sharmi knocks on the wall. "The fire department said he'd had these reinforced, so they were almost fire retardant. I guess he wanted to protect the files he stored for his clients."

She'll have to tell Toby that there may be locals now looking for an accountant, even if he was keen to leave that life behind when they bought the store. Clearly they need the money. Addie goes around the other side of the desk and opens the drawers; apart from some pens and stationery, they are empty.

"We cleared those out. I still have to go through some of the documents that I have at my place. I wanted to get rid of anything personal given how nosy locals can be."

Addie breathes out a laugh. "That would include new locals too."

"There's nothing in here for you to find anymore. So feel free. This land is easy to access—people have already scavenged."

"If you still have any of the tax files for the general store, I'm sure Toby would love to see them. He mentioned Mary had her taxes done by Eddie."

Sharmi nods. "I can definitely have a look. I'll bring them by if I find anything."

Addie glides her hand over the top of the paperwork, again all of it illegible from smoke or water. She flicks through the pile. A familiar receipt sticks out. She pulls it free and holds it up.

"George's receipts. I'd recognize them anywhere with that handwriting."

Sharmi seems distracted, looking back at the front of the house. "George did a lot of work out here over the years. He's pretty much seen the inside of everyone's house in this town."

Addie studies the receipt. *Kitchen* is the only word she can read. "And what about the built-in heater? Who installed that?"

Sharmi looks at Addie like she should know. "Well, George, of course—but it wasn't his fault, if that's what you're thinking. The heater that caused the accident was a portable one. Why it was being used was a mystery, given they had one built into the wall. Everyone knows those portable heaters are death traps."

Addie slips George's receipt into her back jeans pocket, her curiosity piqued. "So no one has worked out why they would need to use a portable heater when they had one already installed?"

"Exactly, if it was in a bedroom or even in here while Eddie was working, you could understand it, but this was in the main living space." Sharmi studies the front of the house again.

"Everything okay? Are you expecting someone else?" Addie scans the driveway for more vehicles.

"No. I just . . ." Sharmi looks at Addie. "I sometimes feel like someone's watching me when I come out here. Do you feel it?"

"I don't, but this place is pretty isolated. I get why you'd feel exposed." A chill snakes up Addie's spine.

"Should we look at the shed and get going? Sorry to rush you but I should head home before it gets any hotter. I don't like riding in this heat."

"Of course." Addie takes in the study, something feeling not quite right.

Sharmi picks up one of the folders as she leaves and places it on the shelf. The gesture breaks Addie's heart.

"It must be hard coming out here knowing what happened to your friends."

Sharmi heads toward the laundry at the back of the house. "Knowing this place will be gone soon is harder. Like they'll be erased."

Addie follows behind slowly, her thoughts on something else. "Sharmi, you said before that the Donollys dying from the gas and not the fire was a theory. What did you mean?"

Sharmi stops, and Addie almost slams into her. "I wondered if you were going to ask me about that."

"Okay." Addie knows when to wait for someone to talk. Or not.

Sharmi turns to Addie and says, "If they were all dead before the fire hit, then everyone should have been in their beds asleep."

Addie isn't sure where this is going. Her research said they were all found in their beds.

Sharmi continues, "So why then was Shell found burned to death on top of the dining room table?"

Chapter Thirty-Eight

Addie drives back to the store, her mind racing.

There is nothing publicly online to suggest that any foul play was a factor in the deaths of the Donollys. All reports state the family members were in their respective beds, where they supposedly perished.

Sharmi said that she only knew about Shell's position because she had been one of the first people on-site after the fire started and had overheard the firemen saying they found a female body on top of a burned dining table.

What had Shell been doing at the time of the gas leak? Sharmi thought her friend had been getting up to grab a drink, often not sleeping well, and succumbed to the fumes quickly, falling onto the dining room table.

It was a theory she had shared with the police, but lately Sharmi has been questioning if Shell got up to a noise and caught someone in the middle of something. A break-in?

Addie knows all too well how quickly things can escalate when thieves are caught midrobbery. She passes the church, soon back at the store. It's quiet and she's glad. She feels like she's leaving the lion's share of things to Toby.

And Clancy—who's due back at school next week.

Her role of playing detective will have to take a back seat. *Maybe that's for the best,* she thinks. Nothing seems to be connecting, and the more she discovers, the less makes sense. At this rate, her big story idea will end up being a total dud if she doesn't discover something concrete soon.

As she walks through the back door of the shop, she makes a mental note to visit Mildred, who is home from the hospital as of this morning. Find out if she saw anyone or anything suspicious at the fair before she almost died. Maybe a fresh lead will help.

Toby hugs her as he joins her in the kitchenette. "Find anything good out there?"

Addie gives him a quick kiss on the cheek, the smell of him making her feel instantly safe. "We ran out of time to go through the shed properly."

Toby shakes his head, laughing a little. "Let me guess, you were too busy snooping around the crime scene or interviewing Sharmi about the town?"

"You got me. How's it been here? Is Clancy around?" Addie sticks her head out front, but the store is deserted.

"She had to go and help her mother get Mildred settled in. She hasn't come back yet. It's been quiet today anyway—after the fair, everyone seems to be hibernating." Toby pulls a mug down from the top of the coffee machine. "Can I make you a coffee?"

Addie smiles. "I'd love one. I was thinking I might see if Mildred wants one too. I'm sure she'd be grateful for the company."

Toby pours milk into a jug, not looking at her. "I'm wondering if you're asking too many questions too early. I thought we were going to ease into this. Be a little more discreet?"

He's right, and she's wondered the same thing, but she's sure she'll find something if she just keeps digging. "I thought you wanted to know what happened to your uncle?"

Toby stops frothing the milk and looks at her. "I *do* want to know what happened. I promised my mother, and I stand by that promise.

But I want to go slow with this, take our time. We may only get one chance to find the truth, and right now this feels like a game to you, like a puzzle you need to solve."

Ouch. Damned if she does, damned if she doesn't.

"I'm sorry, Tobe. I can assure you this isn't a game to me, and I'll be more tactful going forward. I know we have different styles of doing things, and it might seem like I am going too fast, but I'm making progress and I need you to trust me."

He gapes at her. "You found something?"

She can feel the instant change in energy coming off him, like he's a kid at Christmas. She kicks herself for getting his hopes up when she technically knows nothing.

"It's just a hunch at this stage, but the apparent 'accidents'"—she does air quotes around the word *accidents*—"aren't adding up."

Toby nods. "You found something at the Donollys'?"

"Sharmi told me a detail that I haven't seen reported anywhere and needs some further investigation. It looks like Shelley Donolly wasn't in her bed when she died. Which means that she was up and walking around when there was a gas leak."

"Okay?" Toby waves his hand like *keep going.*

"And it got me thinking—"

"No! You? Thinking too much." He chuckles.

She does, too, because maybe she *is* overthinking her theory. "Fair, but what if Shelley was awake because someone else was there?"

"Like a robbery?" He purses his lips.

"Maybe. Or someone she was expecting. Sharmi said she was often awake at all hours because she had trouble sleeping. What if someone knew that and paid her a personal visit?"

Toby gasps a little. "Like an affair?"

"I'm not sure. Maybe." Addie taps the counter with her fingernails like it will help her think. "That's what I want to find out. I'd ask the police about their theories, but they've already shot me down. Without credentials, I'm just a nobody."

She thinks about Dalia and the Kerrindale paper and how they would have all the contacts they need to get the information. The clock is ticking for her to find the answers.

Toby asks, "But if someone else was at the Donolly house that night, wouldn't they have died from the gas leak as well?"

"Not if the gas leak was covering up a crime."

"You think someone killed her and then tampered with the heater? But—" He stops himself.

"Yeah, I know. Those kids. Who could have been that cruel?"

"Wow. If any of that is true, then we have a real sick bastard running around town and breaking into people's houses."

"What if they aren't breaking in? What if they have or had access before?" Addie pulls the receipt out of her back pocket and hands it to Toby. "I found this in their study. It seems George did a whole bunch of work at their place and was the one who installed the heater."

Toby looks up from the receipt. "George? You think he's the one killing people off? He doesn't seem the type."

"I didn't say it was George, but it's worth considering. Sharmi said something interesting when I was out there about how George has worked on and has intimate knowledge of nearly every house in this town. There might be something in that."

Toby frowns, like he's thinking, as he heats up the milk again. "What would George have to gain? What's his motive?"

Addie takes the receipt Toby has left on the counter and puts it back in her pocket. "That's where I'm drawing a blank. There doesn't seem to be one. That or I need to find one."

She watches Toby make the coffees, her thoughts clamoring for attention in her head. Trying to work out why Clancy's father feels important to all this.

Toby hands a coffee to her and sips on his. "Hmm. These new beans really make a difference. I'm glad we switched suppliers. It's a reliable and professional team they have up there."

Addie is half listening, taking her own sip and agreeing that their new coffee supplier provides a much better product than the cheap beans Mary would get in. "You said *team* just then . . ."

Toby waits for her to finish her thought, which she doesn't. "I did. What's going through that head of yours? You want your own team here at the store?"

He smiles a little, but Addie remains serious, still in thought.

"What about George? Does *he* have a team? Surely he can't do all that work by himself?"

"You're right." Toby's eyes go wide. "He must have contractors or tradesmen he brings in for the bigger jobs, which would mean not just George but anyone working for him would have access to those houses."

"Not just the houses but the people inside them." Addie puts down her coffee, the milk making her stomach churn. Or maybe it's the sudden excitement of knowing she's onto something. "Maybe Shelley Donolly knew too much about someone in this town or saw something and she was silenced. Maybe she worked out who the Highway Reaper was."

"That would mean he's alive and well."

"It does." Addie shivers.

"George." Toby clicks his fingers. "He's coming over later to look at some of the pipes that need replacing out back. You know how he loves a chat. I'll find out who he hires. You go and talk to Mildred, and we'll get Clancy to mind the store. Divide and conquer."

Addie leans up and kisses him square on the mouth. "*We* make a great team."

Chapter Thirty-Nine

Even after ten minutes, the smell of Mildred's house takes some getting used to.

Addie can't decide if it's the obvious dust or the suffocating toxic stench of the mothballs spotted around the house. She makes a note to ask Beatrix if they should be removing the balls to save Mildred's lungs from further damage.

Clancy is back at the store, and Beatrix is on a shift at the hospital, so it's just her and Mildred. Oh, and Mildred's dog, Betsy.

He's just like his owner, brutish on the outside and gooey on the inside. A little white ball of fluff who couldn't care less what his name is. Addie pats his curled-up body in her lap beside Mildred's bed.

She has a mountain of pillows behind her and sits up, greedily drinking the coffee Addie brought her from the store. Addie also brought some photos she found in the shed of a young Mildred with Mary and Frank.

"I can't believe the food in that place. What were they trying to do, kill me?" Mildred has brought up the food at the hospital no fewer than three times already since Addie's arrival.

"You look well." It's not a lie. Mildred has color in her skin and seems in fine spirits since her dance with death.

"It's good to be home. Thankfully Clancy looked after Betsy while I was a little worse for wear. He doesn't like being on his own." Mildred sips her coffee and licks her lips. "I miss these. And you've changed the beans. Much better."

"We did. Thanks for noticing." Addie isn't sure how to ask about cheating death, and Mildred is acting like nothing of the sort even happened.

"Get at it, dear. I can hear your questions bubbling from over here." Mildred, as usual, doesn't hold back.

"Am I really that obvious?" Addie smiles as the dog lets out a soft snore.

"You are to me. It's like that brain of yours is only ever in interrogation mode." Mildred gives her a direct look. "You aren't planning on doing one of those ridiculous stories on me, are you? I'm not dead yet."

Addie can't help but laugh. "I might do something about the fair and what happened, but I don't have to mention you by name."

Mildred's straight look becomes one that says: *like that will matter.*

"Anyway, I'm not here for that. I'm here to see how you are."

"Piffle. Just ask me what's on your mind." Mildred settles back into her pillows like Addie's about to tell her a bedtime story.

"Okay then." Addie has missed Mildred's directness. "Did the doctors say anything else about what they think happened to you?"

"Nothing meaningful. It doesn't matter anyway. I know who it was." Mildred looks smug.

"*Who?* Someone did this to you?" Addie wakes the dog up and apologizes by patting him across his scruffy body.

"Of course someone did this to me. Isn't it obvious?" Mildred scoffs, placing her empty coffee cup on the side table near her.

Addie waits for Mildred to tell her who is behind the town's killings, trying her best not to appear too eager. *This is it.*

"You're right about this town being cursed. That's exactly what happened to me. I haven't been to that fair in years because of that woman, and the second I'm there selling my baked goods, she has to come and put a stop to it." Mildred shakes her head, almost spitting her words out.

"A woman? Who was it? And what did she do? Poison you? Put something in your drink?" Addie hadn't even considered a woman doing any of the killings.

"Don't be daft. It's nothing like that. I could see her, pointing right at me. Calling me over like she's come to collect me or maybe whispering some kind of spell. Next minute, my heart stopped."

Addie sighs. Now she knows who Mildred is talking about. Beatrix. Who she believes is a witch. "You know, Clancy and her mother have been nothing but kind to you, and you're still going around gossiping that Beatrix is some kind of witch who put a spell on you?"

"Beatrix?" Mildred frowns. "I'm not talking about her—even if she is a witch. I'm talking about Mary. That woman is haunting this town and is going to take us all with her."

Addie has to take a breath to steady her disappointment. "That's who you think did this to you? Mary's ghost?"

It's not uncommon for a dying person to speak of being visited by dead relatives or friends, even pets, so this doesn't surprise Addie. What is interesting is that it was Mary—her sworn enemy.

"Damned right it was her." Mildred scoffs, flipping through the old photos Addie brought over. "Look at us. So young."

"I wouldn't have recognized you if your name wasn't on the back. It seems like you, Mary, and Frank were always together back then. It must have been hard to lose both of them from your life like that."

Mildred throws the photos on the bed beside her. "Like I said, Mary was at the fair pointing straight at me, mumbling things under her breath. Asking the Reaper to call on me, no doubt. Which he did. Mary never could bear to be alone for too long."

Addie's ears prick up. "The Reaper?"

"Yes, Death himself." Mildred folds her arms over her chest. "He didn't get his way, though, did he?"

"You're stronger than that, Mildred." Addie's thoughts are less on death and more on something else. "It's interesting you bring up the word *reaper*, as I've heard some whispers about another series of deaths that happened a few decades ago. They called him the Highway Reaper."

"Blimey, I haven't heard that name in a while." Mildred recoils a little. "This town was like a different planet back then. You wouldn't even recognize it. *Thriving* is the best way to describe it. Some drifter took advantage of our good fortune and used this town as his hunting ground."

Addie can't help herself as she leans forward a little, careful not to smother the dog. "So you remember the town back then?"

"Of course I remember back then, nothing wrong with my memory." Mildred thinks for a moment. "Why are you asking me about that? Do you know something I don't?"

"I doubt that, Mil—Ms. Whiteman."

"You can call me Mildred. You've seen me in my delicates, so I figure you've earned it." She tugs at her nightie just to drive her point home.

"Thank you, Mildred. I appreciate that." Addie puts the dog at the end of Mildred's bed so she can focus fully, and he curls up and is asleep instantly. "I guess I want to get your take on if all the deaths happening recently could be the work of the same person who did those killings back then?"

Mildred laughs. "I doubt it. For one, it was no local giving us a bad reputation with all those missing backpackers. It was some drifter, like I said. Some ruffian who was here for quick work and to use our sweet town as his personal playground for evil."

Addie mines her information on the Reaper case and says, "Yes, but didn't this happen over years and not just months?"

"If you say so." Mildred seems to be clamming up.

Addie treads carefully. "I don't say so—it's what the news reports from back then say."

"All I know is that a lot of people went missing, but no one could verify they were dead. Most of them were backpackers or hitchhikers, so anything could've happened, and no one can prove it went on here in Boney Creek."

Arguing semantics with Mildred is not going to work. "Okay, but there's a lot of people around town who were here when this occurred. Maybe there's someone you can suggest I talk to?"

"The only person who likes opening his trap around here is Walter. I've seen he's taken quite a shining to you. Ask him."

Addie is surprised. "But Walter said he wasn't here when the disappearances started. He didn't come to Boney Creek until the mideighties or so."

"Is that what he said, is it? Well then." Mildred yawns. She's a bad actress, as it's clearly fake. "I'm tired, might nap like my Betsy there."

Addie kicks herself. She pushed too quickly. Toby will be disappointed in her. "Of course, you must be exhausted. I can come over later and check on you if you like. Bring you another coffee?"

Peace offering, more like.

Mildred fluffs her pillows around her. "No need. I'm right as rain now."

Not great if she can't even bribe Mildred with coffee. *What is she hiding?* Addie wonders. "I'll leave you be. Just call if you need anything, and one of us will come straight over." Addie rises and takes the empty cup.

"Don't bother locking the front door. Beatrix said she'll be over later to see me." Mildred pulls the bedsheets up to her chin. "She comes and goes as she pleases now. Betsy doesn't even make a sound. Can you believe it? That dog barks for any other thing that moves, but not Beatrix. I told you she was a witch."

Addie sighs and turns to leave. "Well, I'm glad you're feeling better. You gave us quite the scare."

"Speaking of scares, if you run into Mary's ghost, tell her to haunt someone else. I've got a lot more living to do." Mildred's voice is muffled from the sheets.

"I will be sure to do that." Addie walks into the hall reluctantly. "Take care of yourself and get some rest, Mildred."

"Call me Ms. Whiteman!"

Betsy's bark hits home that Addie has really screwed this one up.

Chapter Forty

Addie walks back to the store, the sun beating down on her head.

That cow-manure smell is back, and right now it annoys her. She should have handled Mildred more tactfully.

The only vehicle parked at the store is George's truck, which has an open toolbox on the flatbed on the back. That's something—at least George is still here, and hopefully Toby is *actually* getting some answers.

She waves to Clancy inside and goes around to the back of the store, where George is squatted over a freshly dug hole in the ground. His shorts ride low, and Addie can see his butt crack. Charming.

Toby smiles as she approaches, giving her a quick thumbs-up. She's pleased knowing he's getting some answers. She's pissed off that she can't return the favor.

"Hey, George," Addie says as she stands beside Toby, giving his hand a quick squeeze. "How's it all going here?"

George looks up and shades his eyes. "Addie. Good to see you. Can't say it's going well, to be frank. Do you want to tell her, or should I?"

"You tell her." Toby shrugs as Addie looks up at him.

She already knows they are about to spend more money they don't have.

"Most of these pipes are completely shot. Small cracks are affecting the water that is coming from your rain catchments, which is not great. Soon they'll be large cracks, and then you'll have no water at all." George stands and points to a series of green grassy spots leading to the large water tank. "See those bursts of green?"

Addie nods. Toby purses his lips—he obviously knows what George is about to say.

"That's where your leaks are."

Addie groans. There are loads of them.

George continues, "Good news is that I know where your trouble spots are. Bad news is there are too many leaks to fix individually, so my advice is we set about replacing the lot. Maybe go with some copper piping this time, so you don't have these problems."

"Isn't copper expensive?" Addie asks, even though she knows the answer.

"It is compared to replacing your current plastic piping with another plastic. I can quote for a few options, and you folks can see what works best for your budget. How does that sound?"

"Sounds good, George. Has to be done, so we may as well do it right," Toby says.

"Anyway, I'd get onto these pipes quick smart if I were you. There won't be rain for months, and you don't want to lose any more water. It's like gold around here."

Addie follows her eyes along the spots of green, which provide a clear path of where the pipes lay underground—everything else in the yard is bone dry and dead as a doornail.

"Righto. I'll get you that quote, and we'll book you in."

Addie isn't sure what intel Toby already has, but she's not going to miss a good lead when it's presented to her. "Will you be doing the job, or will it be someone else you have working for you?"

She feels Toby tense beside her. Crap, has she put her foot in it again?

"You two seem mighty interested in my crew today. Something I should know? Anyone complaining of bad service or anything like that?" He looks at both of them, waiting for an answer.

Addie answers first. "Um . . . no, nothing like that. I was more curious because you have so much work on, and I worry for you doing all that by yourself."

George frowns. "You don't think I can do it myself? That it?"

Addie looks at Toby, but he's obviously curious how she's going to get out of this one.

"Quite the opposite, actually." Addie pulls her shoulders back, gaining her confidence. "What I meant is that I'd prefer if it was you doing the work, especially if we are getting copper put in. I'd just prefer this job to remain discreet, that's all."

George visibly relaxes, even laughs a little. "Well, why didn't you just say that? Of course I'll do your job, and I agree on being discreet. People will do anything for a quick buck around here."

Addie relaxes as well.

Toby still looks a little unsure. "You mentioned you have one of Larry's kids doing most of the manual labor. Does that mean he'll be coming to do the digging, or do you do that too?"

George considers the question. "I haven't given it much thought, but I imagine it'll be Harrison doing the digging. He's a hard worker, that one. It's better if we do this by hand than by machine—don't want to dig up anything else while we're at it."

"Like what?" Addie gasps.

"I mean electricity lines. Possibly septic, though I doubt it. What'd you think I was talking about?" George asks.

Addie straightens her face, which obviously has a mind of its own. "I was just asking. I can't seem to help it."

"She really can't." Toby softens and even grabs her hand.

"George, can I get you a drink? A coffee? I'm about to make some sandwiches for me and Toby. And your daughter, obviously. You are welcome to join."

George flinches a little, like he's pained. "I'd love to, but I have to head back out to the Donollys' place this afternoon. Sharmi wants me to check on a few things."

Addie's ears prick up. Toby squeezes her hand tightly, already preempting the questioning.

"I was actually out there earlier. It's horrible what happened." Addie blinks as the sun catches on a piece of tin from the shed and blinds her.

"It really is. That poor family didn't deserve what happened to them. Good people." George hitches up his shorts and sighs. "Right tragedy if you ask me."

"I heard you spent a lot of time out there, doing work on their home . . ." Addie leaves the words dangling, hoping George will fill in the rest.

"Oh yeah. I did a lot of work out there. We gutted their kitchen, built a new bathroom, laundry. Redid the septic. Lots of electrical. That place was really taking shape." George looks like he's done talking as he grabs the shovel and fills in the hole that he dug.

"When you say *we*, who was out there working with you?"

George keeps shoveling. "Oh, there was a few of us, depending on the work. Myself, obviously. Larry Jr. most days. Larry came over to help with some demolition, same with his other son, Harrison. Kip's old man, Ken, was there for a bit of heavy lifting."

Addie nods like she's not that fussed with what George is telling her. Just conversation. Toby gives a small nod like this is also the same intel he has gotten.

George pats over the hole with the shovel. "That'll do it then. Can't have anyone falling in that until I'm back next."

"Thanks, George. We appreciate it," Addie says.

Someone clears their throat at the back door, and all of them look to Clancy, who's leaning into the frame, obviously annoyed at something.

"Hey, love. Didn't see you there." George tilts his head at his daughter. "Why have you got that face? What'd I do now?"

Clancy shakes her head at him, scowling. "I can't believe you've forgotten him already."

George looks confused. "What are you on about?"

Clancy stands upright, her face flushed. "You really forgot who was also out there at the Donollys' helping out, huh? It's like he never existed to everyone in this town."

George finally catches on. "You're right, love. No excuse to forget him like that."

Addie doesn't need for them to spell it out. It's obvious who they are talking about that was also out helping at the Donollys' farm.

Kip.

Chapter Forty-One

Addie stands wiping the same shelf over and over.

Her brain is doing that thing where it has many dots and she can't make them connect. The only solution is cleaning. It calms her mind and helps her not get overwhelmed by everything going on in her brain.

Toby sits in back in the kitchen with the laptop. His budget open, trying to reconcile profit with loss. Loss is the clear winner. Like Addie with cleaning, Toby needs his time with his spreadsheet. Playing with numbers until they make sense, his own way of overcoming anxiety.

The store is quiet, listless. Waiting for customers who aren't coming today. There seems to be a weird feeling about the town. Like knowing a storm is coming. Or seeing the smoke before the orange flames of a fire.

Just like Kip kept saying before he died. Did he know what happened at the Donollys' and was trying to tell someone through his cryptic clue? Kip died after the Donollys, so it's highly possible.

Or was Kip the one who tampered with the gas heater and set the house on fire? Is that who Shelley caught that night? Addie has yet to find anyone who actually saw Kip riding away from the Donolly house the night it happened, so was it just a rumor?

More questions.

Addie let Clancy go home early. She was in tears, presumably because of how everyone is forgetting her best friend. It's not surprising.

No one seems to be talking about the deaths that occurred here so recently, or if they are, they are just whispers. Addie said she would pop over to the teen's place later and watch a movie or play a game or something. Keep her company while her mom is working, like she promised.

She picks up each of the candy bars from their box and wipes them with a dusting cloth. One by one, until the box is empty. Then she neatly stacks them again and moves on to the next box. A pointless task, when there are so many other things she should be doing around here, but she needs this menial work to help her focus.

She keeps returning to the fact that Kip was out at the Donollys' doing work. What does that mean? Did he see something he shouldn't have, and someone killed him? Or did he kill Shelley and the rest of the Donollys, and someone took matters into their own hands when they found out?

How did they make his horse, Smoke, kick him if it wasn't an accident? Why not make it look like a suicide?

A suicide.

Like Gale's sister, Janet. With Gale corroborating her sister took her own life, it is the only death Addie can confirm was neither an accident nor foul play.

She opens the Snickers in her hand and takes a bite. The cleaning isn't helping, so maybe sugar will. It's the afternoon after all, when everyone should be doing nothing but taking a siesta.

She chews slowly, letting the chocolate work its magic to help her think. Create a timeline of events.

Janet was the first death in Boney Creek. Suicide.

The Donollys were second. Heater malfunction, leading to a fire.

Kip third. Horse accident.

Mary fourth. Death by choking.

She now knows that Kip was connected to the Donollys and had direct access to their house and land.

Mary had access to everyone, and everyone had access to her. What had her son, Gary, said about locals coming into the rear of the store? That everyone felt welcome back there, even if it was a private area. So anyone had the ability to get to Mary if they needed to.

That just left Janet. Why did she take her life, and how was she connected to all the other deaths? If Gale knows anything, she hasn't said.

And the biggest question of all? How was everything linked to the tragedy of the past, the Highway Reaper killings?

Addie takes another bite and lets the caramel, peanuts, nougat, and chocolate create a perfect storm in her mouth. It's helping. That or it's the placebo effect making her think it's working. Placebo chocolate.

She flicks her eyes to the front of the store, movement distracting her. It's Walter, red and flushed from the sun. She stands up from the milk crate she's been sitting on and opens the door for him before he gets there. "Nice to see you."

He steps in the store and pulls a handkerchief from his jeans pocket, wiping his brow. His *Jaws* T-shirt covered in sweat spots. "Addie. Always a pleasure. Unlike this heat."

"It's not much better in here, I'm afraid. That air-conditioning will have to wait until next summer. For now, stand under the fan, which honestly feels like it's just a rotating oven."

Walter smiles and looks at the cleaning cloth still in her hand. "Getting some chores done? I didn't interrupt, did I?"

"Not at all, in fact an interruption is exactly what I need. Can I get you a drink? Maybe an iced coffee instead of a hot one?"

"I might grab a soda and have it here if you don't mind. I don't want to walk back in this heat just yet." Walter takes a can from the fridge and moves to the table and chairs in the front window, wincing in pain as he takes one of the seats.

"Are you okay?" Addie goes to help him, but he waves her away.

He settles himself, steadying his breath. "I'd love to say yes, but I won't be able to hide it soon."

Addie did wonder if there was something more to his trembling hand. "Is it Parkinson's?"

"That's what I've been told." It's hard to read his expression. "I'll have to face facts soon, but for now I'm content to enjoy the small things. Your company included."

"I'm sorry, Walter. If you need anything, please let us know."

"I appreciate that." He gestures at the other chair across from him. "Come and join me. Looks like you have a lot on your mind, and I'd love a distraction."

"That obvious?" Addie laughs. "I'd love to join you. As you can see, we aren't run off our feet."

Addie grabs a soda as well and sits across from Walter as he sips his. They are silent for a moment, both staring out into the stillness of the main street of Boney Creek. It's like a ghost town, with no cars, no people, no wildlife, not even a gust of air.

"It's been quiet up at the church too. No drop-ins. No one needing a chat or a shoulder for support. It's like the town is holding its breath and waiting for the next tragedy."

Addie taps the side of her soda can with her short fingernails. "I was just thinking the exact same thing. Almost like everyone is afraid to come out after what happened to Mildred at the fair."

Walter eyes her steadily. "You may be onto something there. It's hard to feel safe when death seems to be hovering."

"Isn't that when you ask God for help? Ask for a miracle or something?"

"If it's God's will, then I am not here to question it."

"Seems convenient. Like we have no say in what's happening in this town, or we have no say over our own destinies. I'd prefer to not leave my fate up to something I don't believe in, no offense."

Walter chuckles. "None taken. It is up to each individual to decide what they believe and where they will place their faith."

Addie pulls the half-eaten Snickers from her front pocket; it's already soft and melting. "I place my faith in this chocolate."

"What are you skirting around, Addie? What's really troubling you?" Walter sips his drink, keeping his eyes on her.

Addie glances toward the back and lowers her voice so as not to distract Toby. "I just can't work it all out. All the deaths, the so-called accidents. If they are connected. The timelines. The whys. It's making me a little wobbly."

"I see." He doesn't judge her; there's no shift in his face or eyes. "What makes you think they're connected?"

"I don't know if they *are* connected—that's the thing. Janet's suicide started the chain of events recently, but I know there's something I'm missing there. I just don't have enough information to work out what it is."

"It was a shock to us all, especially Gale. I know things were rough that last year, with the café not doing so well and the accident out at the tree. I worry for that little girl of hers."

"Wait," Addie says. "What accident out at the tree?"

"Oh, I guess you wouldn't know about that. It would explain why you said it was Janet who started the chain of events, but I don't think that's correct."

Addie leans forward. "What do you mean? You said she was the first to die when you showed me the threatening letter Gale gave you."

"So I did." Walter considers this for a moment. "Actually, what I said, if I remember correctly, is that Janet was the first *local* to die."

Addie waits for more, not sure where this is going.

"There was another accident, a year ago. A man called Christos. A tree branch fell on his head when he was out cutting firewood illegally. On your property, mind you, or Mary's back then. If you ask me, that's when things really started getting strange around here."

"Christos? This is the first I am hearing of this." Addie doesn't want any more dots in need of connecting. "Why do you think his death had some connection to what's happening now?"

"Christos was Janet's ex." Walter leans forward. "Myah's biological father."

Chapter Forty-Two

Various snacks and an almost-empty bowl of buttery popcorn sit in front of them as Addie and Clancy finish watching a soppy rom-com where the guy is chasing the girl of his dreams through an airport.

He reaches her just in time, and they kiss. The credits roll.

Clancy groans. "Why do movies always end like that? It takes the guy five billion years to actually realize he loves his best friend, and that's only because she's flying somewhere."

"Movies are not real life, Clancy."

"Would Toby chase you through an airport if he thought he was about to lose you?" Clancy's innocent face looks up at Addie.

"Hmm. Maybe, but only if he didn't have an audience and I didn't force him to talk openly about his feelings."

"That's because he's a Virgo." She laughs. "They overthink things and keep their emotions to themselves for fear of getting hurt."

"That sounds like my husband. Sometimes I have no idea what goes on in that mind of his."

Clancy sighs. "I wish life was like a movie."

"Listen, if the movie kept going, that couple would be sick of each other after a few years." Addie scoops up a handful of popcorn and, seeing how the butter has started to congeal, thinks better of it and throws it back in.

"Yeah, that's true." Clancy has been pensive all night.

Addie figures she is thinking of Kip. "I'm going to wash up. Your mom will be home soon."

Clancy lounges back on the sofa now that Addie is standing. "Mom's doing a double. She won't be back until morning."

"And your father? How is he?" Addie picks up the two empty glasses and stacks them in the popcorn bowl.

Clancy sighs loudly. "Just like you said about real-life relationships, my mom and dad are sick of each other."

So she wasn't thinking about Kip.

"I'm sorry, Clancy. It must be hard."

"Dad's living out in one of the trailers Kip's dad owns in the middle of nowhere. I think he likes it there by himself. No women to annoy him." Clancy doesn't disguise how upset she is.

"I doubt that is true. Your father loves company from what I can see. I bet he misses you more than he's letting on. Haven't you noticed how he finds any excuse to pop into the store to see you?"

"I guess."

Addie picks up the napkins and adds them to the popcorn bowl. "I'm really sorry, Clancy. You've had a tough year."

"The worst." Clancy picks at her lip. "It's like everyone's secrets can't stay hidden anymore."

"What do you mean by that?"

"Nothing." Clancy sits up, suddenly animated. "You know what we should do?"

"Why do I not like the sound of this." Addie walks into the hall toward the kitchen.

Clancy follows like an eager puppy. "We should get the Ouija board out. Talk to Kip."

"No." Addie puts the dishes in the sink and turns to Clancy. "Your mother was very clear about you not using that thing. I was here when she told you, remember?"

Clancy isn't listening, already bounding up the hall.

Addie checks her phone for a text from Toby, but there's nothing. It's still early, and he's probably sitting with a beer in front of the TV in their own home. A pang runs through her; she misses him.

"Why don't we head back to my place. You can sleep in the spare room," Addie calls out. She's yet to do much with Gary's old room, but the bed has fresh linen at the very least.

"Hang on. We can't go yet." A thud comes from up the hall and Clancy curses. "I'm okay!"

Addie can't help but smile.

"I've got it," Clancy says as she comes back into the kitchen with the Ouija board in her arms.

"I thought your mom said to put that in the chest in the shed."

"She did, but then I found something and forgot." Clancy moves a candle and a small vase of flowers from the kitchen table and places the board there instead. She pulls the heart-shaped piece of wood from her hoodie pocket. "This is called a planchette, and this is how we talk to Kip."

"There is no way we are using that. Your mother would kill me, and you in the process."

The teen plonks into the chair and moves the planchette from side to side on the Ouija board. "I just want to talk to him."

Addie is out of her depth. "Why don't you talk to me instead? I can tell you haven't been yourself."

"You wouldn't understand." Clancy puts her arms on the board and rests her chin on them.

"Try me." Addie gets up to put the kettle on and to give time for Clancy to open up. "Do you want some tea?"

"Sure. As long as it isn't the lavender one."

Addie pulls down the Berry Blast flavor and scoops some into the teapot infuser, keeping her hands busy as she talks. "You said you found something before . . ."

"Yep. In Mom's chest. She always has it locked, but she gave me the key." Clancy plays with the planchette like it's a toy car.

"I remember—I was here. She's not going to be happy you didn't lock that board away, though."

"I know, but I don't care." Clancy sighs and leans back in her chair. "I need it."

"Why do you need it?" The kettle whistles as it boils, and Addie's heart jumps a little. The mood has gotten weird.

"To talk to them. Ask questions."

"Them?" Addie stops midpour.

"I meant Kip." Clancy stares at the Ouija board. "Whatever. I thought you'd help me. I thought you wanted answers too."

Addie finishes pouring the hot water into the pot and lets it steep. She needs to tread carefully. "I do want to help, but not like this."

"You wouldn't understand." Clancy has tears in her eyes.

"I do understand." Addie comes over and sits across from her. "I lost my gran a few years back, and I'd do anything to talk to her again, but not like this. I also won't go against your mother's wishes."

Clancy wipes her eyes. "What would you ask your gran if you could talk to her again?"

Addie closes her eyes, knowing exactly what she would say to the woman who raised her. She would say she was sorry. Sorry for not being there when she died. Sorry for not checking on her earlier when her gran wasn't answering her phone. Sorry for leaving her to rot like that when she should have been there; instead a ridiculous story had been her priority.

Only she states none of that to Clancy, instead saying "I would tell her I'm sorry for not becoming the storyteller she wanted me to be . . . and that I miss her."

"You can say that anytime. Mom says that spirits can hear us when we talk, but not to bother them too much. I tell Kip I miss him all the time." Clancy places the planchette on top of the wooden board. "Using this is different, though. This is about trying to get answers."

Addie brings over their tea, wishing she'd made some of the calming one as well. "What questions, Clancy? Tell me what's going on."

"Why don't you speak to your mom?"

"It's not something I like talking about." That's not what Addie wants to think about tonight either. "She gave me up when I was just a baby. She didn't want to be a mom, so she left me with her mother—my gran."

"And your father?"

"I never knew him." Addie studies Clancy. Something tells her these questions aren't about her. "What did you find in the chest?"

"A letter Mom hid from me." Clancy picks up the planchette and holds it flat in her palm. "Do you think if I could talk to Kip, he'd tell me what happened that day?"

Addie is intrigued about what's in the letter Beatrix hid from Clancy, given she's said they don't keep secrets in this house, but Addie doesn't want to push. The teen will talk about it if she wants to, and knowing Beatrix, she already knows Clancy has found something.

"You should talk to your mother, Clancy. Keeping secrets is never a good idea, especially from the people we love."

Addie can hear herself. She has no right to give advice she doesn't adhere to.

"You make it sound so easy." Clancy gets up and puts the Ouija board under her arm, clearly upset.

Addie sighs, pouring tea into their cups in the hopes Clancy will sit back down. "Listen, if you want to talk to Kip, then your mom also said she'd help you do that."

"Mom can't be there when I talk to Kip."

Addie swallows her tea. "Why not?"

Clancy stalks up the hall to her room and yells out before she slams the door, "Because I think my dad had something to do with Kip's death."

Chapter Forty-Three

DAY EIGHTEEN

After the bizarre events with Clancy the night before, Addie doesn't get much sleep and is paying for it now. She knows she needs to talk with Beatrix about what Clancy said but doesn't know how to do that without betraying the teen's trust. Also how does she say out loud that Clancy thinks her father might have killed Kip?

Instead she does what she does best and immerses herself in menial tasks. Thankfully, today is the day most of their deliveries turn up, and there is a massive pile of mail and packages she has to get sorted.

Toby has also woken up in a weird mood and has been strangely silent and surly most of the morning. No amount of coffee or prompting from Addie has helped so far. He can get like that sometimes, preferring to process things internally.

Addie knows to leave him be and doesn't mind sorting the mail. She can let her mind wander as she scans in packages and inserts envelopes into the correlating name-and-address slots—with so few residents, they only take up part of the wall.

She half expects Beatrix to storm in here any minute and berate her for letting Clancy pull out the spirit board, but Addie also knows the likelihood of Beatrix ever stepping into the store is slim to none.

Clancy isn't in today. She went into Kerrindale with her mother to get school supplies. Addie is resigned, knowing that soon Clancy won't be around to assist them at the store unless it's over the weekend.

Her phone buzzes in her back pocket, and looking at the screen, she is excited at the name of the person calling her. Jada Gonzales, her old editor from the paper. Her heart rate picks up as she answers it.

"Jada, hey."

"I see you've left me multiple messages." Her voice is the same as usual, clipped and rushed. Jada has this way of speaking that makes Addie think she's done something wrong.

"Yes, I did. What do you think?" Addie's heart feels like it's beating in her mouth.

"It looks like you may have something there." Jada almost sounds friendly. "I scanned your blog, which needs a lot of work and reads more like fiction, but I'm interested in the story pitch you sent me."

"You are?" Addie lowers her voice, so she doesn't sound like an excited child and repeats herself. "You are. That's great."

"Do you really think those accidents are something more sinister and there's a connection to the Highway Reaper cases?"

Addie shouldn't be surprised Jada has done some digging. Before she was an editor, she was a feature reporter and specialized in murder, missing persons, and cold cases.

Addie knows better than to divulge any of her thoughts that she can't back up with evidence. Jada would see through that in a heartbeat. "I'm not sure yet. I'm still gathering information."

"Don't bullshit me. You know something, or you wouldn't have started that blog and then contacted me." Jada clears her throat. "I agree with you. If you have a story, we should get ahead of it before the paper in Kerrindale scoops you."

Addie can hear a slight excitement in Jada's tone and hopes to take advantage of it. "I've tried the police up here, but they aren't forthcoming on anything beyond what's already been reported. Do I have your permission to say I am working for the paper again?"

Jada is silent, obviously considering. "Not yet. I need something more than what you have before I can commit to anything."

"Listen, I can't really talk about this now. Can I call you back later?" It is partly true. Toby is chatting with someone on the other side of the partition, and she doesn't want him knowing she's reached out to her editor after saying she would never work there again.

"If you find something, let me know." Jada sighs in obvious frustration. "If it's good enough, I'll offer you an exclusive feature, prime position, with freelance credentials—*but* only if it's something concrete and you can back it up with sources."

Addie holds on to the counter in front of her. She's been waiting for this moment for years, and she isn't going to let it pass her by. Even Toby has said if they found the guy who had apparently killed his uncle, she could tell his story and use the personal connection.

"Yes, great!" Addie's heart now bounces around in her chest. "I have a lot of leads, some I am yet to chase, but I know if I keep digging there's a story here."

"This isn't one of your blogs, Addie. I can't go on vibes and questionable prose."

Ouch.

Jada keeps going. "I've told you before that journalism is more than just telling a story. You're a good writer, but I've never been sure you have what it takes to be an investigative journalist."

Addie opens her mouth, but Jada isn't finished.

"Everyone thinks they're a journalist these days with their iPhones and strong opinions. An opinion is not journalism. Reporting before collecting the facts is not journalism. The constant need to be first or to get the scoop or to go viral has turned what constitutes real media into a joke."

Tell that to Dalia.

"I-I know . . ." Addie isn't sure what she did to deserve Jada's mini Ted Talk, but she wants this story so badly. "I'm still connecting a few dots here. I have a lot of leads. I—"

"You said that already." Jada sighs. "Look, I have to go. Maybe we'll catch up when you are back here for your court appearance. Otherwise, call me when you have something I can print."

"Jada. Wait." Addie is whispering now. Her stomach churns as she makes a decision and heads out the back of the store into the morning sun. "I do have something, and it's more than a lead."

"I'm listening."

Chapter Forty-Four

Jada's call has put a fire in Addie's belly so large she couldn't extinguish it if she tried. Now she has a real reason to investigate and get ahead of the story before the local paper in Kerrindale does.

Her old editor is right. If she wants to be a respected investigative journalist, she needs to put in the work. Not be like Dalia, the girl from the fair, sniffing around with her iPhone and the sole purpose of going viral. Addie feels justified in what she just told her editor. If she doesn't tell this story, someone else will. It's that simple.

Her mind races as she thinks about everything she has to do. Addie grabs a notepad and pen and starts making a list of who she has yet to talk to or follow up on. She'll need to get some locals on the record as sources. Get quotes.

Gale is on the list. As is Larry—screw him and his greedy attitude, she is a reporter with a potential story, and that makes her powerful. She knows she'll have to talk to George again. Clancy, too, with Beatrix present. Go back out to the Donollys', take pictures like Jada asked her to.

She'll scan and send through all those articles Mary has about the Highway Reaper to her editor as well. Once Jada receives everything she's got, she'll see there's a story there.

Addie buzzes on adrenaline. Excitement is something she hasn't felt since that night when she almost lost everything. If coming here means she finally gets her wish of being seen as a serious journalist, then maybe the universe had a plan after all. Or if Walter was here, he would say it was God's plan.

Her pen floats in the air as she thinks about the one person she has yet to pay a visit to. Mary's husband. Frank. The recluse. His address is right there on one of the mail slots. With two pieces of mail that have been collecting dust. Perfect excuse for an impromptu drop-in.

Toby has been trying to get a hold of Gary, but he isn't picking up his calls. Not surprising. So now they should take matters into their own hands.

And she has yet to find out about the man who died last year when a tree branch fell on him. That's when things really started getting strange around here, Walter said. If Walter is right, then the questionable deaths in Boney Creek didn't start with Gale's sister's apparent suicide, but with her ex's death.

Addie knows with certainty that this is the dot she's been looking for.

She finishes sorting the mail, whispers to Toby that she has an errand to run, and then leaves the store.

Addie jogs across the road to the café and this time goes straight around to the back. She knocks loudly, knowing Gale is inside because she can hear kids' music playing.

The door behind the security screen opens, and Addie can just make out the scowl on Gale's face. "What do you want?"

"I heard about Christos. Let me in—we need to talk." No more stalling; Addie is tired of skirting the truth.

"Come in then." Gale unlocks the security door and holds it open for Addie. She's in the same grey matching sweats, and her hair is messy around her face. She looks exhausted.

Addie walks into the tiny living area, where Myah is sitting in front of an iPad screening a children's show; the room is filled with boxes. The child turns around, her eyes wide. "It's the stranger danger."

Gale comes up behind Addie. "This one is definitely stranger danger. Well done, darling."

Myah is satisfied and goes back to her show, the dirty doll by her side.

Gale notices Addie staring at it. "Her mother gave it to her. It's her favorite. That's why it's filthy—she won't let me wash it. Says it still smells like her mommy."

Addie's heart breaks for the poor child. "What's with the boxes? Are you going somewhere?"

Gale ruffles the top of Myah's hair as she walks past, then sits down in her chair with a box in front of it. "We're finally getting out of here. I have a job in the city, and Myah is going to start a new school."

"I'm happy I caught you then." Addie is glad they are making a fresh start after everything they've been through. "I have some questions, but I'm not sure if we should be talking in front of . . ." Addie references Myah.

"I knew you'd be back." Gale gets up and grabs some headphones, which she plugs into Myah's iPad, not missing a beat. "You media types just can't help yourselves, can you?"

"I've been asked to do a newspaper feature on what's been happening in Boney Creek." Addie pulls out her phone, hoping Gale doesn't ask her to elaborate on what paper. "Do you mind if I record our conversation?"

Chapter Forty-Five

"What do you think?" Gale frowns. "Of course I bloody mind—put that thing away."

Addie does as she's told, wondering how her editor would handle Gale if she were here instead. Something tells her that there's no way Jada would get Gale on the record either.

Addie decides to dive right in. "Tell me about Christos."

Gale glances at Myah, who is engrossed in her show. "You'll need to be more specific."

"He was Janet's ex, Myah's father, is that right?"

Gale is staring into her. "Someone's been blabbing, I see. Has to be Walter—he was the only one who knew. Janet told him in confidence."

Addie isn't confirming that. "He died a year ago. A tree branch, I hear."

Gale moves a box cutter onto the side table away from Myah and wraps a ceramic bird in some newspaper. "Why are you asking me if you already know all the answers?"

"Was his death an accident?"

Gale stops wrapping. "Cutting trees is dangerous, and he should have known better than to be out there alone."

"Illegally, too, right? Why was he cutting trees without permission?"

"Money. It's always about money. He needed extra cash and was looking for any way to get it." Gale resumes wrapping.

"Gale, we are going to go around in circles at this point. If you're leaving town anyway, why don't you tell me what happened to Christos?" She then adds, "And Janet."

Gale carefully places the wrapped item in the box in front of her. She takes her time, considering what she will say next. "Do you know why I didn't come that first day you opened the store?"

Addie is taken aback. She'd almost forgotten about that. "I don't, no."

"I promised Gary I would be there to help you when you opened, and I wanted to." She picks up a ball of purple Play-Doh from the floor and rolls it around in her hands. "When I saw the whole town there, I just couldn't go in. It felt like the end of one era and the beginning of another, and I didn't want any part of it. Mary wasn't my favorite person, but we'd known each other a long time. It didn't feel right that I helped you."

"It's okay, truly." Addie wishes she'd made more of an effort with Gale, understood her grief instead of being so wrapped up in her own crap. "Clancy helped out."

"She's a good kid." Gale stares intently at the Play-Doh, squeezing it like it's some kind of stress ball. "Kip was a good kid too."

"I've heard." Addie knows the best she can do is let Gale talk. Get whatever she needs to off her chest.

"He came over here just after Christos died. Did anyone tell you that?" Gale looks up at Addie.

Addie leans forward with her elbows on her knees. "No, I didn't even know about Christos until yesterday."

"Kip said he'd been out at Frank's trailer, where Frank was teaching him to shoot. Frank is Mary's husband."

Addie nods. "Yes, I know. Her ex-husband. The recluse."

"For the best, really." Gale's voice is quiet, fatigued almost. "Frank knew where Mary's heart lay."

"Where was that?" Addie asks.

Gale blinks a couple of times, then answers. "With the store of course."

Myah looks up from her screen and gives Gale a wide smile. Gale returns it with a thin-lipped one.

"You were talking about Kip. He came over after Christos died . . . ," Addie prompts.

"I wasn't here, but Janet told me later." Gale hands the Play-Doh to Myah, who takes it and returns to her show. "It's when the café was still open. It was doing badly, and we knew it was a dying business. That's why Christos came back. He was up north at the mines, making good money and sending back what he could for Myah. Janet hadn't been doing well . . ." Gale coughs, then whispers, "Mentally."

"I'm sorry." Addie doesn't ask for more information; she can fill in the blanks.

"She'd attempted a couple of times over the years, but then Christos came to town for some laboring work with Larry. They enjoyed each other's company, had Myah pretty quickly, and I thought all of that was behind her. But raising a kid was hard on her and she ended up pushing Christos away, and he returned to the mines. I was out of my depth by myself."

Addie wants desperately to go and hug Gale, but she's not sure how that would be received.

Gale wipes the edge of one of her eyes. "When she attempted again, I needed help, so I called Christos and told him he had to come back. Help me with Janet. With Myah. He didn't hesitate. He was a good man, rough around the edges but had a good heart.

"He came back and made what money he could. Worked for Larry. For George, for Ken, Kip's father. Stole firewood. He took any job he could get. He tried, and I thought we could all make it work . . ." Gale's words trail off.

"Then he died," Addie finishes for her.

"Then he died," Gale repeats. "That was the beginning of the end. I knew it, even if I didn't want to believe it. The day Christos died, I had a feeling Janet wouldn't be too far behind. I just didn't think she'd use the gun he left here."

Addie feels a stab in her gut at the tragedy of it all.

"That's why we're leaving. Janet's life insurance finally came through. Enough for a trust for Myah, and enough to get us to the city to start a new life. She must have planned the whole thing."

Addie glances at Myah, who is still absorbed with her show. "What do you mean she *planned the whole thing*?"

"She knew we couldn't sell the café for much, so she took out a life insurance policy a few days after Christos died. It had a suicide clause that had a twelve-month waiting period."

Addie gasps, putting it together. "She waited a year? She knew all that time?"

"Seems like it." Gale wipes a tear from her cheek. "I thought she was doing better. She was excited for the fair and talking about renovating the café and adding a bookstore. I thought we were going to be okay."

"So what happened?"

"What happened is she was waiting for that clause to expire, so she could take her life and make sure Myah and I would be okay. She had it all laid out on her bed, the insurance policy, the updated will saying I could have full custody of Myah. Janet had thought of everything."

"Why are you telling me all of this?" Addie asks.

"I have no idea. I don't even like you." Gale clears her throat. "We're leaving this godforsaken town anyway, so why does it matter?"

Addie finally knows what the right thing to say is. "I won't print any of this. You have my word."

"If you do, I'll sue you." Gale tries to be tough and then seems too exhausted to get beyond a release of air. She sits beside Myah on the floor and tucks her into her lap.

Addie leaves, knowing the conversation is finished and before the tears can spill over.

It's not until she's crossing the main road that she realizes Gale didn't confirm why Kip had come over after Christos died.

Chapter Forty-Six

DAY NINETEEN

The GPS tells Addie she's two minutes away from Frank's place.

Not that she'd know it. She's been traveling along a poorly maintained dirt road for miles now, and there's no sign of life out here.

Addie slams on the brakes. Only barely seeing metal fencing jutting off the side of the road due to all the dried overgrowth. She reverses and parks in front of the rusted gate, which is padlocked shut.

Crap. Now what?

Addie scoops up Frank's mail, grabs her water bottle and phone. She figures she'll climb the fence and take her chances on foot. The house can't be too far along the barely there trail. Can it?

The padlock clatters as she not-so-gracefully straddles the gate and jumps to the other side. She's thankful she's in her usual attire of jeans and work boots as she tramples through the dangerously tall pasture, which hasn't had a car down it for who knows how long. If there are snakes in here with her, all she can do is make a hell of a noise so they'll leave her be.

The sun offers no mercy, even with her sunglasses on, and she'll be out of water soon. She checks her phone. It's two in the afternoon, about as hot as it can get. Oh, and she has no cell service. Just perfect.

She doesn't even know what she plans on asking Frank or how she'll broach the subject of him living on their land. She'll cross that bridge when she comes to it.

Her thighs burn, and she's panting as she reaches the top of a small hill. The house below is obvious, as it's the only thing for miles. She stops to get her breath, taking it all in.

She was expecting a run-down, poorly maintained cabin or trailer, but instead it's a decent-size brick farmhouse with multiple sheds and water tanks. It even has some rosebushes lining the circular gravel driveway, where a new-looking SUV sits in front of the property. Two horses graze in the back paddock.

Addie scans the long driveway from the house to a dirt road that is in much better condition than the one she drove up, and when she follows that road all the way to the town, she can see the unmistakable arch of the cemetery.

Cemetery Road.

She curses under her breath, realizing she's come the wrong way, and all this hiking was for nothing.

Addie sighs as she looks back at her vehicle and then down at Frank's house. She should hike back and drive in the right entrance but decides against it. She's not doing that walk again through the long grass with the heat and any hidden snakes.

Instead she treads carefully as she heads down the hill and into the back of the property. There are two large sheds. Some stalls that look like horse stables. Multiple water tanks. And behind the house is a lovely patio area with fresh flowers and a large canopy for shade.

If this is how a recluse lives, then sign me up, she thinks.

Her feet crunch on the stone path leading to the front driveway, and she rounds the side of the house.

Crack.

A shot rings out over her head, and her breath sticks in her throat. Addie cowers with her hands over her head. She has nowhere to hide.

Her heart pounds in her ears, and she tucks herself into her chest. She's a sitting duck out here.

"Who the hell are you, and what are you doing on my property?" The man's voice gets closer, and she has to presume this is Frank striding toward her.

Addie lifts her head and both her arms in surrender, leaving her phone, mail, and bright-pink water bottle on the ground. She hadn't completely forgotten Beatrix's warning that Frank had a rifle at the ready for unwanted guests, but she also didn't think he'd *actually* use it.

Addie doesn't dare look at him as his boots crunch ever closer to where she still hunches over in fear.

"I said who are you and what are you doing on my property?" Frank now stands close by, the rifle pointed directly at her.

"I'm Addie—Addie Clarkson, I bought the general store with my husband." Addie's voice trembles, and she's pretty sure some pee has escaped without her consent. "Please don't shoot."

Out of the corner of her eye, Addie sees him lower the rifle, and she dares to raise her face to his.

His blue eyes stare into hers, sizing her up for potential danger, no doubt. His face is lined but has a softness to it, and for a man in his eighties, he looks downright incredible. He also looks completely different from the young man in Mary's photos Addie found in the shed. He has on a checked dress shirt with tan pants held up by a leather belt with a large metal buckle.

Addie takes him all in, quickly, also sizing him up for potential danger and weirdly not feeling like he is a threat. This is not the Frank that she had in her mind—she was imagining a run-down man to go with the run-down house. Stereotypes of an elderly recluse.

He uncocks the rifle and tucks it under his arm. "Ah, so you're the famous Addie who's been writing that blog everyone's been telling me about."

Addie thinks about UserBC217 and their comments on the blog and wonders if they could be Frank.

No way is that going to be her leading question.

"That's me." Addie stands, her knees cracking as she does. "I didn't mean to creep up on you like I did. I seem to have come in the wrong entrance."

Frank looks past her, toward the hill. "You came up over there? What were you thinking?"

Addie agrees that she wasn't thinking, so says nothing.

He sighs and shakes his head. "Let me get my truck, and I'll drive you back to your car."

"I was hoping I could speak with you a moment." Addie looks down to her feet and bends to pick up the envelopes. "I also brought your mail, which has been sitting there for a while."

She takes a step forward and hands it to him. He doesn't take it or even make a move toward her. Instead he glares at her with his piercing blue eyes. "You think I was born yesterday?"

"I-I." Addie gulps down a dry swallow. "No."

"You think I'm not going to see through that flimsy excuse of you coming here with my mail? I'm not stupid." There's no humor to his voice, and Addie wishes once again she'd thought this through.

"I didn't mean any disrespect. I was honestly here to drop off your mail and thought I would ask you a few questions about the store while I was at it."

"The store? Why would I know anything about the store? Listen, I can't help you. Any problems you are having have nothing to do with me." He turns back to the house and says, "Come on, I'll take you to your car."

"Mr. Peterson, let—"

"Hold up. You think I'm Frank? Christ's sake, no wonder you're making no sense. I'm Ken." He turns around, looking slightly amused. "You really think I'm that old fossil? He's like a hundred."

Addie can feel her face flaming from embarrassment and wishes she could crawl into a cave.

Ken grabs the mail out of her hands and looks at the envelope. "No wonder. That bastard is using my address again. Frank doesn't have one of his own. He lives on the same land that you bought, and the only way you're going to get there without him shooting you is by horse. He trusts anyone on horseback, just like my son used to do. That or go with Walter in his utility vehicle."

Addie swills some water to avoid passing out from the heat bouncing off the gravel.

"Personally, I'd leave him be." Ken laughs. "He won't give a warning shot like I did."

"Thank you for the heads-up." Addie suddenly stops, connecting who she is speaking to. "Ken? As in Kenneth Shaw, Kip's father?"

"And you call yourself a journalist."

Chapter Forty-Seven

Kip's father's SUV glides over the potholes and dirt like it is asphalt.

Addie is so embarrassed by her mistake and can't believe she didn't recognize him—even if they hadn't met.

All she knows of Ken Shaw is what Clancy has mentioned, which was barely anything.

"I am sorry about Kip." It's only the fifth time she's said it now. What she wants to say is: *I am sorry about the blog I wrote about Kip.*

When Ken only nods, she looks out the window at the barren pasture going by. Soon they'll be at the cemetery his son is buried in and eventually her car. After that she might just crawl into a hole and never come out. Being an investigative journalist sounds awesome, but the reality is far different.

"Is everyone in town treating you okay? I hear you've made some good updates to the store." Small talk is preferable to the quiet of the car, it seems.

Addie turns to him. "Yes, everyone has been really welcoming. We had a few teething problems when we first moved in, but that's to be expected."

"I heard about your first day and how everyone decided to be assholes. Kind of funny when you think about it." Ken smiles a little.

"You weren't part of it then? Whatever test the town was giving us?" Addie can't possibly remember everyone who was there that first day.

"I was not. I don't tend to come into the store if I can help it, no offense."

Now Addie is back to question mode. "Why is that, if you don't mind me asking?"

"I find it hard to go in there knowing Clancy might be working. When I see her, I expect Kip to be somewhere nearby." He takes a deep breath. "It'll pass."

Like on cue, they drive past the cemetery. Both of them keep their eyes on the road rather than acknowledge it.

Addie fills the silence. "When you lose someone, you never know what is going to cause you pain. Deliberately avoiding potentially triggering situations is a wise decision."

"That's it exactly." Ken grips the steering wheel. "No point in adding to the misery, as my dad would say."

Addie treads carefully, remembering only parts of what George told her about Ken's father dying when the pub burned down. "Is your father still alive?"

Ken gives her a quick frown as they turn onto the main road. "No. Dad left us a while ago."

"And he lived in Boney Creek too?"

"He did." His hesitation is clear. "Why do you ask?"

They pass the general store, and Addie can see Toby serving someone through the windows. For a moment, she thinks it's Beatrix but knows that's impossible. Yet her car is there, too, probably dropping off Clancy.

Ken lets out an obvious breath when they drive past Mildred's house.

Addie tries to distract him. "Do you like living here? Have you ever thought about leaving?"

"This is my home." Ken stares straight ahead, his back rigid. "My son is here."

"Of course, I'm sorry."

"Stop saying you're sorry. You aren't sorry. My son is just fodder for you. A story. A mystery to solve. You can write about him, but that doesn't mean you know him."

She deserves that. "I want to find the truth, Mr. Shaw. Don't you?"

He pumps the brakes and pulls over to the side of the road next to the nature reserve where the fair was held. Paint markings still line the grass where the stalls were set up.

Addie's heart thumps in her chest. She's angered him, and the last thing she wants to do is cause him more pain. "I can get out here. I'll find another way to get my car. Thank you for the ride."

She goes to open the door, and a loud click sounds through the car. She pulls on the door handle, but it's now locked.

"Mr. Shaw, please let me out. You're scaring me." It's true. Addie hadn't until this moment considered she may be in danger. Addie dares to look at Ken. Afraid of what she'll see. She knows firsthand how a person's eyes can be devoid of emotion.

Only Ken is the opposite of that. He wipes a tear away as he catches her staring at him. He unlocks the car. "I'm sorry, I didn't mean to scare you. I needed a moment and didn't want you leaving just yet."

Addie wants to comfort him but has no idea how. "Take your time. You've suffered a great loss and have every right to be upset."

He wipes his eyes and straightens his back. Addie figures they'll drive away again, only he turns the car off.

This can't be good.

Chapter Forty-Eight

Addie sits and waits, ready for whatever this is about.

"He died right there, you know." Ken moves his head in the direction of the nature reserve.

Addie is confused. She read about Kip's death, and it was at the stables where Smoke was.

He sees her confusion and says, "My father. This used to be a pub back in the day. The heart of the community. Dad owned it, ran it. His 'second home,' he called it."

Addie wonders where this is coming from.

"The pub burned down in the late eighties. The beginning of the end of this town. First the pub, then the highway being built. No reason for people to come through, nowhere for them to stay even if they wanted to."

Addie asks a question she already knows the answer to. "Your father died in the fire?"

"What?" Ken seems distracted or maybe annoyed at her question. "Yes, he died in the fire. Him and two other young lads. They didn't stand a chance when that blaze took off. Some say they were locked in the pool room. Some say the roof caved in and that's why they didn't get out."

"Why are you telling me this?"

"You know why." Ken stares her directly in the eye.

"The Highway Reaper. There's a connection there."

"That's right. I've been reading your blogs. Seeing you make the leap. We all have." He looks back toward the area where a pub once stood. Where his father took his last breath. "You have to understand something about a small town . . ."

Addie waits for him to finish the sentence, having no idea how to finish it herself.

"People think everyone knows everyone in a small town, which is simply not true. You have a lot of loners out here, minding their business and keeping to their own. So when someone comes in and upsets that balance, you're going to make a lot of people uncomfortable."

"Was it you who wrote those comments on my blog?" Addie asks.

"Are you listening?" Ken is clearly annoyed. "We protect our own. The more you dig, the more this town will clam up. So, for your own sake, leave the past where it belongs."

"What are you saying? That you are protecting a predator? A murderer?" Addie can barely breathe.

"I'm saying that you have no idea what you are doing. You think finding the truth is going to make everything better, like it's some kind of midday movie? Not a chance. Finding the truth just leads to more heartache and pain."

"What about closure?"

"Closure is something people bandy about to make them feel better. It's like hope. Both are bullshit."

Addie doesn't know if he's talking about Kip or his father. Takes a guess. "Are you saying that this town knew who the Highway Reaper was and kept it a secret? Or are you saying they took matters into their own hands and got rid of the problem themselves?"

Addie knows she's treading into dangerous territory with her suggestions, but Ken was the one who brought it up and she'd be bonkers if she didn't ask.

Ken chuckles at first, and then his laugh belts around the interior of the vehicle. It's unnerving, and Addie contemplates reaching for the door handle again.

"You think my father was the Reaper?" His laughter continues, like he's in a manic state or something.

"Isn't that why you are telling me this?" Addie can see the church steeple ahead and thinks of Walter. "Some kind of confession, maybe."

His laughter subsides, and his breath is shaky. "I told you because that's when the Reaper died. The night of the fire. Only it wasn't my father—it was two out-of-towners he'd cornered that night in the pool room. They had been coming in and out of town for years, doing seasonal fruit-picking work. Anytime they were in town, someone else went missing or turned up dead. It didn't take a brain surgeon to work it out. They attacked him when he accused them of it. One punch was all it took, and they killed my old man."

Addie is surprised at how calm she is. This is the information Toby has been desperate to find, and now she knows the answers. She can give him closure.

Only . . . something doesn't feel right.

"Why didn't I read about this? I know about the pub burning down, but they said it was bad wiring, and there was no mention of anyone being found after the fire."

"That's because the truth was buried along with my father and those two sickos."

"Someone got them out before the fire started? I'm not sure I understand."

"It was closing time. The only people left were Dad and the two guys he was planning on confronting. Another man had gone missing a few days before, and Dad had had enough."

"What man? Do you know his name?"

"I don't." Ken waves her off. "It's not important—what's important was this town was sick of the lies, sick of the deaths. It was giving Boney Creek a reputation, and not a good one."

"So how did the fire start? How were the bodies moved?"

"Frank Peterson. The man whose mail you have in your hands. He came to see Dad about something. Heard a commotion. Saw Dad lying dead on the ground and who had done it to him. He didn't hesitate. Got out his rifle from his car, came back in, and shot those boys down where they stood. He called a few other locals to help—"

"Who?"

"That you don't need to know. They got Dad's body out, saw that Frank had killed those bastards in cold blood and would be put in prison because of it, then covered up the crime scene with a fire. They knew better than to use an accelerant. Some faulty wiring is easy to fabricate. Mom got a decent payout and had no desire to rebuild, gave the land to the council, and here we are."

"But your dad's body?"

"He was put in his favorite chair at home." Ken lowers his voice, reflecting. "Mom said he'd had a tumble that day and she'd put him there to sleep off a bad headache. As far as anyone was concerned, he'd died in his sleep after suffering an aneurysm."

"And the other two guys? The ones who murdered and took"—*Steve*, Toby's uncle, she almost says—"those innocent people."

"No idea. Buried deep underground on someone's property, I imagine. I don't give a shit."

"We have to tell the police. There are families out there looking for clos—peace."

"You tell anyone about this, and I'll deny it. I'm telling you so you'll give it a rest. The Highway Reaper is some conjured boogeyman who doesn't exist. It was just two sick fucks who had the opportunity and the means and took advantage of a small town and the innocent people who passed through it."

"Is that why everyone shuts up about this when I ask? The whole town is keeping this secret? It would also explain why Frank's son, Gary, called his dad a hero that first day we took over the store."

"Frank *is* a hero. The way he took those bastards out that night after they killed Dad with a coward's punch. He protected my father's body, made sure he got a proper burial. Then he started that blaze, so Mom still got the insurance money. There's been no other killings since that fire, and that's all because of Frank."

Addie's mouth falls open. "But that's not true. What about Janet, the Donollys, Mary . . . Kip?"

"Kip was an accident. Plain and simple." He leans across and opens the door for her. "I've said enough."

Addie doesn't move. "Did you leave that note at my house? Was it you trying to scare me?"

Ken narrows his eyes and looks almost disgusted. "Get out before I say something I'll regret."

The vehicle moves before she's ready, and she stumbles out of the car, covering her eyes from the dust as it speeds off. As she collects herself, her first thought is of her husband.

I need to tell Toby the "Highway Reaper" is dead. That there's no connection to the recent deaths.

And then she has a story to write.

Addie turns around and jogs back to the store.

DECADES OF DEATH IN BONEY CREEK

The first in a series of exclusive reports.

by Jada Gonzales

For decades, a serial killer named the "Highway Reaper" has preyed on innocent passersby in and around the town of Boney Creek.

This person, or persons, was never found or convicted of their crimes.

Crimes that included three confirmed dead and four missing, presumed dead. This number is said to be grossly underestimated by the local police, as they are aware that not every missing person is reported.

It's enough of a mystery to inspire a fictional version in book form called "Murder Highway" and a yet-to-be-released feature film of the same name.

Yet for all of its coverage, only a handful of suspects have ever been named, but no one has been charged due to lack of evidence.

One man, a trucker by the name of Bruce Albury, came forward and confessed to killing twelve people and being the Highway Reaper, but none of his confession could be corroborated with evidence or intimate knowledge of the crimes.

What is known is that all the victims were not locals of Boney Creek. Backpackers, drifters, hitchhikers, and even a newlywed couple; their last known sighting was in the small town of Boney Creek.

So was this killer a local? Taking advantage of a thriving town that was the last stop for three hours as travelers headed north. Or was this about opportunity, or maybe a series of thrill kills committed by more than one perpetrator but had been lumped together into a conflated boogeyman.

One person who believes that the highway reaper is a local is Toby Clarkson, who recently bought the general store with his wife, and previous employee of this newspaper, Adelaide Clarkson.

Toby invested in the Boney Creek general store after its previous owner, Mary Peterson, a long-standing member of the community, was found dead after choking on her morning cereal.

Mary Peterson was the seventh in a series of mysterious deaths to happen in the township of Boney Creek over the last three months—this time all of them locals.

Toby had an ulterior motive for moving to Boney Creek other than running its only operational store. His reasons were personal, as his uncle, Steven Clarkson, was said to have been one of the missing persons last seen in Boney Creek.

To this day, Steven's body has never been found, but

his last known sighting was at the Boney Creek pub, which also operated as the town's hotel. Steven had withdrawn money from the town that day, but no activity on his bank account has occurred since.

Toby Clarkson has recently come to Boney Creek to infiltrate the town, unbeknownst to its residents, and find the person responsible for his uncle's presumed murder. With Toby is his aspiring journalist wife, Addie, who has started a blog on the current deaths in Boney Creek and the potential connection to the gruesome events of the past.

Did the town hide a killer then, and are they protecting one now? It is a fair question and one that this paper will be following as it investigates further.

(ARTICLE CONTINUED ON PAGE SIX)

Chapter Forty-Nine

Addie bursts through the doors of the general store, excited to tell Toby what she learned. Only she stops dead as soon as she gets inside, knowing instantly something is wrong.

So it *was* Clancy's mother she saw here before.

Beatrix looks out of place standing in front of the counter with Toby behind it. She wears a flowy floral dress and sandals, her hair in a long plait.

She also looks upset. *Mad?*

It must be about the other night and Clancy pulling out the Ouija board while she was there. *Crap.*

Addie glances around the room, but Clancy isn't visible. This can't be good. She hopes Toby will be able to make sense of everything, but when she sees his face, she notices that he, too, is clearly upset.

"Is everything okay?" It's the best she has, the mood of the room definitely hostile.

"Where have you been?" Toby can't even look at her.

"I told you, I had to head out for a moment." Addie pulls her T-shirt over Frank's mail, which is tucked into her back jeans pocket. "Then I had some car troubles, so I had to get a ride back to town."

Why she is lying is unclear. It seemingly feels like she has to.

Beatrix hasn't taken her eyes off her, and as usual, Addie gets the sense she is having her soul examined. She instinctively tucks her hand with her wedding ring behind her back.

"Beatrix, it's so nice to have you in here. I hope Toby is looking after you. Do you want a coffee? A tea? I can make you a chai if you prefer." Why is she rambling? Why is she nervous? Should she get ahead of this before Beatrix scolds her about letting Clancy pull out the Ouija board on her watch? Will she be believed that they never used it?

Toby holds up a newspaper and waves it in the direction of the kitchen. "I think it's best if we all speak in here."

Addie's heart picks up even faster. This has got to be about more than the Ouija board. "Where's Clancy?"

Beatrix answers, her tone even but firm. "Clancy is at home. She won't be returning for work."

Toby glares at Addie before he steps into the back with Beatrix following.

Why does this feel like I am in trouble with my parents?

She in turn enters the kitchen, where they are already seated at the table. Toby pulls out a chair for her.

She hesitates at sitting down, hoping whatever this is won't take too long given she has bigger things to discuss with Toby—but first she has to get rid of Beatrix. "What's going on? Beatrix, if this is about the Ouija board, I promise we never used it."

Toby points at the chair, the newspaper he has now folded on the table in front of him. They don't get the papers delivered, as there isn't a demand for it, so she isn't sure what its relevance is. "Sit down, Addie."

She does as he says, now more nervous than she was when she was in the car with Ken. "You are both scaring me. What's going on? Is it Mildred? Did something happen to her?"

"Mildred's fine." Toby looks to Beatrix for confirmation.

"Mildred's fine," Beatrix repeats, her voice now with an annoyed edge to it. "I've already spoken to Toby, but you should hear it from me directly . . ." She shifts in her seat and glances at Toby.

He nods as if he's telling her to keep going.

Addie can't take it anymore. "What? What's going on? Tell me what you told my husband."

Toby flinches as she says *husband*, and Addie's stomach sinks. Has Beatrix told him? *No.* She wouldn't do that. *Would she?*

She wants to cry.

Beatrix clears her throat. "I came past to tell you both that Clancy won't be working here anymore. Not after school, not on the weekends, never again."

Addie is shocked, but also glad because this is something she can resolve. "Beatrix, I really am sorry. Please don't blame Clancy—she just needed someone to talk to."

"Addie, be quiet. Let her speak." Toby barely opens his mouth as he talks.

Addie does as she's told. Exhaustion from the afternoon catching up with her.

"This is not about the Ouija board. This is about the article that came out today and how you've compromised my family's safety."

"Article? What article?" Addie glances at the newspaper on the table, which Toby has his hand on top of.

The newly installed bell tinkles as someone comes in the front door. Toby stands and says he'll be right back.

Beatrix lowers her voice. "You gave an interview saying Clancy thinks George may have something to do with the recent tragedies around here, about her telling you that Kip was scared for his life and his death wasn't an accident—"

Addie cuts Beatrix off. "I updated all of my blogs. Clancy doesn't appear in any of them, and I certainly didn't mention what your daughter and I discussed the other night to anyone. Not even Toby."

The bell sounds again as the customer leaves, and Toby sits back down.

Addie tugs at the newspaper, pulling it out from under Toby's hand. "Is there something in that paper I should be aware of? Something you are both skirting around?"

Unfolding it, she wants to vomit. It's the paper she used to work for in the city. The one Jada, her old editor, called her from. When Addie had divulged information to prove she had something concrete for a story. Jada had listened intently, or maybe that was her taking notes.

I'm going to kill her is all Addie can think.

Then the reality of what they discussed hits her like a brick to the head, and seeing Jada's name in the byline solidifies that their conversation wasn't in confidence as she had presumed.

"Oh my god, Toby . . ." She doesn't even know how to continue.

Toby barely looks at her while Beatrix's eyes drill into her. Addie opens the paper up to a headline that reads: DECADES OF DEATH IN BONEY CREEK.

She doesn't need to read any more. It all floods back to her now. What she discussed with Jada over the phone. An assurance of information for the promise of a feature cover story. How she'd given up Toby's secret and his connection to Boney Creek.

Addie can barely breathe. "Toby, I am so sorry. It wasn't my fault, I told Jada—"

"Whatever excuse you are about to give me, save it. I don't care. You betrayed me, Addie. That wasn't your information to share, not yet. Not until we found out what happened to my uncle."

"Actually, I did find out what happened—" She reaches out to him, but he pulls back.

"Leave it, Addie. I've had enough. I thought we were a team, I thought we had each other's backs. Not only have you betrayed me, but you've also betrayed my family." Toby's voice hitches. "You betrayed Clancy and *her* family. What the hell were you thinking?"

"I-I wasn't. I made a mistake. I'll fix this." Addie stands, the paper in her hand. "I'll call Jada and get a retraction. Go to another paper with what I found out. We'll do this right, babe."

"Listen to yourself. You are still talking about a story when we are both in front of you begging you to stop. Only you can't, can you? Those articles will always be more important than the people you supposedly care about."

Beatrix stands and whispers, "I should go."

"I thought you'd learned your lesson after the break-in . . ." Toby's words dry up.

Addie stops. Frozen. Then she slowly pivots her head to Beatrix. "You *told* him?"

"I didn't say a thing." Beatrix holds up her hands, her voice calm. "Only you can share your truth, Addie."

"What truth? What am I missing here?" Toby is standing now, looking at both of them with his mouth open.

Addie wishes the ground would swallow her whole. This is where she loses it all. This is where he learns how much of a monster she really is. There will be no coming back from this.

She can see it in Beatrix's eyes. In Toby's body language. She wrote the ending to this story the night the intruders came to their door. The night she lost her baby, and it was all her own doing.

Addie opens her mouth to seal her fate, thinks better of it, and runs out the back of the store.

Chapter Fifty

Addie walks blindly until her brain can work out how to fix all this.

She wants to leave. Escape. Go back to the city, get everything out of storage, and start again.

Toby isn't going to forgive her for this. For the article. For the eventual truth of that night and her role in it. How does she fix this when he can't even look at her?

Beatrix will never speak to her again, and neither will Clancy. The whole town will now know about Toby and his reasons for coming to Boney Creek. They aren't safe anymore to hide in plain sight.

Addie's tears blur her vision as she walks on the side of the main road. She's forgotten her water, her hat, her sunglasses. The only thing she has is her phone—which is useless now, given no one will be contacting her ever again.

She contemplates calling Jada. Yelling at her for betraying her trust. Only there's no need. She knows what Jada will say; Addie can pretty much have the whole conversation in her head.

Jada's ruthless. She's good at her job because she does everything for the story—even if that ruins lives. She took Addie's scoop and made it her own.

She wants to kick herself for being so stupid but kicks a rock out of her way instead. What did she think was going to happen? Jada would keep her information safe until Addie finally had a feature to write?

So naive. Such a rookie mistake trusting someone she doesn't even work for anymore, all for a promise of a stupid article.

Was it worth it?

Addie knows the answer is no. None of it was ever worth it. She never had the grit to be a journalist, not a good one anyway. She's too impulsive, too flighty, too . . .

Weak.

Her stomach sinks. That's it. She's weak.

A car blasts its horn as it hurtles toward her. Someone waves as they go past. She doesn't see who it is, but halfheartedly waves back. It doesn't matter, soon she will be gone, and this town and all its residents will be memories.

Was it worth it?

The sign for Cemetery Road is up ahead, and she almost laughs. Of course this is where her feet would take her. To the people who she used as entertainment. A means to an end. She owes them all an apology.

Her mouth is parched, and her head feels foggy with the sun beating down on her as she walks through the arch leading into the cemetery. She cringes as she passes the weeds that she tried to hand off to Gale as flowers.

What an embarrassment.

She follows the same path leading to where Gale was that day. Kip's grave. It feels right to start with him. To ask forgiveness for ruining the lives of his friends and family in trying to get to some ridiculous truth that was never there.

All these dots she tried to connect. Forcing herself to make the leap that the town had another serial killer stalking them. She's like the police when they get fixated on one suspect and don't look elsewhere. She was so busy searching for a killer, she couldn't even contemplate that the deaths could have been simply accidents.

She stands in front of Kip's temporary headstone. It's only his name on a wooden plaque until the real one gets placed when the ground has settled.

"I'm sorry, Kip. You had your whole life ahead of you." Addie clears the grass in front of it and straightens up a fresh bouquet of flowers. "You didn't deserve this."

She sits in the grass in front of his plaque. The tears coming now. For so many lives lost. For her life now in tatters. For betraying her husband in the worst possible way.

She should have told Toby how she was feeling, said she was scared to start a family, have their lives change so dramatically with a child coming. So simple in hindsight and yet so hard when she was back there. Feeling so much pressure to be something in both her professional career and in her personal life. Not realizing she didn't have to make a choice. That she had a loving partner who would have understood her concerns.

Yet Toby hadn't trusted her either. Had he? Their coming to this town was a betrayal of *her* trust. Even as she tries to deflect her own shame, she knows that it isn't the same. Toby understands her, that she would take on his family's tragedy and make it her own. Run blindly toward something she didn't understand or even fully consider.

He knew the story of Boney Creek would be something she would pursue doggedly—which was exactly what she did.

Why hadn't she given him the same opportunity?

"Because I'm selfish." Her voice sounds strange in the quiet of the cemetery. "What do I do now?"

Her tears have dried up. She doesn't deserve this self-pity. Not given where she is. Where people have lost their lives and no longer have a chance at a future, at fulfilling their dreams.

Addie wonders what *her* dreams are anymore. It's like they dried up with her tears.

Her phone buzzes in her back pocket, and she leans forward to dig it out. Her heart skips in her mouth, hoping to see Toby's name.

It's Clancy. She's left a video message.

Addie clicks it open, both anxious and afraid of its contents. Clancy whispers into the camera, her nostrils and lips taking up most of the screen.

"Addie, I am so sorry." She sniffs and wipes her nose with the back of her hand. "Mom told me what happened, and it's all my fault. She found the Ouija board in my room, and I told her you wouldn't let me use it, but she won't let me come to the store anymore or see you. It's all my fault. I'm so sorry. Please don't hate me."

Her heart shatters at seeing Clancy so upset. She wants to call her and explain that it was Addie's fault and not hers, but she knows she shouldn't. It's clear Clancy was recording that video in private, afraid someone would hear her.

Something twigs in Addie's brain. A sense of déjà vu. *Why?*

She stares at Kip's name in front of her, and it comes to her. Kip filmed a similar video before he died, one Clancy sent to her to look for clues. Kip had been afraid, whispering, up close to the screen like Clancy was.

She clicks on the video of Kip. Just like Clancy, it's mainly his nose and lips in the frame. His voice trembles as he talks quietly into the camera, some of his words barely audible, but Addie gets the gist.

"It's me. Kip. I'm gonna be quick because I'm not sure how much (inaudible) I've got to film this." He looks behind himself like someone is there. "Something is going on, my dudes. I don't know what yet, but as soon as I (inaudible) it out, I'll tell you all. The only thing I know is that wherever there's smoke, there's (inaudible). That has to mean something, but I just dunno what." He looks behind him again, and he pulls back the camera slightly, so all his face is in the frame. "(Inaudible.) Gotta go. Love yous all."

Addie pauses the video before it can autoplay again. Kip's face is frozen in a frown as his eyes look directly at her. It's unsettling.

"What was going on, Kip? What were you afraid of?"

She thinks back to her first day in the store when Clancy was adamant that Kip's death wasn't an accident. She was sure her best friend had been murdered.

Addie scans the cemetery. It's quiet. Only a slight breeze causes a hum in the tall grass. She can see Mary's plot from here. Another temporary marking to say who is lying in the recently covered grave below.

Addie looks at the screen of her phone again, covering it from the sun. A chill slowly creeps up her spine as she sees what is behind Kip's head where he was recording from.

It's the stables, and behind him is the grey outline of his horse, Smoke.

This video was posted a day before Kip's accident, when the horse he shared the screen with fatally kicked him.

Addie watches the video again. Something not just niggling at her now but yelling. Kip talks, his voice shaking. He's obviously afraid. Of what?

Of who?

The only thing I know is that wherever there's smoke, there's (inaudible). That has to mean something, but I just dunno what.

Addie pauses it again. What's bugging her about this part? Something isn't sitting right with her.

Wherever there's smoke, there's fire.

The fire part is barely audible, but it's pretty clear what he's saying by the inflection at the end of the word. This phrase meant something to him. It has to be a clue.

Smoke is his horse.

And fire is?

Oh.

Addie stands with her phone in her hand, her heart telling her she's onto something.

She looks at Kip's plaque and says, "I think I know what it is. I understand what you were trying to tell us."

She opens her phone to her recent calls, presses on the number.

Chapter Fifty-One

A hatchback pulls onto Cemetery Road, and Addie knows it's Sharmi.

Addie phoned her, not stating the true purpose of the call, and asked for a ride. Sharmi didn't hesitate.

She opens the door as Sharmi pulls up outside the arch, and the blast of air-conditioning is immediate and welcome.

"Are you okay? You sounded a little breathless on the phone." Sharmi waits for Addie to get in before doing a U-turn back into town.

Addie puts on her seat belt even if it feels pointless on these roads. "I'm okay. Just have a lot on my mind. Thanks for coming to get me."

Sharmi nods and stops the car at the intersection. "What were you doing at the cemetery?"

"I wanted to pay my respects to a few of the people I've exploited lately." Addie hopes that will be enough.

"Oh yeah? Did someone say something about your blog?" The roads are completely quiet, but Sharmi has yet to turn in to town, time having its own currency out here.

"Not directly." Addie is grateful Sharmi hasn't seen the newspaper article yet. "Do you mind if we make a stop before we go and get my car?"

"Sure, did you want to go back to the store first?" Sharmi pulls out onto the main road.

"No, I want to go and see where Smoke is being boarded. Can you take me there?"

Sharmi does a double take, frowning slightly. "I can, although you might need to tell me why."

"There's been something bugging me about how Kip died, and I want to see the location for myself." Addie wants to be honest to gauge Sharmi's response, which is annoyingly neutral.

"Well, now you have me intrigued." Sharmi lets out a breathy laugh.

They pass the empty coffee shop Janet used to own and continue through the town. Addie deliberately looks down as they pass the general store, not wanting to add to that pain right now. If she can prove she's right, maybe she can make it up to everyone. Especially Toby.

"So what's the interest in Kip?" Sharmi asks, her tone still neutral.

Addie watches her, looking for any signs of deception, not answering that question but asking one of her own. "Kip didn't keep Smoke on his own property. Isn't this a little far from where he lives?"

Sharmi agrees. "Kip kept Smoke out this way because the land has been cleared for grazing. A lot of pasture around here has toxic weeds that can be poisonous to livestock."

"And your horse? Blaze, isn't it?"

"Blaze, yes." Sharmi turns onto a dirt road that is in the same direction as the Donollys' place. "I have him stabled on my property."

The car rattles as they drive over small stones and potholes, and Addie leaves Sharmi to concentrate, her first theory already shot. They pull up to a clearing alongside a metal gate with white wooden fencing surrounding an area that's mostly dirt.

"This is it," Sharmi says as she undoes her seat belt. "Did you want to go in?"

"If that's okay." Addie gets out of the car with Sharmi, and they walk toward the gate.

Smoke lifts her head from out in the pasture as she sees them approaching and nickers softly. Sharmi clicks her tongue, and the grey horse trots toward them.

Addie scans the area. The fenced-off pasture has a smattering of trees for shade and a roofed horse shelter that is divided into two sections, one narrow with no door and a larger, walled-in section with access for the horse to get inside. A water trough sits just nearby.

Sharmi lets Smoke smell her flat hand and then rubs her neck. "There's a good girl."

"Will she hurt us if we go in?" Addie never was a horsey girl, and their size petrifies her.

"You want to go in? Why?" Sharmi reaches up and rubs behind Smoke's ear.

"Like I said, I wanted to be sure about a couple of things. Is it okay?" Addie watches Sharmi, but the woman is more focused on giving Smoke cuddles.

"I haven't seen any signs of distress or aggression in Smoke, if that's what you mean. More loneliness. If only we had a way to tell pets what happened to their owners when they die." Sharmi kisses Smoke on her muzzle.

"So you come here often then? With Blaze?" *Slowly now,* Addie thinks.

Sharmi looks surprised. "Of course. Smoke has gone through a trauma, and being with other humans and horses is good for her. I've asked Ken if Smoke can come and stay with me permanently, but I know he comes down here a lot as well."

Sharmi unclips the gate chain and lets Addie in first, then closes it behind herself. Smoke reaches over to smell Addie's hair and then sniffs at her hands as she freezes in fear.

"The key is to not act afraid. Horses are good at sensing what we are feeling." Sharmi comes over and leads Smoke away by her halter. "If I'd known we were coming here, I'd have brought some treats. That's what she's looking for when she's smelling you. Sorry, bud, I'll bring some by later," she says to Smoke.

"I'll take your word for it." Addie walks over to the horse shelter. "Can we go inside and have a look? Whose property is this?"

"It's Larry's, of course. He owns most of the land around here, as you know. My place isn't far from here either." Sharmi points up the dirt road. "Shell's place is just up the road as well, if you remember."

"I do remember." Addie won't be getting the Donollys' place out of her head anytime soon.

Addie surveys the shelter. It's different from what she had in her mind and throws out another theory she was toying with. "I thought this place would be more like a stable, with a door and four walls, so the horse is locked in." Addie steps inside the larger section of the shelter, shifting the dirt beneath her feet.

"No, this is a better setup. The horse has the freedom of being on pasture during the day and comes in for cover during the night."

"And no other horses stayed here with her?" Addie glances back at Sharmi, who is staring at her phone.

Sharmi looks up. "What's this about, Addie?"

It's a good question and one Addie is now asking herself. "I was hoping if I came out here, I could answer some of the questions rattling around my brain."

"And they are?"

"Kip died while grooming his horse." Addie steps into the wooden walled-up section of the shelter. It's warm, but not as bad as outside.

"That's right." Sharmi sighs and comes inside with Addie, Smoke sticking her head in behind them. "I don't have long. You might need to get to the point."

Addie knows her next line of questioning might hit a nerve, so she takes her time. "Kip said something in his videos before he died: *Wherever there's smoke, there's fire*, and I think I know what he might be saying."

"I don't understand."

"You told me your horse's racing name was Strident Moon, but you just call him Blaze."

Sharmi nods. "Racehorses often have a racing name and a barn name that the horse can recognize."

"So if Kip knew your horse was called Blaze, then that could be what he was talking about in his videos and not about the Donolly fire like everyone thought."

Chapter Fifty-Two

Sharmi winces a little, but Addie isn't sure if it's because she's onto something or because she mentioned the Donolly fire. Or both. "Addie, you've lost me."

Addie paces as she's talking, to help her focus. "What if Kip was saying that wherever Smoke was, so was Blaze. I wonder if there's a reason. Like maybe . . ."

Sharmi glares at Addie. "Like maybe what?"

"Like maybe Kip saw you when he was out working at the Donollys'? Maybe he would ride Smoke over there and you rode over on Blaze. Put the two horses together. Maybe you were having an affair with Eddie and Kip saw you—"

"I'm going to stop you right there. Firstly, I would never do that to Shelley, and neither would Eddie. Never. Secondly, you think I killed my friends and then Kip? Have you completely lost your mind?"

Now that Addie is talking out loud, it does feel like a stretch. "It was just a hypothesis and obviously a ridiculous one."

"I understand you are trying to help Kip and his family, but making wild accusations won't help. Yes, Kip would ride Smoke over when he was helping George with the renovations at Shell's place . . ." Sharmi rubs her mouth and pauses. "He was there often just before he died, but that doesn't mean anything. Kip died here, not at Shell's place."

"Wait." Addie spins around the open area of the shelter. "There was plenty of space for another horse to be in here with Kip. What if it wasn't Smoke who kicked him but someone else's horse."

"Like Blaze?" Sharmi looks exhausted all of a sudden. "I can assure you that neither myself nor Blaze were anywhere near here the day of the accident. I'd just lost my best friends, for Christ's sake."

"Yes, of course. I'm sorry." Another dead end. Addie really thought she was onto something.

"Besides, Kip was in the next stall when he died. Not this one."

Addie wants to get outside to look at the narrow stall, but Smoke is obstructing the exit. "What do I do?"

Sharmi is clearly losing her patience as she nudges Addie out of the way. "Here, let me show you so you can stop all of this grasping at straws. You'd make a terrible detective."

Addie shrugs. Totally fair.

Sharmi leads Smoke over to the narrow stall, and she resists for a beat but then backs in, lining up with two metal loops on either side of the stall. "This is where a horse can be crosstied. So Smoke would have been clipped in that day, with ties on either side of her. It's a safer way of grooming, especially when you are working with a horse's hooves like Kip was. The hoof pick he was using was found near his body."

Addie realizes there is no way two horses could be in here at the same time. There is only enough room for Sharmi to be beside Smoke, which means Smoke must have done the kicking. Not another horse, including Blaze.

Sharmi pulls at one of the loops on the wall, and Kip's horse doesn't flinch. "Smoke was still tied up when Kip was found later in the day."

Addie is taking everything in, something not sitting right. "So something spooked Smoke, and in the process Kip was struck?"

"That's it. Exactly as you described in your blog. No foul play, just an unfortunate accident. Besides, if someone tried to attack Kip, he had a perfectly good weapon in his hand with the hoof pick he was using.

As far as I know, there was no blood or signs of him having to defend himself."

"So something must've spooked Smoke. What or who could have done that?" Addie needs some air. The idea that Kip died just here making her queasy.

"It could've been anything. A loud noise. Another animal. Horses can be unpredictable at times, especially when they are tied up like that with restricted movement." She releases the halter from Smoke, who is content to stand where she is, showing no signs of distress.

"I really thought I was onto something with the Blaze reference, no offense. I thought if I found out Blaze was there that day, I'd find our killer."

"Me, in other words. You really need to get a better bedside manner, Addie." Sharmi almost smiles. "You've got to stop thinking of everything as a conspiracy. Sometimes bad things happen to good people."

Addie shivers as she looks back into the stall, sure she's still missing something but having no idea what it is.

Chapter Fifty-Three

Addie returns to the general store after Sharmi dropped her off at her car.

She's dreading talking to Toby since running out. If he says he's leaving her, she won't be surprised.

It's now late afternoon, and the place is quiet, save for Mildred, who is sitting at the table and chairs at the front of the store. Any other time, Addie would be happy to see her up and about, but right now she just wants time to make amends with her husband.

Addie comes through the back door, taking a deep breath as Toby glances up from the laptop in the kitchen. His face is unreadable, but he puts his finger up to his mouth meaning: *shhh*. He then nods his head to the front, where Mildred is seated.

Addie nods back, understanding her husband doesn't want her talking loudly for their regular customer to hear. She comes around instead and whispers in his ear, "I'm sorry."

He pulls her ear to his mouth. "I know. I'm sorry too."

Addie looks at him, confused.

He brings her ear back to his mouth again, his warm breath comforting as he says, "We've both made mistakes. It was my fault we came here. I made you look into all of this."

Addie whispers back, "I would have agreed to come, and you know it. I would've done anything for a story—there's no denying that. Please forgive me. I never meant to hurt you."

"We both made mistakes, and we both paid for them." She feels him draw in a shaky breath beside her ear. "What's done is done. We'll figure it out."

She doesn't deserve his forgiveness. Not when she hasn't told him everything. Not when she has compromised their role in this town.

"I'll make this up to you and to everyone I hurt. I promise. I'm just not sure who I am anymore, and I was looking for validation in all the wrong ways."

"Let's talk about it later." He brings Addie's lips to his and kisses them lightly. "Remember, as long as we're together, we can do anything."

Addie's breath hitches, and she's determined not to cry. Not now, not when she needs to fix all the mistakes she's made.

"What's with all the whispering back there?" Mildred yells.

Toby and Addie laugh quietly, but she knows this isn't over. "We can talk more later, okay?"

"Later sounds good. I know there's more we need to discuss." He may have verbally forgiven her, but the sadness in his eyes tells her Toby knows there are more secrets to come.

She kisses him again as her stomach clenches. Soon he won't forgive her quite so easily. She'll tell him everything later and will live with the consequences.

Addie joins Mildred out front. She is in a bright-blue floral dress and has a crossword puzzle book in front of her, with her tri-cane beside her. Mildred's face isn't as pale as it was the last time Addie visited, but that might be the heavy-handed blush currently on her cheeks.

"Hello, Ms. Whiteman. It's good to see you again." Addie sits across from her. "How are you feeling?"

"Not bad. Not good. Just another day." Mildred has an empty coffee cup in front of her.

Addie references it. "Can I get you another one?"

"No, dear. I've already been sitting here too long. I should get back and feed Betsy."

Addie stares at the slowly sinking sun with the country backdrop through the glass windows. It's a sight she'll never get tired of, and part of her knows she might have to say goodbye to it soon if Toby asks her to leave.

"You two have a little tiff?" Mildred bobs her head in the direction of the kitchen.

Addie nods. "We did."

"Clancy told me about the article. It was a real shock to hear about your husband's uncle and what that bastard did to him."

"Yes. Toby was trying to get some closure, and instead of helping him, I exposed him." Addie can feel her eyes welling up and doesn't know how to stop it. "I was so busy looking for answers about everyone else's lives, I lost sight of my own."

She expects Mildred to be upset about their coming to town under false pretenses and claiming she couldn't have recognized Toby when they first arrived, but to her surprise, Mildred reaches her hand out and places it over Addie's. "We all make mistakes, dear. It's how you handle them afterward that matters."

"Thank you. I appreciate that, and I hear you loud and clear." A tear falls down Addie's face, and she wipes it away. "I think I needed this all to unfold to know what is important."

"And what's that?"

"Him." Addie looks toward the kitchen. "The family we will hopefully have one day."

"Good girl." Mildred pats Addie's hand before pulling away. "You learned that lesson a lot quicker than me."

Addie studies Mildred's face. There's a slight peakedness under the makeup from being sick, but also a sadness too. "Are you talking about Frank?"

If Mildred is surprised at the question she doesn't show it. "I made a lot of mistakes when I was young. I thought things would stay the same, even if you pushed someone or said the wrong things. I learned the hard way that people can become ghosts well before they are taken from this world."

Addie wipes her eyes.

"It's worse when they are still here. Haunting you with their close proximity." Mildred sighs deeply. "I should go, dear. I've overstayed my welcome."

"Why don't you come back?" Addie places her hand over Mildred's this time. "We'll be having dinner in a few hours, and we'd love for you to join us."

Mildred smiles, and it's genuine.

Addie knows inviting Mildred over will delay her chat with Toby, but she also knows it's the right thing to do after everything Mildred has been through. "If you don't want to leave your dog, Betsy is welcome to have dinner here too. I haven't seen Gravy for a while, so I think we're safe."

Mildred sits back. "Gravy? The cat?"

"Yes. He seems to come and go as he pleases. I'm just not sure where he ends up."

Mildred crosses her arms over her ample breasts. "The cat goes to Frank's place. He loves that thing. Spoils it rotten."

Addie is wide eyed. "You talk to Frank?"

"No, but I keep an eye on this place, and I know he did, too, before Mary passed." A look of sadness washes over her face. "Betsy yaps nonstop when someone is creeping around, but I'd know Frank's smell of tobacco from anywhere, and I always know when it's him."

Addie needs to ask. "Who else has been creeping around?"

Mildred purses her lips. "Some lowlifes who caused problems for Mary."

"What do you mean by that?" Addie leans forward. "Causing what problems?"

"Mary was having bits and bobs go wrong for quite some time, small things at first, like someone breaking into the ice freezer or deliveries going missing. Then they'd get bigger and more expensive. Over time she stopped fixing them as her money dried up. Same thing was happening over at the café Janet used to run. When those fuel lines stopped working here, though, that's when Mary admitted defeat."

"Admitted defeat?"

"She knew this place was going under, and she couldn't bear to see it crumble. That's why she had her will changed."

"Wait, what do you mean she had her will changed?" Addie asks.

"It said that under no circumstances was this store to go to Larry or his sons—no matter what price they offered. She knew it was Larry's boys who were sabotaging this place so he could snap it up for a steal."

Addie pulls back her chair. "I need to tell Toby this—hang on a minute."

"It's okay. I'm listening." Toby steps into the front of the store with them. "No wonder Gary couldn't take the better offer on this place. It had nothing to do with his morals but was because he couldn't legally."

"Mildred, how do you know all of this? I didn't think you spoke to Mary." Addie grabs Toby's hand as he comes next to her.

"I-I guess I must have heard it from . . . let me think . . . Shelley Donolly. Yes, that's it."

"Shelley Donolly?" Now Addie is really confused.

"Shelley would pop in when she came to the store. She was such a lovely person. That's who redid Mary's will. I'm sure of it."

Addie is reminded that Shelley Donolly also changed her own will when she had kids and Janet had her will updated before taking her life. *Strange.*

Mildred continues, "Mary was telling everyone around town about her will, that Larry wasn't going to get her store. She was really proud of that fact. She loved provoking people, seeing how far she could push them. Trust me, I know."

Addie squeezes Toby's hand, grateful for his proximity. "Do you think someone hurt Mary that morning when she apparently choked? Someone like Larry who had a vendetta against her?"

Toby moves his hand to her shoulder now, and it feels heavy there. She realizes she's doing it again. Asking questions, still trying to find the story.

Mildred licks her lips. "Lots of people have threatened to kill Mary over the years, and she's responded *Over my dead body* more times than is normal. Hell, she's said it to me more times than I can count. But someone actually kill her? I doubt it. It was her time, plain and simple. Just like it'll be mine soon enough."

Toby says, "You're too tough for that."

"Once upon a time, maybe, but now I know it's coming. Truth be told, I knew all day at the fair that something wasn't right. I could feel it in my bones. I was just having such a good time, I didn't want to believe anything was wrong." Mildred reaches out for her crossword puzzle. "They say you see a light, but all I saw was Mary coming to collect me. Then she was gone, and I'm still here . . ."

Addie watches the old lady shrink into herself like a great sorrow has consumed her. She doesn't quite understand it.

Mildred grabs her cane and pulls herself up with a groan, and Toby moves around to help her. "I'll walk you home."

"I won't say no to that." Mildred takes his arm with obvious pleasure. "Is that dinner invitation still going?"

"Of course. One of us will come over to help you back here with Betsy." Addie gives Toby a look that means *sorry.*

If he's upset with her, he's doing a good job of hiding it as he walks Mildred to the door.

Addie thinks about Mildred's dog, can't help herself and has to ask "The morning Mary died, did Betsy bark?"

"Of course not," Mildred mumbles. "Like I said, it was her time to go."

Chapter Fifty-Four

When Toby doesn't return from Mildred's after ten minutes, Addie knows he's probably done the polite thing and is having a cup of tea with her. She knows she'd do the same thing if the roles were reversed, only for very different reasons.

She's still processing that someone, most likely Larry's boys, was sabotaging the store and that Mary had changed her will because of it.

The wills.

Addie knows there's something there. Mary changed her will before she died, Janet changed her will because she *knew* she was going to die, and Shelley Donolly had changed her will when she'd had her children.

Shelley Donolly.

There's the connection she's been looking for—she knows it—but she just can't make something stick. Did Gale say who had updated Janet's will? *No.* But the chances of it being Shelley Donolly were pretty good.

Toby will be home soon, and then they will close the store, have dinner with Mildred, and Addie will tell him everything when they are alone. It will be up to her husband what happens next, and either he will forgive her, or he will divorce her—there will be no in-between.

Whatever happens, her days of sniffing out a story will be over. It's for the best. She gave up so much for a career she thought she wanted when it has given her nothing in return.

Yet. There's always a *yet*. A *but*.

She has to know. She has to know what happened over the last few months.

On the table, next to the computer Toby was working on, are some ratty folders. He told her Sharmi had dropped off Mary's paperwork from the Donolly place, so this must be what he's sorting through. That's not what she's looking for, though—what she needs is the pad and pen.

On a clean piece of paper, she scribbles a message that she's going to see Gale to say goodbye before she leaves town. It's partly true, even if she has no idea when Gale plans to move with Myah.

She places it on the table so it's visible, locks up the front doors to the store, and closes the back door without locking it. As she walks to Gale's, she texts Toby to repeat what she wrote on the note but also adds that she left the rear door open and will be back to make dinner.

He replies with a thumbs-up as she walks past the café to Gale's place. The faded CLOSED FOR FUNERAL message has been taken down, and in its place is a brightly colored sign saying **FOR SALE BY OWNER**.

Addie knocks on Gale's security screen with a heaviness in her stomach.

Gale's face is an open scowl as she comes to the door and looks through the mesh. "I have nothing else to say to you."

Addie swallows. Gale's demeanor is always off-putting. "I wanted to say goodbye before you head off."

"Like hell you did."

Addie can just make out Gale's features through the security door, and it's clear she's not letting her in this time.

Looks like our friendship was short lived.

"I have nothing else to say to you." Gale locks the security door and grabs the open door behind it.

"Wait, don't go. I just had one more question. It's about Shelley Donolly doing Janet's will."

Gale freezes, and Addie wishes she could see her face clearly, although she knows she's right. She knows it was Shelley Donolly who also updated Janet's will before she chose to take her life.

"Who told you that?" Gale spits out. "Because it sure as hell wasn't me."

Addie feels a pump of adrenaline at being right for a change. "It was a hunch, but you just confirmed it."

"Think you're smart, do you?"

Yes. "No, of course not. Listen, there's got to be a connection there, Gale. Did you know Shelley also updated Mary's will not that long ago?"

"That's none of my business. And, honestly, I don't care. I'm getting out of here, and I'm not coming back."

"Please, can I come in?" Addie pleads. "Just for a moment."

"No. I am about to get Myah ready for bed." Gale leans closer to the mesh. "Give it up. You're looking for something you are never going to find."

"Why were you putting flowers on Kip's grave that day? Why did you tell me Kip came over to see Janet after Christos died?" Addie also steps closer, her voice low. "You know something, don't you?"

"Flowers?" Gale lets out an exhausted laugh. "You're like a dog with a bone, only it's so far up your ass, you'll never sniff it out."

"What the—"

"Get off my property, and leave us the hell alone."

The door slams closed behind the security screen just as Addie's phone buzzes with a message. It's Toby telling her to take her time because Clancy is about to visit the store to get her last paycheck. He'll text Addie when she's left.

She heads to the main road wishing she could say sorry to Clancy in person and make it better, but she has to apologize to Beatrix first.

Her feet take her in the direction of Beatrix's house, and she starts composing the apology in her head. It sucks. She sucks. Beatrix won't forgive her. Then in a few hours, it will be dark, and Toby won't forgive her either.

She needs a miracle.

The church steeple peeks through the trees ahead of her, and she takes it as a sign.

If anyone knows about miracles, it's got to be Walter.

Chapter Fifty-Five

"Why did you tell me about Christos?"

Walter looks up from a bag of groceries he's packing into the back of a utility vehicle. "Addie, hello."

Addie has limited time before Toby says she can come back and wants to get to the point. "Forgive my directness, but it's been a day, and I need answers."

"I've heard some whispers going around town about you and your husband." Walter leans against the vehicle. "What's on your mind?"

"Christos, Janet's ex. Why did you tell me he was Myah's biological father when Janet told you that in confidence?"

Walter frowns. "Where is this coming from, Addie?"

Addie paces beside the vehicle. "Did you tell me for a reason? So I'd follow some kind of lead? Just give it to me straight, Walter. No more half truths."

"Half truths?"

"You lied about when you first came to Boney Creek to live. You said you weren't here when the Highway Reaper started hunting, but you were." Addie keeps pacing, her thoughts all over the place.

Walter steadies his hand. "Why don't we go inside and make a cup of tea. You seem agitated."

"I *am* agitated." Addie stops. "This town is a tough nut to crack, and you aren't helping. Why did you lie about when you came to Boney Creek?"

"If I did lie, it wasn't deliberate. That time was very complicated for me, Addie, and my memory isn't what it used to be. If you are asking me if I am the Highway Reaper, I am not."

"I already know it wasn't you." Addie wrings her hands, trying to calm her nerves. "Sorry, I have a lot on my mind."

"I can see that." Walter walks over to a set of chairs under a large evergreen tree. "Please sit down. You're making me nervous."

"I think better when I keep moving. Did you tell me about Christos for a reason?"

Walter sits hesitantly on one of the chairs. "How do you know Janet said anything to me in confidence?"

"Gale told me."

"You've been speaking to Gale?"

"Yes." Addie sighs, feeling like a ticking clock is hanging above her head. "Gale told me Janet had her death planned soon after Christos died. Did you know that?"

It's Walter's turn to sigh. "I did not, no. Janet was having a rough go of it—I knew that. We spent a bit of time together because of the fair, but what she did . . . well, that was a shock."

"And Christos? Tell me what you know about him."

Walter must see she isn't here for bullshit and answers with some reservation. "I knew he was Myah's father without her even telling me. When he first came to town for work, he spent a lot of time here at the church, helping out with odd jobs and maintenance. Janet took a shine to him and would come by while he was here. She was pregnant not long after that."

Addie pauses, thinking. "Then he left."

"He did. I know he wanted to stay and start a family with Janet, but the town forced him out."

"What do you mean the town forced him out? According to Gale, Janet pushed him away. What did Christos do?"

Walter holds his trembling hand in his lap. "There were a lot of rumors swirling about Christos when he was here. Why he was spending so much time at the church, especially out in front, with a perfect view of young Clancy's house."

"What?" Addie gasps. "Did they think he was a pedophile or something?"

Walter nods. "That was what her father was going around saying. George gave Christos work, too, but he sniffed something out that he didn't like, and there was a massive brawl because of it."

"Gale obviously never mentioned any of this."

"You're still an outsider here, Addie. No one's going to spill their guts just for the sake of it."

Ken did when he told me about who was doing the Reaper killings, though, she thinks, wondering why.

To control the narrative.

"It makes sense that Gale wouldn't mention the rumors about Christos. She wants to shape my very public opinion and make sure his reputation is untarnished for Myah's sake." Addie gets that the town has played her as much as she's tried to play them. "So you told me about Christos because you knew I'd start digging. You don't think his death was an accident, do you?"

Walter thinks about it, then nods. "I guess I did. You were doing those other blogs, but I knew no one would tell you about Christos. He's like a breeze that blew through once." Walter gets up, grabbing his back as he does. "The branch from the tree killed him, there's no doubt about that, but there was talk of some gunshots up that way on the day of his death. If someone was a crack shot, they could've easily done some damage without anyone being the wiser."

Crack shot. Where has she heard that before?

"What about George? I'm sure he was not happy Christos had come back to town after all those years."

"George? He has a temper, but murder? I can't see it."

Addie checks her phone, but there's nothing from Toby. She hasn't even discussed what she came here for, putting off her own problems in favor of other people's per usual. "Walter, how does confession work?"

"Confession?" Walter turns and stares at her. "I didn't think you were religious."

"I'm not, does that matter?"

"It doesn't. Confession is anyone's right. I just can't give you absolution if you aren't baptized."

"I don't deserve absolution," Addie spits out.

"I'm happy to help where I can, Addie." Walter shuffles back toward his cottage to the remaining groceries on the ground. "Anything you say to me in confession is strictly confidential."

Addie doesn't move. "So if someone confessed to murder, you wouldn't be able to tell anyone?"

Walter stops but doesn't turn around. "That is correct."

"So . . ." Addie takes the bags from Walter and places them in the utility vehicle. "So someone in this town could have confessed, and you'd have to keep it a secret."

"If you need to talk to me, I am here for you."

Addie picks up the case of beer, her mind racing as she places it near the groceries. "Where are you going?"

"Frank's place." Walter straps everything in. "It's Friday night, and we like having a beer together. Also gives me an excuse to drop him off some supplies."

Frank. The recluse who will shoot anyone he doesn't know. The man who Beatrix said is a crack shot.

"I'm coming with you."

Chapter Fifty-Six

The sun descends into the skyline as Addie sits beside Walter in his utility vehicle. It handles the rough terrain without issue as they drive over the remote pasture leading to Frank's trailer.

A bright-orange flag flaps wildly above their heads, Walter telling Addie that it's to let Frank know it's him and not another unwelcome guest.

All this land being hers and Toby's is not lost on her, and it brings an ache to her heart knowing what she still has to confess later tonight. This might be the last time she gets to explore Boney Creek.

The off-road vehicle rattles and shakes, its engine loud in Addie's ears, making conversation impossible. The helmets they both wear also preventing any kind of chatter, which suits Addie just fine.

She keeps checking her phone, but there's nothing from Toby, and she wonders what he could be talking with Clancy about for so long. She shoots off a text to tell him where she's going, but there's no reception and it doesn't go through. Maybe it'll be too late for them to have the talk tonight. One more day of living with her lies.

Walter waves his trembling hand ahead of them, while the other stays on the wheel. She squints and can just make out the trailer in the distance.

As the structure gets closer, it's exactly as she pictured it. Run down, with various faded annexes coming off it. Camp chairs sit around an inactive firepit, given it's fire season.

An elderly man steps out from the trailer, the utility vehicle having sounded their approach. He tucks a long-sleeved shirt into his jeans, which hang off his angular frame, and pushes down his stockman's hat onto his head. It doesn't take him long to spot that Walter hasn't come alone, and Addie can feel Frank's eyes on her as they pull up beside his trailer.

If he has a gun, she can't see it.

Frank doesn't move from where he is, just stands watching them as Walter turns off the vehicle, takes off his helmet, and yells out, "I brought a guest with your groceries."

"Nothin' wrong with my eyesight." Frank nods at Addie.

She waves as she gets out of the vehicle, her heart pounding a little. "I'm Addie. It's so nice to meet you."

Walter collects the bags of groceries from the tray at the back of the utility vehicle, and Addie follows with the beer, which she puts on a table under one of the annexes.

As Frank puts away the groceries and beer in the fridge, Addie takes everything in around her. There are various tanks of water and solar panel sheets scattered around the place. The property is run down, but obviously well loved and kept neatly. She scans the horizon for signs of the Boney Creek township but can't see any.

Frank ties up a bag of rubbish and puts it in the back of Walter's vehicle. It looks like they have a system.

Walter grabs three beers out of the fridge and holds one up to Addie. She takes it just for something to do as she waits for someone to fill the silence. Frank flicks on a floodlight, and they all sit around the dormant firepit. Everyone taking a sip of their beer.

Frank speaks first. "I expected you a while ago with an eviction notice. Is that why you're here?"

Addie is grateful for the night closing in so he can't see her blush. "It's not, no. I didn't even know you were out here until recently. It's a good setup."

"It's home," Frank says pointedly, rolling a cigarette.

"Addie wanted to ask you some questions, didn't you?" Walter looks to her.

Yelp. She had expected to ease into it. "I mean, I did. If that's okay."

"Depends on what the question is." Frank lights up his smoke.

"I wanted to ask about the day Christos died and if you remember anything?"

Frank picks a piece of tobacco off his tongue and talks to Walter. "That the guy stealing my firewood?"

"That's right. About a year ago, branch struck him." Walter sips on his beer.

"What's that got to do with you?" Frank's eyes are barely visible, with his hat still on and the shadows of the night creeping in.

"She's a reporter," Walter says.

"I pretend to be." Addie tries at a laugh, but her heart isn't in it. "I'm hoping to tie up a few loose ends for a blog I'm writing."

If Frank knows about the blog, he doesn't say. "And what's your question?"

Addie picks at her beer label. "I want to know if you saw or heard anything the day Christos died."

"Like what?" Frank ashes on the ground. "Ask what you wanna ask."

"Did you hear a gunshot that day?"

Frank takes a long drag of his rolled cigarette. "Hear it or shoot it? You're like a book over there."

Addie tugs at her mouth, annoyed she is so obvious. "Fine, did you shoot at Christos the day he was killed?"

Walter clears his throat as Frank chuckles. "The answer to that is no. I heard his chainsaw, got my binoculars out to see who would have the balls to come on my property, and then sent the kid out to give him a bit of a scare."

"The kid? As in Kip?" Addie looks at Walter. "Did you know about this?"

Walter shrugs, giving away that Kip might have spoken to him.

"So what happened?" Addie directs this to Frank, who is already onto rolling another cigarette even though he hasn't finished the first one. "Kip fired off a shot to scare Christos?"

"Can't say, but he must've scared the guy off because his chainsaw stopped soon after. What do ya think happened?"

Addie can sense he's holding back on something. "Could the shot have hit the branch that fell and killed Christos?"

"Sure," Frank answers without thought.

Addie looks to Walter for backup. "Is that why Kip was so distressed a year before he died? Do you think he might have accidentally killed Christos?"

Neither of them say anything. She knows she's right.

"It would explain why he went and visited Janet, maybe to apologize. Confess?" Again, Addie looks to Walter.

He sips on his beer, his face giving nothing away.

"Kip was a good kid, and he knew his way around my rifle, but he would never have done anything to hurt anyone." Frank lights his freshly rolled cigarette. "If anyone is to blame, it's me for giving him the gun. Although everyone knows that chopping down trees is a dangerous business, and no one's to say how that branch came to strike him."

"It was God's will," Walter adds.

Addie isn't so sure. "Did Kip say anything to you, Frank? Did he act strangely after that?"

"It's not my place to speak for the boy," Frank says, a hitch in his voice now.

Addie puts her beer on the ground, the couple of sips she's had making her queasy. "Kip would have known about the rumors surrounding Christos, though, about him taking an interest in Clancy. Maybe it *was* deliberate?"

Both men say nothing.

Addie stands. "I need to go and talk with Clancy."

"Leave it be, Addie," Walter says. "That girl has been through enough."

Addie wants to shake him. "Don't you see? Kip had a motive to kill Christos."

Frank frowns, or what Addie could discern of a frown with all the shadows on his face. "The boy didn't kill that man. A branch did."

"You gave a teenager a gun and sent him off to *scare* someone. You should be ashamed of yourself." Addie looks around, everything outside the light pitch black. A sense of dread fills her. "I want to go back to town, Walter."

Franks stands and takes off his hat.

But it's Walter who says, "You're not going anywhere."

Chapter Fifty-Seven

Addie thinks back to her first day in Boney Creek, when she wondered if anyone could hear her scream out here. She prepares herself for testing that theory.

"Sit down, drink your beer," Franks says, rubbing his barely there hair back and forth.

"I'd prefer to stand." Addie steps behind her chair, ready to use it as a weapon if need be. No one even knows she's out here. If only her text to Toby had gone through.

"So . . ." Frank's eyes narrow, his expression plain to Addie now that he's not wearing his hat. "You're married to Toby then?"

"Um, yes. What has that got to do with anything?" Addie steadies herself on the back of the chair.

"I remember him from when he was a kid. His old man did the taxes on the store for Mary and me." Frank sits back down on the chair.

Addie had almost forgotten their connection. "Did someone show you the article in the paper?"

"Show me?" Frank laughs lightly, his teeth a slight yellow color. "No, Walter told me all about it."

"You have a phone?" Addie is surprised, then comprehends. *You have a phone.* She pulls hers out from her back pocket and checks the signal. There's still none. Even if Toby was trying to get a hold of her, she's unreachable.

Walter says, "We have walkie-talkies, in case of emergency."

Addie tries to keep her voice steady. She can't quite gauge what the mood is here, but it's apparent how she's compromised herself. "I understand if you are both mad. Toby didn't mean any harm by moving to Boney Creek. He just wanted to know what happened to his uncle."

"I'm not mad at the kid. His father was a good man, and Mary and I were sorry to hear what happened to him." Frank finishes his beer and lets out a belch. "Trouble is, there's going to be all those media sorts sniffing around again, thinking there's something here when there's not."

Addie drags her chair farther away from both Walter and Frank and sits down. She's suddenly exhausted. "It's not Toby's fault—it's mine. I leaked the story, so any issues you have are with me."

"Wanna 'nother one?" Frank asks Walter, holding up his empty beer. Walter holds up his half-full bottle as a no. Frank looks down at Addie's full beer still sitting on the ground where her chair used to be. "You gonna drink that? Beer should never be wasted."

"No, help yourself." Addie slaps the back of her neck as a mosquito bites her. "Look, I'm sure we can work this out."

"Too right, we'll work this out," Frank says as he picks up Addie's beer. "We can't have people thinking the past is something to dig up."

"I know what happened back then. Ken told me. I can write all about it. Clear it up once and for all."

Addie notices the look Walter and Frank give each other.

"Ken Shaw? That's who has been shooting off his mouth?" Frank looks to Walter again instead of Addie.

Addie answers, "Yes, that Ken. He told me about how you were a hero that night, Frank. About the two guys who would come in for seasonal work and how you took matters into your own hands. I know there's no connection to back then and what is happening now."

Both men are quiet.

"What am I missing? It's clear you are both hiding something." For once she isn't the only open book around here. "Was it one of you who wrote those comments about the Highway Reaper on my blog? Warning me of something."

"With what?" Frank scoffs. "Walter read me out those half-baked pieces you wrote. You really have some nerve writing about my Mary like that."

Addie is done defending herself. Tired of saying how sorry she is. The blog was a mistake; her investigating was a mistake. She gets it.

And . . . *What is that?*

She leaps back at the animal rubbing against her legs, sure it's something from the dark about to attack her. Only, it's just Gravy. The missing cat.

She takes a deep breath at cheating death and strokes his back. Gravy gives a soft meow and purrs as he rolls over on the dirt.

"You scared me," she whispers, rubbing his belly.

The two elderly men watch her with interest but seem content to not continue the conversation, which suits Addie just fine.

Gravy walks off toward Frank, and Addie stands, swaying slightly as vertigo hits. Or is it nausea? She's so tired, she can feel her eyelids getting heavy.

"You don't look so good. Did you want to go lie down?" Frank says as he finishes off the beer he took from Addie.

Addie very much does want to go and lie down. Unsure if she's about to faint or vomit or both.

What's wrong with me?

Walter gets up. "You're as pale as a ghost, Addie."

"I don't feel so good . . ." Addie reaches out for something to hold her up. "What did you do to me?"

She finds nothing but air as she hits the ground.

Chapter Fifty-Eight

Addie slides her hand across the sheets, rubs her head.

Ouch. Why do I have a bump there?

"Toby?" Addie sits up, squints in the dark at the strange room.

Where am I?

It smells in here. Like tobacco and mildew. There are whispers outside, and she remembers. Walter and Frank. They drugged her. She pulls back the covers of Frank's double bed in his trailer. She's fully clothed, her boots still on.

She sighs with relief.

Her head pounds as she swings her legs off the edge of the bed, trying to blink away the vertigo. She needs to stop the room from spinning so she can work out how to get out of here.

Someone laughs outside, and she gulps down a breath. What are they planning on doing with her? No one knows she's here. No one is coming to save her.

Gran, help me. What do I do?

The night of the break-in flashes in front of her like a disjointed movie. The blow to her head reverberates around her skull. It echoes the pain she feels now from when she fell. Or did they hit her too?

Someone comes into the annex area just outside where she's sitting, and she hears the clink of more beer being pulled from the fridge. She holds her breath and waits for the door of the trailer to open. Only it doesn't, and the talking continues outside. She can't hear what they're saying, what they're planning.

She needs to find a weapon. Be ready for when they come for her.

The trailer is small. She can see the whole thing from where she sits, the floodlight from outside spilling through the blinds that are open at the other end of the trailer. Below the blinds is a table with wraparound seating, the door to freedom, and a narrow kitchen across from what looks like a wardrobe or bathroom. Everything feels heavy with dust and cigarette smoke, but the place is surprisingly tidy.

She has to stand. Get moving. Make a plan for how to get out of here. There is no way she's going to be another statistic of Boney Creek. She steadies herself as she grabs the edge of the wardrobe, her knee striking an open cupboard as she lurches forward.

She inhales a gulp of pain and covers her mouth, sure her staggered breathing is so loud they'll be able to hear it from outside. She barely squeezes past the doors and limited kitchen, having no idea how Frank lives in such a claustrophobic space.

The accordion door is the only other possible way out of here, and she pulls it across slowly, revealing a toilet and small sink. No shower. No window.

Damn. She has no means of escape.

She tucks herself into the tiny space and checks the back of the accordion door, which has a lock. It won't hold for long, but it may give her precious moments until they decide to come and get her. She just needs a weapon, or better yet, the gun that she knows Frank owns.

The only place it might be in here is the wardrobe, which has a single sliding pocket door. She takes a couple of steps, and it opens easily, without noise, and she pushes aside the hanging clothes to inspect behind them.

Her eyes are scouting for a gun, but she isn't prepared for what she actually sees on the back wall of the wardrobe. It's covered in articles about the Highway Reaper and aged photos of people she vaguely recognizes from a time now past.

Frank holding an axe with a ribbon announcing he won the wood-chopping competition, with Larry wearing a second-place ribbon and a scowl. Mary and Mildred looking to be in their early twenties, sitting at the edge of a swollen creek in their one-piece swimsuits. Schoolkids all sitting on the back of a large stock horse.

Addie untacks this one from the wall and puts it into the light coming from outside. She knows these young faces: Beatrix, Ken, and George—doing rabbit ears behind Beatrix's head. There is a black question mark above Ken's head written in marker. She puts the photo back exactly as it was and notices a map covered in red crosses farther down the wall. It's of the town and the surrounding area.

Addie's heart pounds, and her head thrums. *What is this?* Some kind of murder wall or is it literally a murder map? She glances behind her, the door still firmly closed, but outside is eerily quiet.

Ken told her what happened back then, so why does Frank have this? Is Frank the Highway Reaper? And what about Walter? There are no old photos of him as far as she saw.

Had Kip's father told her a tall tale to distract her?

To control the narrative.

But why? Had someone else recognized Toby from all those years ago and known all along why they'd come to town? Was Ken getting ahead of something?

Addie pats her back pocket for her phone, but it's gone. Of course it is. No way to take photos and look at them later. *Later?* Will she even have a later?

She has to get out of here. She's not safe, and Frank can't know she's seen all this. Addie pulls the clothes back across and slides the wardrobe door closed.

A stab of pain shoots up the top of her spine and through her head. She flinches. The vertigo is back, and her stomach churns. She's going to vomit. She gags, covers her mouth. There's no holding it in. She spins and throws up in the kitchen sink.

It's painfully loud, and she knows she's done for.

Whispers come from outside, and there's movement. She waits for the trailer door to open, for her fate to be sealed.

"Well now, look who's awake," Frank says as he comes inside.

She puts up her fists, ready to fight if need be. Is Frank laughing at her? He sounds so far away with the buzzing in her ears.

The room spins as Frank steps toward her.

Chapter Fifty-Nine

The church steeple is above her, swaying. The night sky and stars surrounding it.

Is she dead?

Addie lifts her head up. It hurts, and she reeks of vomit. Why is she wearing a helmet? She's . . . she's in Walter's utility vehicle. There is no sign of Walter. Or Frank.

What is she doing outside the church? Where is Walter taking her?

She wonders if she can stand. What is wrong with her? She is so dizzy. They must have put something in the beer.

A noise comes from above her. It's a crow. Staring at her in the dark. Maybe a sign. A warning. She has to get out of here, get to Toby, call the police. Her fingers tremble as she fumbles to unbuckle the seat belt holding her in place. It unclips, and she slides off the seat and onto the ground, then leaves the helmet behind.

If there is anyone after her, she can't hear them and she doesn't trust herself to look, knowing her sense of balance is barely existent. The crow flies away, and so must she. Beatrix and Clancy's house is just there, a light is on.

She can do this. One step at a time until she is safe.

The small gate leading into the house groans as she opens it. Addie wants to groan with it. She closes her eyes and waits for the footsteps to sound on the road behind her.

It's quiet.

She doesn't knock on the front door, where the porch light will expose her, instead shuffling around the side of the house, using its walls for support. Passing the kitchen window, she looks inside. The light is on, but no one is there. She goes to tap on the glass, then stops herself.

She's sure she heard a knock coming from the front door.

It has to be Walter or Frank, looking for her.

She crouches down and closes her eyes, willing herself to stay calm, quiet. To not pass out again. She hears the front door close and then voices as they come into the kitchen.

It's Walter, talking with Clancy. Addie can hear them like they are standing right next to her. Clancy had mentioned something about listening to private conversations from under this window.

"No, I haven't," Clancy says to Walter's question about if she's seen Addie.

"She's not well, and I'm worried for her welfare," Walter replies. "I called an ambulance, but that'll be of no use if we can't find her."

Lies.

"I can run up to the store if you want—she's probably gone up there." Clancy.

Walter. "How about we call Toby and see if he's seen her. She can't have gone far . . ."

Nope, not far at all.

". . . I'm worried she has a concussion."

Concussion. Drugged. Tomato. Tomahto.

Addie has to get out of here. Warn Toby.

Clancy says, "Let me call Mom at the hospital, and I'll ask her what to do for a concussion. Don't worry, we'll find her."

That's her cue to get the hell out of here. The only person she trusts right now is Toby.

Chapter Sixty

The rotary phone is ringing as Addie opens the back door to the store. It's unlocked, and there is a light on over the oven as she enters the kitchen; the place is quiet.

"Toby," she yells up the stairs, already sensing he's not here. Where would he have gone? Has someone taken him too?

She puts on a light and sees dots. After grabbing her headache tablets from the cupboard, she takes two with a glass of water. She lets the phone ring out, knowing it is Walter trying to get a hold of Toby.

Two mugs and a pot of tea are near the sink from when Clancy was over talking with Toby. She inhales the strong lavender smell coming from the open teapot. Frowns. Clancy doesn't drink that tea; she hates lavender. So who was here?

If she works that out, then she'll know who he's with. There's a pile of papers on the table and some handwritten notes on a pad. They are hers, about the Highway Reaper, the locals dying.

Toby has underlined Kip's name and written beside it: *Sharmi says horses can be protective in certain circumstances.*

Sharmi. That's who must have been here. Had she figured something out after the conversation at the stable? Possible, given Toby was making notes for Addie to follow up.

She glances around herself and wakes the laptop to see what's on the screen. It's an article on how horses can be protective and possessive of their owners. Addie scans it quickly, understanding immediately why this would spark Toby's interest. This could be a reason why Smoke lashed out that day.

But why would Smoke hurt Kip, if the horse was protective of him? It has to mean something.

It has to mean something.

She's heard that before, coming directly from Kip's mouth.

The screen is a little fuzzy in front of her, and she sits down, her heart hammering as the phone on the wall rings again. It's deafening in the quiet of the room.

She'll call Toby when it stops, but first she needs to check something. Addie opens up a file on the laptop with the video of Kip the day before he died. She presses play.

"It's me. Kip. I'm gonna be quick because I'm not sure how much (inaudible) I've got to film this. Something is going on, my dudes. I don't know what yet, but as soon as I (inaudible) it out, I'll tell you all. The only thing I know is that wherever there's smoke, there's (inaudible). That has to mean something, but I just dunno what. (Inaudible.) Gotta go. Love yous all."

She plays it again, this time focusing on the parts that are inaudible. It's hard to hear Kip at times because he's so close to the screen, but it's easy enough to fill in the gaps of what he was saying.

Addie knows now where they've been going wrong. That bump on the head may have knocked some sense into her. She presses play on the video. This time she closes her eyes and just listens to Kip's words.

It's muffled but obvious now that she's paying attention. She hears what Kip has been saying all this time, the phrase that they all thought they knew because it's the only thing that made sense.

Wherever there's smoke, there's fire.

Only he's not saying that at all. Instead he's saying a name Addie knows all too well.

Myah.

Wherever there's Smoke, there's Myah.

Chapter Sixty-One

Gale.

Of course. There was always something off about her.

That must be where Toby is now. Addie left a note saying she was going to Gale's—which means he may be in danger. She doesn't hesitate, leaving the store and crossing the road. Her head still a little foggy but the vertigo gone at least.

The town is ominously quiet. No cars, no one walking the street, calling her name or looking for her. Good. They won't think to come to Gale's house.

A floodlight almost blinds her as she walks past the café. She holds up her hand so she can see, conscious the dizziness may not be far away. Parked in front of her is a hatchback with the trunk open; inside are some boxes. The security screen unclicks, and Gale steps out with a box of toys in her hands. She stops as the door swings closed behind her.

"Going somewhere?" Addie says, the floodlight making her blink.

Gale scowls and brushes past her.

"I didn't realize you were leaving town tonight." Addie follows as Gale puts the box in the car.

Gale shuffles other packed items to make room, her tone clipped. "Change of plans."

"Did I have anything to do with that?" Addie steps beside the car so the light doesn't obstruct her view.

"Leave me alone. You've done enough damage." Gale stalks back to the screen.

"Stop." Addie grabs Gale's elbow. "I know what you did."

Gale pulls her arm away and reaches for the handle.

Addie cuts in front of her and blocks it. "I've called the police. I've told them everything."

There's a slight twitch at the corner of Gale's eye, but otherwise she keeps her expression neutral. "Get out of my way. I have nothing to say to you."

She isn't going anywhere, especially now that Gale is making a run for it—Addie's instincts are obviously right about what she speculates. "Was it when I asked about the wills and if Shelley Donolly changed Janet's? Is that when you got spooked?"

"Get out of my way," Gale hisses.

"Or what? You're going to make me?" Addie puffs out her chest, remembering something about making yourself bigger in the face of danger. Or is that when being confronted by a predator? Same, same.

Gale glares at her, not saying a thing but the bubbling anger obvious. They are so close, Addie can feel Gale's breath on her face. She really should have thought this through.

"I know you killed Kip," Addie states.

"What—" Gale steps back. Her mouth slightly open. "Why would you say that?"

"You confronted Kip when he was grooming Smoke. Then when he tried to get away, that horse kicked out at you and struck Kip instead. I saw how small that area was—he didn't stand a chance."

Gale doesn't say anything, but Addie can see her chest rising and falling like she is trying to control her breathing.

"It took me so long to connect it all, but when I finally heard what he was trying to say in that video, everything started to piece together."

"What video? I deleted—you have no idea what you're talking about." Gale eyes Addie, sizing up how she can get past her, it looks like.

Addie leans against the security screen. She knows Myah is in there and Gale will not go anywhere without her. "Did you kill Shelley because she helped your sister plan her will? Is that it? Did you kill Kip because he saw you there?"

All the theories Addie is connecting are flimsy, but she knows she's right. She knows Gale is the key to all this; she just needs to lock it all down.

"I'm leaving, Addie. Let me go . . ." Gale takes a deep breath and releases it slowly. "For Myah's sake."

"You know I can't do that." Addie rubs the back of her head, her stomach feeling queasy again.

Gale steps forward. "You don't look so good."

Addie puts out her hand. "I'm fine. Don't come near me."

"Why? Do you think I'm going to hurt you?" Gale looks offended or smug; it's hard to tell.

"Why did you do it, Gale? Why did you kill all of those people?" Addie needs to sit down.

"You wouldn't understand."

"Try me."

Kip's iPhone video recording.

. . . as you can see, Smoke lets me lift her hind leg with no problem. It's important to keep the horse calm while you handle their hooves. That's why I've got Smoke in this contained area and tied up. This here is a hoof pick, and I'm going to use that—

"Who are you talking to, Kip?"

Gale! I . . . um. I'm making a reel for my socials.

"Why can't you kids speak English."

[horse nickers]

Steady on, girl. It's okay.

"Control that horse of yours, Kip."

You're making her nervous. Don't crowd her while she's tied up.

"It's you that looks nervous. Something to hide?"

I don't want any trouble.

"What's in your hand?"

It's noth—nothing. A hoof pick.

[horse stamping]

Easy, girl . . . easy. Listen, Smoke's getting restless—maybe we can do this later.

"We'll do this now, while I have my wits about me."

Where's Myah? Isn't she going to say hello to Smoke like she always does.

"Are you getting smart with me? You know I don't like her around that thing."

Smoke isn't a thing. She's my family, and she would never hurt Myah. You've seen how they are together. Out at the Donollys'—

"Enough. Don't mention Myah again."

[muffled response]

"Today we're going to get a few things straight."

Like what?

"Watch your tone, Kip."

[muffled response]

"Just be honest and we'll never speak of this again."

Yeah?

"You have my word."

Okay, cool. What do you want to know?

"Let's start with the big one, shall we . . . Why'd you have to tell Janet what you did to Christos? Why couldn't you leave it?"

Oh, um . . . I-I guess I wanted her to know it was my fault, that I was sorry for what I did . . . I said I'd go to the police. But—but your sister said not to worry, that accidents happen.

"Bullshit."

I—I'm not lying. I needed her to know it was my fault and *only* my fault. That I deserved whatever she wanted to do to me.

"Only she did jack shit. She said it was a sign. It's because of you Janet did what she did."

I'm really sorry—I really am. We can go to the police right now if you like.

"Fuck that. They won't do anything. You know it and I know it. That's why I'm here, because we need to get some things straight. Work out exactly what you saw—"

I didn't see anything, promise.

"I know you saw me out there. How could you not? Myah was like a moth to a flame with that horse of yours."

Wherever there's Smoke, there's Myah . . .

"What the hell is that supposed to mean?"

Nothing . . . look, I was only helping out at the Donollys' because they asked me to. I needed the extra work. I was cheap and had nothing better to do.

"What did you see? Tell me straight."

Just that you were suddenly there. I'd never seen you with Shelley Donolly before. I thought maybe she was looking after Myah for you, but that wasn't it because Myah was always out with me and Smoke . . .

"And?"

And that's it. That's all I know.

"You know why I was out there—don't lie. I know you were listening in, spying on us."

Not true. I was there to work, and that's all I did. Except when I was looking out for Myah . . . because you weren't.

"Don't get smart with me. You know as well as I do what Shelley did. She could have said no. She could have told Janet she wasn't going to help her. She could have told *me* what my sister had planned, but no. She may as well have handed Janet that gun herself."

Gale, I—

"Do you know how many cups of tea I had to sit through to get any information out of that woman? Do you know how much I hated sitting across from the snake who abetted the suicide of my sister? She knew I knew. Spouting lawyer-client confidentiality or some shit—"

I should really get going. Clancy is expecting me.

"You can leave when you answer this last question."

Really?

"Just be honest and we can pretend none of this happened, okay?"

Yeah, okay then. Alright.

"The night of the fire, you were there."

Um . . .

"No lies, Kip. You owe it to Janet to tell the truth."

[rustling sounds]

Yeah. I was there.

"See, that wasn't so hard . . . it was late, Kip. What were you doing out at the Donollys'?"

I liked it out there. They were a real honest-to-goodness family, and I watched them sometimes like they were a movie.

"And?"

And I fell asleep in the barn where I put Smoke, and I only woke up because Myah was there, wanting to play.

"Ahh . . . she was supposed to stay in the car."

I came looking for you and saw you inside with Shelley. Mrs. Donolly. I didn't want to bother you. I don't know what happened after that because I put Myah in your car and rode Smoke back home before my dad knew I was gone. That's it—that's all I know. Honestly.

"Bullshit. I know you saw what I did to Shelley."

No, I didn't. I rode back on Smoke . . . I don't know anything else. I swear. I have no idea what you're talking about.

"She brought it on herself, Kip. You need to know that. All I wanted was for Shelley to admit that she updated Janet's will. Helped her with the insurance policy. Had a hand in assisting my sister with doing what she did."

I'm really sorry about Janet—I really am—but I told you the truth, and now I need to go.

"You stay right where you are . . . and keep that horse calm."

[loud bang]

Gale, please! Don't come any closer, and she'll settle down. There's a girl—you're okay.

"Stay where you are, Kip. You need to hear this because it's all your fault. What you forced me to do."

Please just let me go. I won't say a word.

"About what? You don't even know the full story, Kip. About what that woman did. Shelley thought she was so smart, not witnessing any of the documents herself. Putting everything under a company name I didn't recognize. I tried to be polite, be friendly and get the information from her by visiting all the time. Then, I found her business card when I was going through Janet's things. Shelley had written a cute little note on the back saying she'd help any way she could. How sweet."

[muffled noises]

"That vile woman put grand ideas into Janet's head, helped her plan it all so she had no choice but to follow through. Not once did she come to me. I could have stopped it."

[heavy breathing] Please . . . I just want to go home.

"I went out there that night to confront Shelley. She was warming herself with the portable heater while her family slept. Silly woman said something about using the household heater and how it was a waste of money. It made me so mad. Here she was in her big house with her perfect family, and she was worried about a heating bill? How fucking dare she."

You—you killed her.

"I had to. You don't understand. I had no choice. When the life drained out of her as my hands squeezed her perfect little neck, do you know how good it felt? My grief *finally* had a purpose. Killing is easy when it's justified. You know all about that, don't you, Kip?"

No—I . . . you have no idea what you're talking about. What happened with Christos was an accident.

"I tell myself the same bullshit, kid. That what happened next was also an accident. How did you feel when you knew you killed someone?"

I—didn't kill anyone. Not like that.

"I killed Shelley, but not that family. It wasn't my fault that no one was there to switch off that heater. I didn't kill those kids. That's not on me."

[horse stamping]

"You killed an innocent man, Kip. Left Myah without a father. Without a mother. You took everything from me, and now it's your turn—"

Gale, don't come any closer. You're scaring me.

[rustling, loud bang]

"Ow! That fucking horse just bit me."

Don't come back here, Gale.

[horse stamping, whinny]

"What the fuck. Control your animal."

Smoke, it's okay, it's—Gale, please, please, I'm sorry—watch o—

[loud bang, muffled noises]

"Kip? . . . wake up, kid . . . bloody horse . . . What the fuck? It's . . . recording the whole time? What a fucking mess. How the fuck do I delete this? How do I—"

[Video deleted]

Chapter Sixty-Two

"I said, *try me*," Addie repeats.

"And I said get fucked."

Gale walks to her car and closes the back. "I'm going to check on Myah, and don't you dare try and stop me."

Addie is still in front of the security screen, and now she doesn't know what to do. This is where Gale is supposed to confess to everything and tell her why she killed Kip and the Donollys. And Mary—Addie hasn't worked that part out yet.

"Just answer me this: When did you decide to kill Kip? The day he came over and confessed to Janet that he'd fired the shot that killed Christos? Or later, after the Donolly fire that you started?"

"You killed Kip?" Feet crunch on the dirt, and the two of them turn to see Clancy holding out her phone in front of her with the flashlight on. "Addie, are you okay? I've been looking for you."

"Clancy, you need to go back home. It's not safe here."

"What's going on?" Clancy looks to Gale, confused. "Did you really kill Kip?"

Gale shakes her head. "I didn't touch him, Clancy. I promise you that."

"But—but . . . maybe it was me." Clancy searches the dark like she's looking for answers.

"Clancy?"

"What if it was me, Addie? He said not to tell anyone I was there." Clancy now has tears in her eyes.

Addie steps closer to Clancy, keeping her eye on Gale. "What are you talking about? Where?"

"The day Christos died. Frank didn't give him the gun to scare anyone. Kip was out there shooting rabbits. I know because I was with him."

"You were *with* him?" Gale whispers almost to herself.

Clancy's lips tremble. "Kip told me to come and keep him company, bring him some snacks. So I did. Then we got in a fight."

Addie waits for more, although she thinks she knows where this is going.

"I told Kip I was seeing Christos that afternoon because he had something he wanted to tell me."

Gale leans forward. "This is news to me."

"I didn't tell anyone," Clancy explains to her. "Well, except Kip, who said there was no way I was going to be alone with Christos. Then we heard a chainsaw nearby. Kip looked through the scope on the rifle and saw who it was. He said he was going to confront him. I tried to stop him, but he's stronger than me, so I pulled the gun off his shoulder. It went off."

Addie glances over at Gale, who is standing motionless, looking numb.

"Kip quickly looked at where the shot went, and then he fired another one. I didn't really understand why—it all happened so fast. Then he took off back toward Frank's place and told me to go home and not to tell a soul that I was there that day."

"He was protecting you," Addie says.

Clancy nods. "I didn't know why until later, when I found out that a branch had hit Christos, and I would never get to find out why he wanted to talk to me that afternoon. Kip told me never to tell anyone, not even Mom, that I was there that day. That by not saying anything, I was protecting Kip from getting in trouble. Only . . ."

"That kid protected *you*," Gale says. "It was your shot that hit its mark. Kip fired another one to cover up what you'd done. So you wouldn't know it was you."

"I know that now." Clancy looks to Addie. "Do you know who that man is? The man that I killed?"

"Christos?" Addie asks.

"He was my dad."

"What?"

"What?"

Gale and Addie both speak at the same time.

"I'm sure of it." Clancy wipes her face. "That's why he kept watching me—that's why he came into town to get to know me. Then Dad, George, thought it was because he was a perv and ran him out of town. But Christos came back again, and I was supposed to meet him that afternoon—I think that's what he was going to tell me, that he was my father. I figured it out when I found that letter to Mom. I told Mary in confidence that he wanted to chat. I think she already knew, like she knew about everything happening in this town. She gave him a free brownie that day, the day he died. I don't know why she told me that."

Clancy has officially run out of steam.

"So if Christos was your dad, that means Myah is your . . ." Addie looks to Gale, but she's gone. "Clancy, where did Gale go?"

"I don't know," Clancy sobs. "Did Gale really kill Kip?"

"I think so, yes."

The floodlight flicks off, and Addie waves her hand to switch it back on. Only the sensor isn't working.

"Clancy, I need you to listen to me. Run to the store and call the police."

"But—but, I—but what's happening. Did I say something wrong? Is Gale going to kill me too?" Clancy is getting hysterical. "I'm calling

Mom—she should be here soon. Kip. Poor Kip. It's all my fault he's dead. It's my fault my real dad is dead."

"Clancy, listen to me." Addie grabs her by the shoulders, shaking her slightly. "You didn't do anything wrong. Just get to safety, and I'll be right behind you."

Clancy hesitates, then runs to the store.

Addie takes a breath and heads toward the security screen.

Chapter Sixty-Three

Addie pulls down the metal handle, not at all surprised it's open.

Gale has nowhere to run, and she's probably waiting for what's coming to her.

Addie understands what it feels like to wait for something that is inevitable no matter how much you run and hide. Or cover your tracks.

The house is dark, and after the glare of the floodlight, she can barely see. Her hands wave in front of her as she shuffles toward the living room, trying to remember the layout of the place.

"Gale?" she whispers. "Gale, let's just have some of that scotch together before the police arrive, hey? One last hoorah."

Her voice gives away her lie and how scared she is, not knowing what Gale will do next. What she's capable of. Addie needs to get Myah out, make sure the girl is safe.

Addie stops as she comes to the opening of the living space. Her eyes slowly adjusting as she makes out a shape in Gale's favorite chair.

"Don't come any closer." Gale's voice is without emotion.

"Where's Myah, Gale?"

"You think I would hurt her?"

"I would hope not, but we do strange things when pushed. How about I get her and make sure she's safe, and then we can have a chat."

Gale puts something in front of her that looks like a floor lamp or—

Addie squints. *Oh shit. Is that a gun?* "Listen, Gale, we can sort this out. There's no need for anyone else to get hurt."

"Would you just shut up. All you do is talk and talk and talk, thinking you're the hero of your own story. Everything was fine until you got here." Gale readjusts the—

Rifle. That is definitely a firearm. Christos's. That Janet used. Addie knows the nausea now swirling around her is fear of death and not just because of her recent fall.

All Addie has now is her words. "*Was* everything fine before I got here? Really? You didn't seem like you were doing okay to me. That note you left Walter was a cry for help, wasn't it? You wanted someone to know it was you. Why were you in front of Kip's grave when I first met you when you could have easily gone to someone else's? You *wanted* me to dig deeper. When I was here you were practically bursting to tell me what happened, but then reality caught up with you, and the closer I got, the more you didn't like it. You called the store late at night to scare me. You left comments on my blog, so I'd think it was the Highway Reaper. You—"

"You know nothing." Gale adjusts herself in the seat, putting the rifle between her legs.

Addie can see clearly now that her eyes have adjusted to the dark. It's weirdly surreal watching Gale pick up the firearm and point it directly at her, so close she could reach out and grab it. She waits for adrenaline to kick in and for her to run, but she's rooted to the ground. Maybe this is what being paralyzed by fear means.

"Just tell Toby that I love him and I'm sorry."

Gale watches her from behind the barrel, her expression lifeless.

"It's okay, Gale. I understand—"

"How long until the police get here?" Gale sounds almost resolved.

Given Addie never called them, she has no idea. She really should have done as Gary said on the day they first arrived and called on the locals for help. "Don't you want to confess before you kill me? It might make you feel better."

"Shut up."

"I think I've worked out what happened to Kip and Shelley, but I'm a bit stuck on Mary. Was she onto you as well—was that it?"

"Shut up." Gale glances behind herself to Myah's room.

"How did you do it? Shove her breakfast down her mouth to shut her—" Addie stops and listens. It's a child crying.

Gale hears it too. She looks back at Myah's room, and fear, no, sadness washes over her face. Addie can feel the question reach her as Gale asks it silently.

What will happen to Myah?

Gale puts her finger on the trigger, looks up to the ceiling, and whispers, "It was all for you."

Addie puts up her hands, waiting for the shot.

Gale pulls the trigger.

Chapter Sixty-Four

Addie closes her eyes, waiting for the bang, the pain.

Death.

It doesn't come.

"Do you really think I'd have ammunition in the house after what my sister did?" Gale laughs, but it comes out more as a sob. "Although I'd give anything for one now. My kingdom for a cartridge."

"You don't mean that. I know you don't want to hurt me."

"You? Not everything is about you, Addie. God!" Gale closes her eyes.

Myah's crying has now stopped, and with the silence comes the distinct crunching of feet on the driveway outside.

Addie breathes out a sigh of relief; someone has come to save her. Gale looks around the room in a panic, lays the rifle on the floor, and picks something up from the table beside her.

"I'm in here!" Addie shouts out as she turns toward the front door.

It opens as Walter steps inside, shadows hiding his face in the dark.

"Oh shit, you," Addie says as Walter's eyes go wide. She feels a hard tug at her neck and is dragged across the room from behind.

"Addie?" Walter comes into the room and flips on a light. "What the—Gale?"

Addie blinks away the glare—only it's a flash of metal on the side of her neck. In Gale's hand is a box cutter.

Walter steps forward. "What is going on here?"

"Don't come any closer." Gale takes the words right out of Addie's mouth.

"Gale," Addie whispers, the blade now pressing against her skin. "He's dangerous. You have to let me go so we can get out of here."

"Me? *I'm* dangerous?" Walter points to his *Halloween* T-shirt that says *Everyone's entitled to one good scare*. "Addie, you're clearly concussed, confused. What's going on here? Gale, please take that blade away from Addie's throat."

"Stay back." Gale's breath is warm in her ear. "I need to think."

"You drugged me," Addie murmurs. "You and Frank."

Gale chuckles and loosens her grip ever so slightly. "I always knew you were a shifty bastard, Walter."

"Drugged you? Why would we drug you?" Walter balks. "You fainted. We let you sleep for a bit but realized you must have hit your head when you fell. You were stumbling, slurring your words, vomiting."

"You drugged me . . ." Addie doesn't sound so sure. "The wardrobe. There's a map."

"Addie, you aren't making sense. We didn't drug you. You fell, hit your head. I spoke with Toby, and he said that you'd been struck before in that exact same spot. Addie, we need to get you to a hospital. Gale, whatever Addie did, we can work this out."

"I didn't do anything. Did I?" Addie feels like her mind is betraying her. "Gale killed Kip. And Shelley."

Walter frowns. "Gale, is that—"

They all stop. Sirens. Getting closer. The police.

"That's the ambulance," Walter says, looking toward the front door.

"Ambulance?" Gale asks. "So there's still time."

"Time for—" Pain shoots up Addie's arm, and she looks down, instantly nauseated. A deep cut. Bleeding heavily. Blood. So much blood. Like the attack.

Maybe this is a nightmare?

Addie grabs her arm, warm liquid spilling through her fingers. Her legs fold, and she's on the floor. Walter rushes toward her, pulling his T-shirt off.

Gale shoots past them with Myah sleeping in her arms.

"Walter . . ." The room is spinning.

"Let her go. She won't get far." He wraps the T-shirt around the cut, winces on her behalf. "Just lie still. I'll go and wave the ambulance down."

Addie lies back, her eyes closing. "Where's Toby?"

"Toby's at home with Clancy."

Home.

Chapter Sixty-Five

DAY TWENTY-ONE

Addie curls into the corner of the old sofa Toby has brought outside the back of the store for her to lie on while she recovers. It's just her and Gravy sharing it right now. The absent cat is taking up the other corner, the late-afternoon sun warming them as they sit.

It's Sunday, two days after Gale was chased down by police and taken into custody. Word has it she's confessed to killing Shelley and being a party to Kip's death. She has yet to admit guilt concerning Mary, though.

Addie opens her eyes as she hears Beatrix come from inside. "How's my patient? Anything I can get you?"

"You don't have to keep checking on me," Addie says with a smile.

"You know I do." Beatrix puts the cat in her lap as she sits down. "Between the head trauma and the cut, you're lucky they released you already."

"I got the all clear." Addie rubs her eyes. "It's mainly all the media attention getting to us now."

"Will you write about what happened? I know everyone's desperate to hear your story."

"Careful what you wish for, hey?" Addie wants to laugh, but there's nothing funny about it. "The short answer is, I don't know. I'm not sure what I want anymore."

"You've been through a lot. Give yourself some grace." Beatrix's words are as calming as her tea.

They sit and stare at the barren land stretching out in front of them. Gravy purrs heavily in Beatrix's arms. Addie contemplates how she will get the next question out.

"Ask what you want to ask, Addie," Beatrix says lightly.

Addie turns so she's facing Beatrix. "You were there the morning Mary died, weren't you?"

"That is common knowledge, yes." Beatrix tugs at the bumblebee necklace around her neck.

"I don't mean you calling it in—I mean before that."

Beatrix studies her, looking bemused. "You're the one telling the story, Addie."

"There was the necklace I found and the fact that Betsy doesn't bark when you're around. I thought maybe you'd come over to confront Mary about something. I didn't know what until Clancy told me that Mary knew something about Christos." Addie pauses and shakes her head. "But that still didn't feel right. I can't imagine you hurting someone, and even if Mary had accidentally choked when you were there, you would know how to save her."

"Go on," Beatrix says.

"Someone else was there, before you arrived. Did they call you? Did they try and help Mary themselves, but they weren't strong enough to get that cereal from her throat?"

"Choking is one of the leading causes of death in the elderly, and it's not just food but liquids too," Beatrix says plainly.

"Liquids like milk?" Mary's bowl was swimming in milk according to who? So many locals have talked about Mary's death.

Beatrix continues. "Milk, medications, foods. All of it can be fatal. It's called dysphagia, and it's likely that's what Mary suffered from as she had her breakfast that morning."

Addie lets it all click into place.

"It was Mildred who told me about the milk," Addie says, looking at Beatrix. "She was there, wasn't she? That morning. Like she was every other morning baking those goods for Mary."

"We only see what we want to see." Beatrix strokes Gravy's head.

What is she missing?

"Leave it, Addie. Mildred did everything she could to save Mary that day. They have a lot of history. A lot of love. A lot of pain."

"But why would it matter if people knew Mildred was there? That they were actually friends? It was an accident—even you could attest to that . . . oh . . ." Addie scratches her bandaged arm, understanding now. "A lot of love . . . for each other."

Beatrix smiles her knowing smile and says again, "Leave it, Addie. Not everything needs to be a story."

Doesn't she know it.

"Fine, then I'll ask how it went with Clancy instead."

Beatrix tugs at her necklace again. "I told her everything, and she took it better than I thought. George was there too. I wanted him to be part of hearing the whole truth. He deserved that."

"Do you think you'll get back together?"

"No. We love each other, but not like that. Not anymore. I betrayed him and Clancy. And Christos. I was young and only thought about myself, not about the consequences."

Addie knows a little something about that, and it'll be her turn next to tell Toby the truth when things finally settle down. "How did you meet Christos?"

"The hospital. His mother was one of my patients when I worked in the cancer ward—she had terminal cervical cancer. We connected through trauma. I was struggling to have a child with George, and we'd separated because of it. Christos was a comfort to me, and I was a comfort to him. When his mom passed and he went back to the mines to work, I figured that was it."

"But you were pregnant?"

"Yes, with Clancy. By then I was back with George, and in my mind, Clancy was always his. When she was around ten or eleven, Christos came back to find me. I think he knew Clancy was his. George took his interest the wrong way, and there was a fight. It got nasty. I asked Christos to leave, which he did."

Addie leans her head against the couch. "But he was also with Janet then?"

"That's right. I encouraged him to find someone new. I wanted Janet to be happy as well. And when she got pregnant, it all got a bit complicated. It wasn't until he came back for that final time that George finally realized what was going on. He'd had suspicions, but Christos wanted a paternity test—he wanted to know Clancy. After he died, I didn't do so well. I ended up telling George everything, and he moved out."

"Do you know what will happen to Myah?"

Beatrix sighs. "I don't, not until we know what will happen to Gale. But I plan to petition to get custody, as she's Clancy's half sister."

"I'm sure Christos would have liked that."

"I believe he does." Beatrix tugs at the necklace.

"Is that how you talk to him the right way, through that necklace?"

Beatrix chuckles lightly. "Leave it, Addie."

She does. Preferring to close her eyes again and let the quiet settle in. The quiet pain they both share.

She knows her pain isn't over.

Not yet.

Chapter Sixty-Six

EIGHT DAYS LATER

Toby gives Addie's hand a squeeze before he starts the car.

"You ready?" he asks.

She isn't but says yes anyway.

The sun is only just surfacing, and the store is closed. No one will open it today, and a sign in the window says that any mail can be collected tomorrow. Toby has timed the drive perfectly for the court appearance.

Soon Addie will have to get up on the stand as a witness and tell the whole truth and nothing but the truth. The thought makes her want to vomit.

Toby blasts the air-conditioning, reminding her of their first day here and how much has changed since then. How much has also stayed the same. Her lies are still festering inside her.

Soon they will be out. Of her own mouth or from the young attacker from that night. Either way, Toby will know soon.

She looks at him, and he smiles as he tunes the radio to a sixties station. Maybe the same one Mary listened to on those early mornings. She and Mildred, probably dancing together while the world slept.

I'll tell Toby on the way, she decides. Prepare him for what she did before it comes out in front of everyone in a courtroom. Her mom will be there too. Of course she will—she's never around, but when Addie doesn't want her there, she decides to show her face. Addie knows it's just another opportunity to talk about her gran's money and how she can get her hands on it.

Her mother is as predictable as her cycle.

Hmm. Addie considers when the last time was she had her period. She's late. Which means . . . *Oh shit.*

It would explain some of the nausea, the dizziness. Why she fainted at Frank's. Beatrix even mentioned something, but Addie shrugged it off, other things on her mind. She should have known right away given she felt the same way before.

It makes sense, she thinks. She was pregnant the last time she saw the guy who attacked her. Is this life's idea of a cruel joke?

"You ready?" Toby repeats, not waiting for a reply and turning the car around. "Soon this will be over, and we can get on with our lives."

If only.

"Oh, and I forgot to tell you that Larry dropped off a money order yesterday for all the damage his boys have done around the store." He doesn't add the emotional damage, including prank phone calls and a threatening letter. "That money will come in handy."

Along with Frank's nominal rent, they may just get ahead.

Toby finally went out there to visit his old friend and see for himself what Addie had discovered in the wardrobe. Only it had all been taken down. Addie's phone was found in Frank's bedsheets, but no murder wall. Addie knows what she saw, and she's going to get to the heart of what Frank has been hiding when they return.

She owes it to Toby to find out what really happened back then to his uncle—not for a story but so he gets closure.

One thing at a time. For now she has to get through this day.

Addie tries not to cry. Toby grabs her hand and squeezes it, sensing she's not okay.

"Don't worry, babe. As long as we're together, we can do anything."

"Toby, I have something I need to tell you . . . ," she begins.

"As long as we're together, we can do anything," he repeats.

Tears fall down her cheeks. "After I tell you, you're never going to say that to me again."

Toby grips onto the steering wheel and takes a breath. "It's okay. I know what you did."

Addie can barely breathe. "What did you say?"

"You heard me."

"But how?"

"Your gran's inheritance money. I noticed part of it missing from the term account, along with who it had gone to." He seems calm, just like he was when they drove into town that first day and saw the funeral.

"Why didn't you say anything?" Addie wishes she could open the car door and not have to deal with the shame she feels.

"Because I was angry and needed to be sure."

"Sure of what?"

"What you were capable of."

Addie's stomach churns, and she wants to be sick. "And now you know what I am capable of?"

"Yes." He glances over at her, his face not giving much away. "Everyone does things when they feel trapped, and I know you were like a caged animal back in the city—hell, we both were. I had no job satisfaction, and you loved your work to the point of obsession. You hired those boys for a story, and it backfired."

Addie can't believe how composed he is. "I never meant for anyone to get hurt, especially our . . ."

"Let's not talk about that. You and I have lost enough in our lives and made many mistakes. We'll have a family when the time is right."

She instinctively holds on to her belly. Maybe they'll be okay after all. "Toby, I—"

"It's okay. You don't have to explain yourself. I already forgave you." He squeezes her knee. "After my father took his life, I not only promised my mother I would find out who caused our family's grief, but I promised myself I would never abandon my family like he did to us. No matter how hard it got."

She isn't sure how to respond, so she makes her own promise. "I'm going to find out what happened to your uncle. You have my word."

"I know you will." He gives her a quick smile.

She holds back the tears that threaten to come. From joy, from heartache, from how much she loves the man beside her and how similar they actually are. Weeks ago, they drove in disconnected, and now they leave as a united team.

She leans her head against the window and says a silent prayer to her gran. *Thank you for looking out for me. I'll do better.*

They travel over the bridge, and the dried creek bed the town is named after.

As they pass the rear of the sign announcing the town, Addie looks back. The red spray paint has been removed, and the white letters shimmer in the morning sun.

BONEY CREEK
POPULATION 217

◆ ◆ ◆

Acknowledgments

I can't believe I'm writing another set of acknowledgments already! Thank you so much for reading my sophomore book, *Boney Creek*. This was a beast to write alongside scrambling to release my debut, *Original Twin*. I had to have quite a few huddle-in chats with my characters at not knowing who the killer was and if anyone was going to step forward. What a time. The pain of getting this book done was worth it, though, as I am truly proud of how it turned out and can't wait to revisit this town and all its secrets.

I would like to thank my agent, Gwen Beal, from United Talent Agency. I dedicated this book to her because I wouldn't be here without her. Every day I feel blessed that the universe got its shit together and granted me such a fabulous agent. Other special mentions from UTA include assistant extraordinaire Geritza Carrasco, and my film/TV agent, Orly Greenberg.

To everyone at Thomas & Mercer. Thank you again for helping me shape this book into something I can be truly proud of! I'm so grateful to have such a powerhouse team looking after me. To my editor, Jessica Tribble Wells, thank you for allowing me to write this book even if I didn't know any of the reveals or twists—having someone trust my process is such a blessing. Extra-special thanks also to my fabulous developmental editor Dee Hudson, superstar copyeditor Alicia Lea, proofreader Jenna Justice, cold reader Angela Vimuttinan, promotional-text writer Katie Majka, production manager Andrea Nauta, marketing manager Andrew George, author-relations managers and absolute legends Darci Swanson and Heather Radoicic, art director Michael Jantze, and the ever-talented cover designer Jeff Miller.

Thank you again to the amazing writing community and all the incredible authors I get to call my friends. Special mention to my early readers, Sonja J. Kaye, Britney Brouwer, Megan Davidhizar, Marlee Bush, Carmen Marton, and Catriona Macleod. And to my sounding boards, Keshe Chow, Roselyn Clarke, Jessica Conoley, Lora Senf, #2024debuts, and Submission Slog Comrades.

Thank you to the authors who blurbed *Original Twin*: Sally Hepworth, Katya de Becerra, Tracy Sierra, Ashley Tate, Marlee Bush, and K. T. Nguyen.

To my friends who love me even if they never see me anymore: Christina, Kate, Lucy, Catty, Carmen, Caroline, Jack, Safwan, Rachel, Jim, and Janaya.

To my family for always believing in me and being my biggest fans (even if they don't read my books. LOL). Glen, thank you for helping me launch my first book and being such a constant champion. Dad, BJ, and Lara, thank you for cheering me on from afar—it means the world.

And, obvs, Mum! Thank you for always being there as my first reader and wise council as I continue to navigate the wild ride that is publishing. If I could dedicate all my books to you, I would!

Thanks to everyone who read and reviewed my debut, *Original Twin*. You constantly made my day with your kind messages and words of support. I hope you like this one just as much. Thank you also to my local supporters, Tracey and the staff at Collins Booksellers Ballarat on Lydiard, and Rosemary and staff at the Ballaarat Mechanics' Institute.

To my German shepherd, Atreyu. We are in your final days as I write this, and I am not sure what I will do without you by my side. You are my world, my heart, and my bestest boy. Thank you for allowing me to be your mum and best friend.

And to my sister, Kristie. I'm sending you Atreyu. He gives the best cuddles just like you did. Take care of each other and know you are always missed.

About the Author

Photo © 2020 Larissa Hubbard

Paula Gleeson writes mysteries and thrillers for all ages, usually with complicated females at the helm. Her debut novel, *Original Twin*, was released in 2024. Gleeson is also an award-winning filmmaker, screenwriting finalist, and nominated nonfiction writer. She lives just outside Melbourne, Australia, and can often be found in her pj's, drinking tea (wine) and watching horror movies snuggled between her doggo and a large cheese pizza.

To learn more about the author and her work, visit her website at https://paulagleeson.com.